BEING A GIRL

Chloë Thurlow

nexus

This book is a work of fiction.
In real life, make sure you practise safe, sane and consensual sex.

First published in 2007 by
Nexus
Thames Wharf Studios
Rainville Rd
London W6 9HA

A catalogue record for this book is available from the British Library.

www.nexus-books.com

Typeset by TW Typesetting, Plymouth, Devon
Printed in the UK by CPI Bookmarque, Croydon, CR0 4TD

The paper used in this book is a natural, recyclable product made from wood grown in sustainable forests. The manufacturing process conforms to the regulations of the country of origin.

ISBN 978 0 352 34139 6

Distributed in the USA by Holtzbrinck Publishers, LLC, 175 Fifth Avenue, New York, NY 10010, USA

For Dave

Master and so much more

Contents

1

The Casting

I hate my step-sister. I really do. I could have killed her when I put my name down for a summer job at a casting agent's and then found her name written in her big rounded letters on the list. The interview happened to fall on the same day as I was sitting my History A level, and that was just typical. I was confident that I'd done well in Italian and Theatre Studies, but I needed a good mark in History to be assured of my place at Cambridge.

Things *always* work out for Binky and it's just not fair. She's a year younger than me and had suddenly shot up with long perfect legs that she was showing off like an absolute tart in a little pink suit, a white, high-necked top with a gold cross on a fine chain, everything demure and charming, and so much bare flesh streaming out from below her skirt. Her interview was at 2.00 and I watched her leave school, a Burberry bag swinging from her shoulder and her long silky legs like scissors striding down the drive towards the West Gate. She turned with a little skip and a feeling of doom touched me as she vanished from view.

With her delicate features and deep-green eyes, Binky had only recently become aware of the effect she had – on men, on the nuns, on the world – and was making up for lost time. Her name when we were small had been shortened from Roberta to Berta and familiarised to Binky. Everyone, just everyone, adored my little sister. But then, they didn't know her.

The placement was supposed to be for someone in the *upper* sixth and Binky, in the *lower* sixth, wasn't weighed down with ghastly A levels. Our only rival was Virginia Ward, a really nice girl who thought her red-framed glasses were cool and still didn't have *anything* to put in her white cotton bra. Virginia was the sort of girl you did prep with and avoided on Saturdays when we were allowed to go into town.

Once Binky had disappeared through the school gate, I went back to my last-minute revision, memorising dates, names, battles. It seemed as if all of life was one big battle and Binky was ahead in the charge. I read one last time through my notes on the English victory over the French at Agincourt and raced upstairs to the exam room where four other girls were already at their desks, crisscrossing their legs and sweeping the hair from their eyes. We exchanged nods and good lucks and I realised I was going to miss Saint Sebastian's. The convent had been my home for the last five years and I didn't think I was ready for the real world, we had in truth been so coddled and protected.

Once the exam started, I pushed Binky from my mind, and just concentrated. I can do that, really focus on one thing and put everything into it. The afternoon was warm. My underarms were damp and you could smell the tension in the air with five girls sweating over their papers.

The moment the exam was over, I blew kisses to the others and ran. We had started twenty minutes late and I bolted down the drive, along the busy high street and down into the tube without even combing my hair. The convent is at the furthest point on the Piccadilly Line and it was already rush hour by the time I squeezed into the packed carriage. The Underground smelled like a charity shop and I always had the feeling that someone was pressing against me rather harder than they should have been.

At least I didn't have to change, although by the time I reached Leicester Square, I was totally stressed and had decided if Binky got the job with the casting agent I would never speak to her again. Never. This was going to be my job and I would do *everything* I could to get it.

At least the lavatories at Leicester Square were clean. I pulled the band from my ponytail and brushed my hair as best I could with my fingers. That's another bone of contention, actually: Binky's yellow locks fall from a neat centre parting to her shoulders, glossy and perfect, and it's true what they say, men do prefer blondes. We have by coincidence the same green eyes, but like my father, an Italian, I am dark and provocative; at least, that's what matron says, while my step-sister is fair like her English mother. Binky didn't have my figure, but she had those long legs revealed halfway up her thighs, while my plaid kilt fell to the prescribed two inches below the knee. Like so uncool. It wasn't fair and I hiked the skirt up at the waistband and hid the folds of material by pulling out my blouse. Now, I just looked scruffy. I sighed despondently as I took off my socks and hid them in my backpack.

The agency was in one of those little passageways running into Chinatown. I had printed out a map on the web. It was easy to find, although I was so late when I finally got there, the thought crossed my mind that it was more than likely that everyone had left for the day. Binky had got the job and I was going to have to kill her when I got home. I gloomily pressed the buzzer and let out a sigh of relief when a deep voice came on the entry-phone. I was in luck.

'Yes?'

'Camilla Petacci,' I said and the door clicked open.

Inside the building it was dark and, as I climbed the stairs, I don't know what came over me, but I did something utterly mad. It was just silly really, immature, on the spur of the moment, but had consequences that I would ponder long into the future. I was hot in my blazer. The bag of books weighed a ton. Perspiration was trickling between my shoulder blades and, without thinking, I opened the top button on my blouse. Finally, I could breathe.

As I made my way up the second flight of stairs, as if there were some mathematical prerogative in this, some hidden equation, I undid the next button. My heart was pounding and the soft creamy mounds of my breasts were rising and falling as I caught my breath and tapped on the door.

'Come in.' The voice was muffled and seemed far away.

I entered and found Jean-Luc Cartier facing away from me glancing through a pile of photographs. I waited and he slowly turned in his swivel chair, looking me up and down, as I suppose an employer would, and I felt foolish in my school uniform, my blouse stupidly half undone, the backpack like some terrible punishment on my shoulders. I felt like the wanderer in *Pilgrim's Progress*.

'I'm so sorry to be late . . .'

'I was just leaving . . .'

'I had an exam . . .'

I'd blown it.

He glanced at his watch, then at a sheet on his desk. 'It was your sister I saw, the same name, of course.'

'Roberta.'

'Yes, that's right. Binky,' he said, and smiled as if from a pleasant memory. I was livid.

I smiled back through gritted teeth. It was even hotter in the office than it had been on the stairway. I felt another bead of sweat run down my back. Jean-Luc Cartier was fresh in a white shirt and jeans, a heavy watch that he moved around his wrist as he stood and sort of circled me. He wore a look I took for disappointment as he gazed at my school uniform, the bunched-up material around my middle, the backpack with a heart drawn in red felt tip. How pathetic.

As I glanced down at my throbbing chest I realised another button had popped open by itself. I did consider doing the buttons up again, but that would only have drawn attention to my breasts and Mr Cartier seemed to have been reading my mind anyway, and was now focusing the full weight of his gaze down my front.

'You know all about computers, that sort of thing?' he asked, addressing my breasts.

'Yes,' I said. 'I got an A in IT . . .'

'*Très bien.*' He smiled and I pressed my fingernails into the palm of my hand. *An A in IT.* What an idiot.

He looked up from my breasts into my eyes and I blushed under his gaze. I felt hot. Baking hot. My throat was dry. I was so nervous when he reached forward and brushed a lock of hair away from my eye I just didn't know what to do. It was just a gesture, but I had never met this man before and it seemed too weird, too intimate.

'You finish school soon?' he then asked.

'Yes, in a couple of weeks. I've applied to Cambridge,' I said, immediately regretting it.

'Cambridge?' he repeated.

'To read the history of art and theatre.'

He glanced around at the portraits decorating his office. 'You are an actress?' he asked.

'Oh, well, you know, yes, sort of. I would like to act, but I want to get a good education.'

'Just in case?'

I nodded and felt foolish. He was looking me up and down as if I were there for a casting.

'It needs a strong sense of discipline to be an actress,' he then said.

'Yes, I know.'

'Do you have that discipline, Camilla?'

'Yes.'

'*Très bien*,' he said again. 'Come, we should see the nerve centre,' he added and pointed to the corner. 'You can leave your bag.'

I shrugged it off my shoulders. I was going to do up my blouse but, before I could, he stretched his hand out to me. I wavered for a second and when I took it he squeezed really quite hard and led me down a narrow flight of stairs with wooden rails on each side, the space between them so narrow we were pressed together like two people descending on the escalator to the Underground.

We entered a room with four big flat screens pulsing a pale-blue light along one wall and a row of tall filing cabinets opposite. He clicked a loose mouse and brought up the face of a famous actor I'd seen on TV many times but whose name at that instant escaped me. Was he doing this to impress? I wasn't sure. I was just hot and tense. I was in a world that fascinated and frightened me at the same time.

Below a row of tensor lights at the centre of the room was a square glass table that for some reason made me think of Alice when she found the golden key that would take her to Wonderland.

'This is where we lay out the goods for the directors,' he said, and turned to the banks of filing cabinets. 'Most people are on file, but more are going straight to computer now.'

The room was stifling. The computers hummed and Jean-Luc Cartier's voice with its faintly accented English made me feel drowsy. I had worked so hard on the exams I was exhausted. My stomach was squeezed against the waistband of my skirt, my blouse was sticking to my back, and my breasts were rising and falling immodestly with each breath I took. Everything was tight, constricted. I was bursting from my clothes, as matron had said, but it was so close to the end of term it would have been a waste to buy a new uniform.

Mr Cartier didn't say anything but he must have known I was hot and filled a big glass of water from one of those plastic fountains, the bubbles making vulgar noises as they exploded on the surface. I guzzled the water down so quickly, it splashed on my blouse, and I felt like a complete idiot as I handed back the glass. He wedged it under the tap.

'Take off your jacket,' he said.

It was like an order and I obeyed without thinking, hanging it on the back of the chair where the actor was still staring from the computer screen with a faintly mocking expression.

Mr Cartier approached with the glass refilled, but instead of giving it to me, he held it to my mouth and

I was so thirsty I opened my lips. He stared at me and I watched his eyes as he tilted the glass, the water gushing out, drenching my school blouse and running down my front. He kept tipping the glass until all the water had gone and it seemed like a game but he wasn't smiling. This was a new sort of game and I didn't know the rules. I was panting for breath, hot still, and he was standing so close, a wave of panic coloured my neck and cheeks.

Now he spoke in the same soft hypnotic way, kindly, with force, pointing with a sort of impatience at the wet blouse.

'You should take it off,' he said.

We were silent. I swallowed. I couldn't understand what he meant. Had I misheard?

'What . . .'

'It's wet, Camilla,' he added. 'Slip it off.'

'But Mr Cartier . . .'

But what? I didn't know. I didn't have the right words. I could smell sweat under my arms, a feeling of fear, even excitement, like I was in a horror film.

'I can't do that,' I finally managed.

'You can't?'

I shook my head.

'If things are going to run properly it's important to follow instructions. Do you understand that?'

'Yes, of course I do.'

'I thought you had a sense of discipline . . .' he said, pausing, and I wondered if he was trying to remember my name.

'Milly,' I said.

'Then don't let me have to tell you again, Milly.'

Now he waited, staring at me, at my breasts rising and falling, and I don't know if it had been the tone of his voice or some furtive yearning inside me but I

8

wanted to prove that I would do as I was told if I got the job, that even if Binky had long gymnast legs my breasts in their white cotton bra were as pretty as two little flowers. Actually, quite big flowers.

He sighed as he glanced at his watch and, while I was daydreaming about Binky's legs skipping along the drive at Saint Sebastian's, my fingers were nervously doing my thinking for me, releasing the last few buttons on my blouse until it was completely open down the front. The blouse was soaking wet, so it did make sense. Sort of. That's what I was telling myself, anyway.

'Come along,' he said.

I shuffled the sleeves down my arms and clutched the material to my chest. He turned his watch around his wrist and then held out his hand, motioning with his fingers. The actor with no name was staring across the room, daring me, and I gave Mr Cartier the ball of damp material.

He shook out the creases, straightened the sleeves and placed it neatly over another chair. He hadn't looked at me at all, but glanced back with an irritated expression.

'Come along, Milly, and that please.'

He was pointing at my bra. I sort of shrugged and tried a smile. It was ridiculous.

'Oh, but I can't.'

'There is no such thing as can't. Not in my language.'

He held out his hand but I remained defiant. 'Mr Cartier, I'm not going to.'

'But why?'

'Well, I'm just not.'

'Milly, what did I tell you about obeying? Are you going to obey?'

9

'Yes . . .'

He pointed at my blouse. 'You have done very well. Now, off please.'

I felt a tremor run through me. Nothing like this had happened before. It was embarrassing, humiliating, but sort of exciting. He was testing me and I suppose I was testing myself. I was Alice falling, falling, falling down the rabbit hole.

He glanced at his watch and shook his head. I'd blown it. My little sister was going to get the job. She'd be strutting around with the soap stars showing off her long legs. I sniffed back a tear. I didn't mind taking off my blouse. It was hot, and I was rather proud of my breasts if the truth be told. It seemed sort of logical, natural. My blouse was wet and, anyway, breasts are *everywhere*, in every magazine, in the daily newspapers, on every ad in the tube; starlets and weather girls. Breasts were in – or, out rather. They were public property, but no one except the girls at school had ever seen my breasts completely uncovered. Another bead of perspiration slipped down my back, the horror and the shame and the thrill of standing there hot and breathless was just too much to bear.

'Mr Cartier . . .'

'Yes.'

'I just can't.'

But my voice had weakened with my resolve.

'Milly, I think you can. And I think you want to.'

What did he mean by *that*?

'I don't. Honestly.'

And it was true. Almost true. I didn't want to, yet while I felt nervous and self-conscious, my body was tingling with new sensations. After the months of study and stress I wanted to cast off everything, be naked, run naked through the streets, exhibit myself to the world. I liked being on stage. On show.

Mr Cartier had moved back to the chair. He picked up my blouse and held it towards me.

We were silent. The computers were blinking. The lights were bright and I thought about Binky in her pink suit. My breath was beating so fast it was as if I was running a relay race. Mr Cartier held the blouse pegged in his fingers, waiting for me to move towards him and put it back on.

I tried to move but I was rooted to the spot. My knees trembled and the slope of my tummy was knotted against the roll of material at my waist. I opened my throat to suck air into my constricted lungs and his eyes remained on mine as I angled my arms awkwardly up my back to unfasten the metal clasp. I heard the snap. It was loud in the silence.

He nodded and I felt ashamed as I lowered the thin white straps from my shoulders, first one, then the other, being provocative without meaning to, sliding the straps over my elbows, and cupping my breasts with my palms. I continued clutching the bra, but Mr Cartier put the blouse back where it had been hanging and came towards me, his eyes never leaving mine. I dropped the white tangle of cotton in his outstretched hand and he tossed it over the chair.

As he approached me again, I moved back instinctively, my legs knocking against the glass coffee table.

'There, that wasn't so terrible, was it?'

I shook my head.

'Well, come along then, let's have a proper look, shall we,' he said and he sounded like the biology teacher before we peered in turn down the microscope.

It wasn't really a question or a suggestion. Now that I was exposed so fully it was as if my will had left me. I dropped my hands, arched my back, and the most incredible thing happened. As I looked down, the soft plains around my nipples darkened from pink to cherry red, the little buds had sprung out rigid and were prickling. The beat of my breath hastened. I lifted my hands to cover my shame but mechanically took those erect nipples between my thumb and fingers and rolled them hard. I had thrown back my head and although I tried to control it, I realised I was panting.

'*Très bien.* There, you didn't need that little bra at all. They stand up so nicely on their own.'

He placed his hand flat on my ribs, below the undercurve of my breasts, and it was true, they were round and full, the little teats on fire beneath my fingers. His touch was firm, and the awful thought flickered through my mind that I wanted him to cup my breasts in his hands, take them into his mouth and bite me hard. The vision sent shivers up my spine.

The bend of my legs was level with the edge of the table. As Mr Cartier put his free hand against my shoulder, I folded as if the bones of my body were soft rubber and lay back, propping myself up on the glass surface. He drew back the hem of my skirt and we both gazed spellbound at the rising mount pushing up from my white knickers. He looked into my eyes. I think I smiled. Everything was happening so fast it was hard to catch my breath.

When he placed his hand on my knee, I locked my legs together and it was like seeing a car drive uncontrollably towards a cliff edge, his hand moving up my thigh, across the plump muscle at the top. I had stopped squeezing my nipples. My breasts were bobbing about. The heel of his hand brushed against my sex and he slipped his fingers over the band of my knickers.

He pulled at the elastic as if to peek into a closed box, lowering the front and revealing a wisp of dark hair. My mouth was open. I was observing what was happening as if it had nothing to do with me. I wriggled but his hand was firm. The white cotton material was bunched up. He pulled again, just softly, staring into my eyes and, I don't know why, but for the briefest moment I lifted my bottom from the glass table and watched him lower my knickers slowly down to my knees.

We both gazed in quiet astonishment at the dark curly patch of pubic hair. It was lush and silky, an unspoiled lawn. I knew I was to blame for allowing this to happen. I had lifted my bottom from the glass surface of the table. I was wicked and shameless and felt oddly vibrant, totally alive, as if school had been stifling me, drowning me, and I was breathing freely for the first time. I squeezed my nipples and the pressure pushed out a dewy dribble from the lips of my vagina. Nothing like that had ever happened before. It was humiliating with the scent of arousal in the room, and I couldn't understand why I was all wet between my legs.

Mr Cartier placed the palm of his hand on my stomach, warning me not to move, and ran my knickers down my legs and over my shoes. I felt so ashamed as he studied the yellow stains in the gusset, and my mouth literally dropped open when he held the cotton to his nose. I had no idea why anyone would want to do such a thing and I watched in a trance, this strange man with my damp knickers pressed to his face while he inhaled.

'Mmm,' he said.

He nodded with approval and it was a relief when he put the knickers to one side. He looked back at the wayward patch of my pubic hair. I could feel myself leaking. After drinking all that water I wanted to go to the lavatory but didn't dare say anything. I was sweating. The lights were hot. My underarms were wet and my breasts seemed to have grown huge, billowing out like sails in the wind. I cupped my breasts to still them.

Gently but firmly, like the nurse checking for sprains after hockey, he wedged his hand between my knees and eased my legs apart, just a little, and it was as if my will had gone as I watched. I had no idea how this had happened, how it had gone so far, and I couldn't help wondering if Mr Cartier had tested Binky in this way and, if he did, just how far he had gone. How far she had let him go. She had already gone further than me with her boyfriend. Much further.

He now took my hand and slid it from my breast, over my ribs, my tummy and down to the sticky bush of my pussy. He folded my fingers into the moist pink opening, and I couldn't have stopped myself slipping them inside even if I had wanted to. I peeled back the inner lips of my vagina and the warm pad of my fingertip caressed what the girls call the magic button, the little hot pulsing point that no one but me had ever touched.

I was moaning, swirling my hips, unsure how I had come to be masturbating like this with Mr Cartier watching, and pushed back, raising my legs from the floor and resting the soles of my feet on the surface of the table.

'Are you a virgin, Milly?' His voice was a whisper, almost breaking the spell.

'No,' I gasped.

Even this was shameful, humiliating.

'You are, aren't you? You must tell the truth.'

I sniffed back another tear.

'Yes,' I admitted.

'That's lovely. That's why you're so wet.'

He ran his hand under my pussy and showed me his fingers slicked with juice. Below me there was a puddle of drool and Mr Cartier did something so weird I would remember it always. He scooped up the creamy liquid on a fingertip and rubbed it over his teeth. I was truly mortified and flushed a shade of crimson.

I had brought myself to a state of terrible excitement but it ebbed away when Mr Cartier sat on the edge of the table and pulled at my hand. I thought it was over. I had shown I could obey. I had got the job and felt pleased that for once I'd got one over Binky. I scrambled to my feet, my skin squelching on the glass. He swung me round in front of him, his hands running under my skirt to the globes of my bottom. He smiled and I felt – I don't know – safe, confident in being me.

'We don't need this, do we?' he said, and fanned the air under my skirt.

I shrugged and shook my head. Was this the last test? I unrolled the fabric at my waist, lowered the zip and he removed his hands from my body to allow the kilt to fall to the floor. I stepped away from it. I was naked, completely exposed, my breasts warm and full, my pussy wet and smelly. A few hours ago I'd been a schoolgirl taking an exam and I couldn't even remember what it had been about. I looked around the room, at the old TV star staring from the computer, the water fountain, the skirt on the floor, my knickers on the table.

15

Mr Cartier held my thighs and looked up at me with a small smile.

'Now, Milly, over you go,' he said.

I didn't know what he meant. Over where? He was turning me sideways, a hand on my stomach, another on the small of my back. He applied pressure and my bones turned to sponge as my thin body folded over his knees. I spread my hands flat on the floor and realised that I was revealing myself in a way I never imagined I would reveal myself to anyone.

He stroked my bottom for a long time. It was terrifying but it was nice at the same time. He dipped the tip of his finger into my pussy, not far, just enough to make it wet, and then he did something so rude I can't believe I let it happen. I wriggled and squirmed but not so much. I didn't scream out. I felt new things, new sensations. He was making his finger wet and pushing it against my bottom, right over the hole, pushing just softly back and forth and I heard soft popping noises and fidgeted with shame.

'Don't,' I said weakly.

'Shush,' he replied.

And he kept on, dipping his finger into my pussy, then tapping it against the hole in my bottom. I would never in a million years have imagined anything like this happening, being stark naked, stretched over a man's knees, my breasts full and swinging, my pink nipples tingling and hard. I had gone beyond remorse or embarrassment. My body was singing. I pushed myself up and out. The golden key turned and I sucked his finger inside my bottom.

He moved in a spiral, round and round, back and forth, slowly, smoothly, teasing all the nerve endings, the pressure touching my magic button and bringing me back to that oozy feeling that had ebbed away. I panted for breath, his finger greased with my own juice running up inside this dark exquisite place, in and out, in and out. I was naked, naked, my breasts pounding, my bottom in the air. I was coming. I could feel contractions. I could feel a wave inside building up, rolling through my body . . .

Then, just as I was on the point of making it, he slid his finger out, clean out of my bum, and I just wished he'd have kept going for another few seconds. The wave retreated and Mr Cartier now did something that shocked me more than anything else.

He spanked me.

He removed his finger from my bottom, lifted his hand, and brought it down on my soft skin. I screamed and wriggled. But he was strong and the more I wriggled the tighter he held me. He lifted his big hand back in the air and brought it down with a thunderous clap that made me gasp.

'No, no, no,' I cried.

'Yes, yes, yes,' he replied, and smacked me again, three hard smacks one after the other.

I was panting. Tears were streaming from my eyes, snot fell from my nose. His left hand was pressed down on my back. I writhed and yelped as his right hand came down again and again, spanking my soft cheeks and sending tremors of unknown pain and unexpected pleasure coursing through me. I could feel the heat in my bottom spreading down my thighs and up my spine.

He stopped to massage the globes of my bottom, pounding the cheeks like dough and, when the smarting began to ease, he smacked me again, and it didn't feel so hard now. The pain had gone. I was numb. I was all sensation. I was alive. I gasped for breath and waited for the next one, a loud hefty wallop, and as he lifted his hand from my burning flesh the wave inside me started to rise again. The heat on my poor bottom was warming all the liquids inside me. It was like all the taps in a house had been turned on and the juices rolled and tumbled through all the channels and passages of my body, building in volume, and I started to gasp for breath. The gasp became a scream. I screamed and kept screaming, and as another great spank came scolding across my bottom I screamed through the tide of an incredible orgasm.

My first.

And it was glorious. It was better than anything the girls at school had described because it is really indescribable. It is as if you have lost your physical form and become pure essence, pure feeling. You are one with the universe. For just a moment it is like you are flying through space on your way to heaven.

That big wonderful orgasm, my very first, pulsed down through my loins and reverberated through my body like an echo. I rocked and quaked. I shifted and squirmed across Mr Cartier's knees. I pushed out my bottom and I swivelled my hips and felt ashamed, so ashamed, and so pleased with what I had done. I was naked on a strange man's lap and I loved it. I had let him spank me. I had wriggled and writhed and, although my first impulse had been to try and get away from having my backside spanked, a deeper instinct yearned to feel the weight of his hand on my bare flesh. That first spank had been painful and shocking, but with each roaring thunderclap across my bottom the pain just became pleasure and the pleasure just grew and grew until it all erupted in that bounteous climax.

I was still wriggling like an eel and slithered slowly

to a stop. I hung over Mr Cartier's knees, spent and exhausted. My breasts were hanging heavily with their own weight, and I raised my two hands from the floor to give them a good hard pinch. I groaned. I was wet and warm and my bottom was like the mouth of a volcano pulsing with hot lava. Mr Cartier stroked my back from the nape of my neck, down over my waist, over the rising hill of my tender bottom and I kept thinking: I've done it, I've had an orgasm, I've had an orgasm, and I was dying to tell Binky I'd got the job.

Now it was over I did feel ashamed. I dragged myself shakily to my feet and Mr Cartier held my bottom, pulled me towards him, and I felt so embarrassed as he rubbed his face over my drenched pussy. He then stood and really smiled for the first time.

'*C'est colossal. Magnifique*,' he said, and I wanted him to kiss me, but he didn't.

He retrieved my knickers. I rested my hands on his shoulders as he pulled them up. He pulled at the front to take a last peek at my drenched pussy and let the elastic snap back. He did up the bra at the back and then watched with what I thought was a look of encouragement while I buttoned my blouse right up to my throat. I zipped myself into my skirt and grabbed my blazer. I was waiting for him to tell me that I'd got the job but even when we walked upstairs he didn't mention it. He lifted my backpack for me and I slid my arms under the straps.

'Did I, you know . . .'

'No,' he said. 'I'd already promised the job to, what's her name . . .'

'Binky?' I gasped.

'No. No. No. The other one.'

'Virginia Ward?'

He nodded. 'She'll be perfect around the office.'

'But what about me?'

'I'd never get any work done,' he said. 'Once a girl has been spanked she is never satisfied. She just wants more and more and more.'

'That's not true.'

'How do you know?'

I didn't answer. I didn't know.

Mr Cartier went to a drawer and took out a business card which he tucked into the top pocket of my blazer.

'Just in case.'

'In case of what?' I said impatiently.

'The right part comes along for a young actress.'

2

Men in Kilts

I suppose Binky and I have always had a strange relationship. My mother died shortly after I was born and her father died shortly after she was born. Our two stray parents getting married and Binky taking our family name must have seemed like the perfect solution, but Daddy I'm sure had no idea Binky was going to shoot up like a tree with killer legs and the shortest skirts in London. We were born to be rivals and, in our race into the adult world, she had taken the lead. At least, that's what she wanted everyone to think.

Added to her porcelain skin and classic good looks, my step-sister had the self-confidence of those who *always* get their own way. She was *a real cutie*. That's what her driving instructor said when he called her and spoke to me by accident. I thought she was an awful driver but she had managed to pass her test first time after only five lessons and had acquired a pink VW beetle with 'African violet trim' from a friend of the driving examiner. The plot thickens.

Anyway, she hunted me down in Notting Hill one Saturday when I was supposed to be looking for a summer job and almost crashed into an elderly gent in an electric wheelchair. Binky zoomed into a vacant parking spot, gestured hopelessly towards the poor old gentleman and rushed me into the King's Head for a buck's fizz, her latest discovery.

She strolled up to the bar in her pink Doc Martens and behaved as if she wasn't enjoying the heads turning to watch the sway of her perfectly round bottom. If anyone was a little tart it was my sister Binky.

She turned her shoulder to one side as she cast her green eyes on the barman.

'Two buck's fizz, please,' she said in her plummy accent.

'Here, you old enough, darling?' I heard the barman say.

'What a cheek,' she replied, and the barman grinned as he added orange juice to the champagne flutes.

Binky since the start of the summer hols had gone retro with her gelled hair, a slashed T-shirt and a little skirt that would have made our poor matron turn in her grave, if she were dead of course.

'You're becoming such a slut, Binky,' I hissed as she set the glasses on a vacant table.

'You can talk,' she said, and I blushed.

I had told Binky *everything* that had happened that day in Monsieur Cartier's office and I wasn't sure whether she believed me or not. When I looked back, I didn't quite believe it myself, although a rosy glow had stained my bottom for ages and when I closed my eyes and pictured myself wriggling naked on his lap my insides went all watery.

While I was squirming on the hard wooden seat, Binky was pressing a finger to her lips and I could almost visualise all the little cogs whirring around in her mind. She leaned forward and looked deadly serious.

22

'Have you found a job yet?' she asked.

'No,' I answered.

Her eyes grew big. 'We're going to go away for a holiday,' she said, 'and if you don't come, Milly, I'll never speak to you again.'

I took another sip of champagne and the bubbles made me giggle as they went up my nose.

'I don't want to speak to you anyway,' I said, and she drummed her nails on the tabletop until I continued. 'All right,' I added, 'where?'

'As far away as possible,' she said breathlessly. 'Let's go to Scotland.'

'Scotland?'

'Yes, Scotland. We've never been there,' she said. 'You like doing things you've never done before, don't you?'

She turned sideways in her seat and slapped the side of her bottom.

'Only if it's fun.'

'Well, you never know unless you try.'

'I don't know . . .'

'Please, Milly, please. I'm dying to try out my car . . .'

'Have you had it serviced?' I asked. I was the practical one.

'Yes, *matron*, everything's ticketyboo.'

She placed her pink boots up on the bench beside me and her skirt slipped over her thighs.

'Everyone can see your knickers,' I said and she sighed contentedly.

'They're new,' she replied, and sipped her buck's fizz.

We were supposed to be looking for summer jobs, but Daddy had gone back to whatever it was he did for the EU in Brussels; Mummy was having an affair, and in the midst of these passions she didn't mind what we did as long as we didn't make any noise. Anyway, I deserved a break after the exams and raised my glass in a toast.

'To Scotland.'

We finished our drinks and I felt quite tipsy as I watched Binky skip between the cars back across the road to her pink Volkswagen. I had an interview for a job in a shoe shop and thought I'd let the *fickle finger of fate* decide on my future: if I got the job I would stay in London and, if I didn't, I would go on an adventure with my little sister.

I wandered off to the tube thinking about smelly feet. I was ten minutes late for the interview and was told by the woman who called herself Madame Dubarry that I was obviously 'spoiled' from having gone to boarding school and didn't have the right 'attitude' to devote myself to the shoe trade.

She was shaking her head and peering unpleasantly at my chest. 'Selling shoes requires a certain discipline,' she said. 'You are clearly cut out for other, *better* things.'

'I'm sure I am,' I said sullenly and had a real spring in my step as I marched off to the map shop in Long Acre.

During the coming days, I plotted the route, and Binky acquired a pair of pink flares to go with her Doc Martens. We set off the following weekend from Chelsea, up the motorway, and over the sea to Skye, which really was as beautiful as I'd imagined. We had a two-man tent and planned to camp, although I did have my doubts about Binky roughing it with her long nails and creamy white skin, much of which was on display in her Che Guevara T-shirt.

I had dressed appropriately in walking shoes and a heavy sweater. Binky had made fun of my get-up on

24

the long drive, but it turned out that I had made the right choice. We had left London early to avoid the jams and crossed to Skye just before six. It had been warm and sunny all day, but Scotland, we discovered, had its own way of doing things.

We were driving west between high stone walls, the narrow lanes curvy and deserted. The sky grew darker and when the clouds ripped apart in a flash of lightning, we screamed as great hailstones the size of tennis balls started beating on the windscreen. The car misted up. The wipers were slowing and, when the engine conked out, the wipers froze solid and we couldn't see a thing.

We sat there for an hour. Binky wriggled into her sleeping bag and we watched the hail turning gradually to rain. The storm was passing, but when my sister went to start the car, it was dead. We got out and peered at the engine, the jumble of wires and rubber tubes sitting there all wet and cold, a complete and absolute mystery.

'Typical!' I said.

'What is?'

'African violet trim,' I mocked. 'Where did you get this car from, anyway?'

'You know perfectly well where I got it from.'

'How much did you pay for it?'

'I exchanged it . . .'

'What for?'

'I'm not telling you.'

She didn't need to tell me. Her cheeks were as red as her T-shirt. Binky really had grown up, and you didn't have to be a nuclear scientist to know why.

'I knew this would happen,' I said.

'How did you?' she demanded.

'Because something like this always happens.'

'I thought you wanted to have some fun.'

'This wasn't what I had in mind when we left.'

'I did,' she said, and looked back at me with a scornful expression. 'You're such a virgin, Milly.'

I took a deep breath. She had made her point. It was only a breakdown, after all. We had set out in search of adventure, and this was where it all began.

Binky slammed the lid shut and tried the car once more. Nothing. She slipped her arms into her Afghan coat and pulled her big woolly hat over her eyes.

'Are you ready?'

'For anything,' I said, and she smiled.

We glanced back along the lane, but couldn't remember having passed any houses for ages and it was too boring to retrace our steps. I zipped myself into my sensible parka and we set out in the direction we'd been going. We had our mobile phones but weren't sure who to call.

Further along the lane, we saw a building in the middle of a field. It had started to rain again and we were afraid the storm was returning. 'Come on,' Binky said, and she was already climbing the wall. I did have a faint hope that it was a farmhouse where an old lady with her hair rolled into a bun would be busy making scones, but it turned out to be a stone barn, the doors securely bolted. The sky had darkened and the rain was getting heavier. We walked around the outside of the building, but the windows were small and too high to reach.

'What are we going to do?' I said, as Binky vanished around the corner.

She came back carrying an enormous rock and loomed over the new padlock.

'Don't,' I screamed.

But it was too late. She brought it down cleanly on the hasp and as the silver lock sprang open she turned to me with a look of wonder in her green eyes. We were standing close and Binky did something totally unexpected: she leaned forward and pressed her lips playfully to mine. It wasn't a snog, just a peck, but she had never done anything like that before. Her lips were soft but firm and left a sweet taste that lingered on my senses.

'That's disgusting,' I said.

'Liar,' she shot back.

I pulled the door open and we shared the thrill of entering the unknown. The barn was dry with bales of hay stored in steps around the walls. Binky in one swift movement sprinted the length of the barn, vaulted a pile of bales stacked three high and landed perfectly, feet together. Binky was a good gymnast and had never quite seen the point of team games like hockey and lacrosse where the praise was shared. I clapped my hands and, as Binky caught her breath, we stood there in silence, not quite sure what to do. The slate-grey sky was lit by golden streaks of lightning and the sound of the rain running off the roof reminded me that I had not been to the bathroom since the motorway services.

'I'm dying to use the loo,' I said.

'Me too.'

Binky grinned. She was turning the breakdown into an escapade, and that old sense of fun came back to me as we squatted down on our private bales of hay.

I peed for ages.

'Wow, I needed that,' I gasped.

'So I see,' she screamed, and it was totally embarrassing because she was standing there staring at me

27

as I was still peeing. 'Look at the steam. Or is that Scotch mist?'

She spoke with a Scottish accent, and while we erupted in fits of giggles, the shock of a flashlight shining on me before I could pull up my jeans came as such a surprise I tripped and fell back in the hay. Binky laughed as she wriggled into her flares and we turned, blinded by the light.

'What have we here then, some vagrants?'

It was a man's voice, the tone stern but melodic, his rrrs rolling poetically. The torchlight ran over us like eager hands.

'We're lost,' Binky said in her little girl voice. 'Our car broke down . . .'

'You're trespassing on private property.'

Binky dropped her head to one side. 'Can you help us?' she pleaded.

'Just the two of you, are there?' the man asked, the flashlight probing the corners of the barn. 'No other vagrants hiding in the hay?'

'No, just us.'

He shined the light on me. 'You're the quiet one, are you, the dark horse?'

'No . . .'

'Well, now, we'd better see what the Laird has to say. He knows how to deal with young girls.'

'We haven't done anything,' I said.

'Aye,' he replied as he led us out and closed the barn doors.

He pocketed the broken lock. We climbed into the muddy Land Rover parked outside, and I thought at least we were going somewhere safe and warm. We sat in the back holding hands. The man was whistling to himself, and drove for ages over dark fields that looked like the sea at night, on and on, and it was a relief when a big manor house came into view in a dip between the hills. There was a warm light behind the ground-floor windows and I squeezed Binky's fingers to show her I was enjoying myself.

The man opened the car. He urged us up the steps and we passed through the high arched doors into a wood-panelled hallway. He hung his waterproofs on the stand, and I noticed now that he was wearing a kilt, the pleats swaying hypnotically above sturdy calves as we followed him along the passage below the glassy eyes of numerous stags' heads. He stopped at a closed door and rapped with his knuckles.

'You can wait here,' he said.

He went in and we looked at each other. Binky grinned and, as she raised her thin shoulders, I knew she was busy inventing some excuse for breaking into the barn.

When the man opened the door, we entered a baronial hall dominated by a big log fire roaring between pillars of marble. There were various pieces of dark, heavy furniture: chests, a sideboard, a black piano. The extended dining table was framed by tall windows, and wood smoke clung in the defiles between the beams on the ceiling. Crossed swords and old blunderbusses decorated the walls among portraits of stern men with red beards and dour women who gazed out with severe unforgiving expressions. Above the fire was a life-sized painting of a beautiful woman with dark hair and dark unfathomable eyes.

Like the men in the portraits, the man in the winged armchair at the fireside was red-bearded, his hands dwarfing the leather-bound book he was holding. He showed no interest in us as we stood before him. He finished reading to the end of the page before closing the volume. He stretched out his long legs, his feet crossed at the ankles. He was dressed in the classical Scottish way with a short black jacket, a dark plaid kilt and a ruffled shirt. His laced shoes nestled in the fleece surrounding the hearth and the sporran resting in his lap was the size of a small dog.

'Are you related by any chance to the Laird Hamish of the Black Watch?' He spoke quietly and seemed genuinely puzzled.

We shook our heads, and he raised his voice.

'I didnae hear you. Are you deaf?'

'No.'

'No.'

'I didnae think so. I'm the Laird Hamish of the Black Watch and I didnae believe you had naught to do with me.'

'We were just . . .'

Binky started speaking, cooing in her little voice, but he cut her off, holding up a huge hand the size of a dinner plate. 'Can you kindly speak when you're spoken to,' he said, and turned to the other man. 'Byron, did you get those logs in like I asked you?'

'You know I didnae, Milord.'

'Then what are you waiting for, mon? There's no time like the present.'

Byron nodded meaningfully in our direction. The Laird opened his book and we scurried towards the door.

'And one more thing,' he called, 'will you have Mrs McTavish find that mobile phone. Damn thing's got a mind of its own.'

We were led through to the back of the house and set to work carrying logs from the pile at the end of the yard into the shed attached to the kitchen. It wasn't at all polite to be treated in this way. In fact, it was very rude indeed and should have warned me what to expect. It did go through my mind that we should make our way back to the road, but it was a blustery night and we were miles from anywhere.

We caught a glimpse of Mrs McTavish fussing about the big iron range and the smell of the food rising from the pots made my tummy rumble. We'd had a sandwich at lunchtime and I was famished.

'Do you think he's going to invite us to dinner?' I whispered, and Binky was as confident as ever.

'Course he is. He's just making us do a bit of work first,' she replied. She hefted up a big pile of logs. 'Builds up the appetite.'

'We mustn't antagonise him, though,' I said, but she was wandering up the path, and if she heard she didn't answer.

When the job was done, we trooped back to the hall. The fire had been built up and Mrs McTavish was setting three places at the long table.

'What shall we do with these two young criminals, Mrs McTavish?'

'What?'

'I said what shall we do with these two?'

'There's nae need to shout,' the woman said angrily.

'If I didnae shout you wouldnae hear. You're as deaf as a post, woman.'

'I know what you said, mon, and you know what I think: girls who are disobedient need discipline.'

'That's what my father taught me, Mrs McTavish.'

'Aye,' she said darkly, 'and me an' all.'

Her words hung in the air and the Laird nodded, considering the remark. 'Thank you and bless you, Mrs McTavish,' he then said, and held up a mobile phone that looked about the size of a postage stamp between his enormous fingers.

31

When she left, Byron returned, closing the door. The Laird was warming his backside. Byron was tall, at least six foot, but the Laird must have been several inches taller. He continued to look at us while he spoke to his servant. 'What's wrong with you, mon, don't we have a place to hang coats in this hoose?'

'Aye, that we do.'

Byron approached as we removed our coats. He glanced at Binky's hat, she pulled it off, and he hurried out with everything in his arms.

'I suppose you expect Mrs McTavish to clean up after you, do you?'

'No.'

'No.'

'Then take off your shoes and put them by the fire.'

I did so, standing on one leg. Binky was wearing her pink boots; she sat on the floor to pull them off, the Laird watching as if she were performing a trick. We put our footwear and damp socks by the fire where we'd been told and stood with our backs straight like naughty schoolgirls.

'Now, yoo, blondie, what's your name?' asked the Laird.

'Roberta,' said Binky formally.

'So, Roberta, what's this?' he asked, producing the broken padlock from his sporran.

'It was an accident.'

'You destroy my property and call it an accident.' He glanced at Byron, back now at his position by the door. 'You hear what they're telling me. It's my fault for having a locked barn.'

'That's the English, Milord.'

The big man stood back as if he'd been struck. 'So, you're from England, now are you?' He was concentrating on Binky, terrorising her.

'From London,' she said in a whisper.

'Look, we haven't done anything,' I said firmly, and he cut me off.

'Yoo, lassie, you speak when you're spoken to.'

A shiver ran through me as he focused once more on my sister. 'I went there once and I didnae like it. Everyone tearing aboot.' He stared down at her flares. 'You call those bell-bottoms, I suppose.'

She nodded.

'Can you see what they're doing to my polished floor?'

She looked down. 'Dripping a bit,' she answered.

'Shall I call Mrs McTavish to come and clean up after you?'

She shook her head and swallowed. 'No, of course not . . .'

'Then take them off, lassie, and hang them here where they can dry.'

She stood there for a long time, eyes down, afraid to look at the Laird with his sharp eyes on her.

'It must be that terrible traffic doon there in London that's made you deaf,' he roared, and Binky glanced at me, trembling as her hands went instinctively to the low-slung waist of her flares. She released the belt, unpopped the buttons, and wriggled her bottom as she pulled them down, sliding one at a time out of the legs and hanging the flares by the fire.

The Laird spent like an hour studying her long white legs and then pointed to a straight-backed dining chair. 'Sit,' he said, and she did so.

He turned his concentration to me. 'I suppose it was your idea to climb my walls and trespass on my property. Did you break the lock on my barn?'

'No. Yes. I mean . . .'

'You're not even sure. You gained entrance to my wee barn and what do you do, you soil the hay with your piddle.' I hung my head. 'Now, lassie, what would you do aboot this criminal behaviour on our wee island if you were in my shoes?'

I looked down at his shoes. They were huge; he had the biggest feet I had ever seen. His kilt was the same colour as the flames climbing up the chimney, fiery red with maroon stripes running across vertical lines the same shade of African violet as the trim on the car. I could smell the heady scent of pine and wood smoke. Steam was rising from Binky's flares. I looked up with a hopeless shrug.

'I don't know,' I finally managed.

'You've committed a crime.'

'I didn't mean to.'

'Ignorance is no excuse in the eyes of the law, lassie,' he said. 'You may be able to get away with this behaviour in London. Not here.'

He turned to warm his big hands and I felt a tingle of fear run up my spine, fear and déjà vu. The Laird turned back and faced me again, feet apart, hands behind his back, the pose of an old-fashioned policeman.

'Take your blouse off, lassie.'

The words entered the room as if from a distance. Of course Mister Cartier that day in his office had started out saying the same thing. That's where it had started; that's where it always starts, I imagined. But it was different this time. There was no escape. We were in the Laird's clutches. He could do whatever he wanted. My throat felt constricted and my heart was hammering inside my chest.

'Please,' I said eventually. 'I'll pay for the lock.'

'You'll pay?'

'Yes, of course. Anything.'

'You hear that, Byron: anything, she said. Do you believe her?'

34

'I wouldnae like to say, Milord.'

'I will. Honest.'

Again we were silent. His eyes drilled into me. 'Take off your blouse,' he said. His voice now was melodious, almost playful.

'I didn't mean that . . .'

He laughed. 'Ah, you see, Byron, you were right. You've never been right before, but this time you're right. You should write it doon in your diary.' The Laird recovered his mobile phone from somewhere inside his kilt. 'What's the number of Sergeant Doyle?'

'It's in the phone, I told you. You just press the letter P.'

'Why's it P and not D, for heaven's sake, mon?'

Byron didn't answer.

The Laird stared down at the machine, his huge digit hovering over the keyboard. I wasn't sure how things had got to this position, and the last thing I wanted was the police to get involved over some silly offence, ruining my chance of going to Cambridge before I'd even been offered a place. He pressed the appropriate key and lifted the phone to his ear.

'Please,' I said.

He stared back at me, his brow crinkled, a smile emerging from his beard.

'Ah, there you are, mon. It's Hamish the Black Watch . . .'

He listened.

'Aye, and a good evening to you, Sergeant. I wanted to report there's a couple of trespassers on my property, a couple of lassies . . .'

He watched as my fingers hurried like scuttling insects for the buttons on my blouse, unhooking the first.

There was another pause.

'We can probably handle it in the normal way.'

I undid another button while he nodded into the phone. Then a third.

'Aye, mon, and a very pleasant night for it,' he said, and closed the machine.

The Laird sat back in his winged armchair, watching me. I had undone all the buttons on my blouse and stood with my hands clasping the front together. I glanced at Binky. She was staring at the floor. It was typical that my step-sister had broken the lock and I was standing there half undressed. The fine hair on her legs was golden in the firelight. I suppose in a way it was because she had taken off her flares that I had agreed to the humiliation of removing my blouse. Not that I had taken it off yet. I looked automatically back at the Laird and it was like he could read my mind.

'Aye, lassie,' he said.

He spoke softly, kindly, his voice not booming but soothing, a chant. The room was lit by an orange glow. The sky outside was slowly darkening, the long July day turning to night. I peeled the blouse from my shoulders, down my arms and held it in front of me.

'Over here,' he said, pointing at the mesh grille around the fireside.

I hung the blouse beside Binky's flares.

'What's your name, girl?'

'Milly Petacci.'

'So, you have the hot blood of a Latin in your veins, do you,' he said, and thought about that for a moment. 'Why did you do it, Milly? What possessed you?'

'What?'

'If you were caught short you could have gone

36

outside. But oh no, you have to piddle on my property.'

'I'm sorry,' I murmured.

I knew it didn't matter what I said. The Laird of the Black Watch had power over us and was enjoying it.

'So you're sorry, are you?'

'Yes, really.'

'And you'll do anything?'

I didn't answer and he glanced again at Byron.

'I did hear right, or am I going deaf like Mrs McTavish?'

Byron sniffed and changed positions. 'I'll do anything. That's what I heard.'

'It's just an itzy wee thing, Milly. Indulge an old hill farmer who doesnae understand your London ways.'

He didn't say what the itzy wee thing was. He didn't need to. He was just a dirty old man. He wanted me to take off my bra, but if that wasn't bad enough, what I couldn't understand was that the fear had made my breasts swell and my nipples had hardened. I could feel them tingling, pushing against the soft fabric. My breasts were betraying me. My breasts were traitors.

A log broke and sparks chased up the chimney. It gave us something to watch, but once the fire settled it was like the interval in a play was over and the curtain had risen again. My mouth was dry, and mechanically my skinny arms doubled behind my back, my damp nervous fingers slipped the hook from the hasp, and the straps of my bra fell from my shoulders.

No one spoke, but the room appeared to sigh. I went of my own accord to the fireside and dropped the little white fold of fabric on top of my blouse. When I went back to where I had been standing, my first instinct was to slump forward in shame, but I didn't. I straightened my shoulders and even bowed my back a little, stretching my sides. My breasts stood out proud from my chest, high and rounded, the rosy buds so painful I wanted to reach for them, soothe the ache, and it was only willpower that kept my hands modestly behind my back.

The mood had changed. The fire seemed warmer. The Laird stood. Byron moved forward, and the two men studied my breasts as if they had never seen breasts before. I really wasn't sure why men had this obsession.

'Now, lassie, doesn't that feel better?' the Laird asked. His tone was soft, rhythmic, the voice of someone used to being obeyed.

I don't know why I nodded my head but I did, and he appeared so pleased I thought I'd scored a valuable point. I hated being exposed like this, my breasts being scrutinised, but the absurdity of the situation, even the faint awe in the faces of the two men, calmed my nerves and made me feel vaguely superior. Binky was sitting on the edge of the chair, staring at me intensely. The Laird observed her gaze, and when he turned to her it was obvious what was going to happen next.

'Now, lassie,' he said. 'What are you hiding down that wee shirt of yours? You havenae been swiping my antique snuff boxes while I wasnae looking?'

She shook her head.

'Then let's not delay more than's necessary. Off it comes, girl. On your feet.'

Her cheeks were flushed. Her flat tummy was going in and out as she stood, her breasts throbbing. It was

38

odd but, like the Laird, like Byron, I was now waiting in the same salacious way to see her strip down to her underwear. She shrugged, trying to look blasé, and, as I'd always been good at reading my sister, I had the impression that she was competing with me, that she didn't want to be outdone in any way.

She stretched her arms to pull the T-shirt over her head. She shook her blonde hair free and, as she placed the shirt by the fire, the Laird raised his bushy eyebrows, nodding just slightly. There was no escaping his meaning.

Binky lingered for a moment, slipped the bra straps from her shoulders and lowered the strips of material over her elbows. She turned, not really meaning to wiggle, and her breasts quivered seductively as she unhooked the clasp. Her heart, I knew, was pounding, and it made her white breasts tremble all the more.

She dropped the bra on the pile and stood at my side, fragile and defenceless wearing nothing but little knickers, the few wisps of hair escaping from around the elastic all the more endearing. The Laird approached and stood towering over us, legs apart, hands on hips, his eyes flicking between our breasts.

'Now, isn't that better, girls?' he said, but he didn't expect an answer. 'What do you think, Byron, have you ever seen finer titties? It must be something in the water they've got doon there in London.'

Byron stood at his master's side, gazing at our breasts in the same studious manner. The room was hot, the fire roaring. I was perspiring. I could smell fear and anticipation on my skin. I had no idea what this big man was going to do to us and I realised at that moment he really could do anything he wanted. No one knew where we were. We were lost on a dark night and my breasts tingled, my nipples pointing at him like two accusing fingers. I looked up into his eyes and he smiled as he scratched the thick red hair on his cheek.

'Look, now, mon, we have a dark one and a light one.' He leaned back and shook his head. 'Same height, too.'

'That's useful,' said Byron, nodding with approval as he glanced up at the beams on the ceiling.

Later I would know what they were talking about. The damp on my back formed a bead of sweat that ran down my spine. The fire roared. My breasts were full and heavy, my breath threading the silence like a needle passing through silk. I glanced down: my pink nipples had turned dark like ripe plums and hummed as if with a charge of electricity. I was wet and tremulous, the Laird's soft voice like a prayer when he spoke.

'Slip those trousers off like a good girl, now. Just like your wee friend.'

I swallowed hard. I didn't want to, but Binky was standing there in nothing but her knickers and I rationalised that it was only fair. I looked up into the Laird's eyes and got the odd sensation that I was about to sit on a mat at the top of the helter-skelter, and once I pushed off I would slide into oblivion.

'No,' I said, softly, without conviction.

'I don't want to fight you, lassie. Be a good girl and do as you're told.'

I didn't want to, but how could I have refused? I was trapped. We were rushing towards something new, unexplored, incomprehensible. It was like watching the view from a moving train, seeing everything without quite being a part of it. The room was still except for the crackle of the fire. Binky was staring at me, willing me on. Our eyes met and, as I

40

slipped the button in my waistband from its place, I felt a rush of wind as I went spiralling down, down, down into nothingness. I pulled at the zip, shuffled my jeans over my bottom, and eased them down over my knees.

'You should lend your wee friend a hand, girlie,' the Laird said to Binky, and she looked back at him.

'She's my sister,' she said, and he smiled as he cast his eyes over us once more.

'Sisters,' he said. 'Of course, I knew there was something.'

'Same eyes,' said Byron.

'Aye, green as emeralds,' the Laird said. 'Come on, let's be getting a move on.'

Binky helped me keep balance as I pulled my jeans over my feet. I was wearing pink panties with tulips embroidered in the elastic, flimsy and feminine. They seemed to hold great interest for the Laird and he studied the swell of my pubis for a long time before turning again to Binky.

'You did that very well, lassie, very well. Now, help your sister, do this last teeny wee thing for me.'

The horror of what he was suggesting made the breath catch in my throat. Up until then it had seemed almost innocent. He was punishing us for damaging his property. We were a couple of city girls, and he was a hill farmer making fun of us. I'd thought about old Mrs McTavish making dinner in the kitchen and had felt safe with her there. Binky was trembling, unable to speak.

'Don't,' I said, my voice a whisper.

He turned from Binky to me, his blue eyes like fire. He was about to speak, but took a great gasp of air and, in one movement, his left hand was around my back, and with his right he grabbed the front of my

41

knickers and pulled them down to my feet. The breath went out of me. I was naked. Completely naked. My armpits were damp, my breasts were swollen and my nipples really hurt.

'There now,' he said, as if something had been proved, and folded his arms.

What self-respect I had left disappeared as Byron slipped my knickers over my feet and stood, staring into the gusset. I knew they were sticky and felt so ashamed as he held the damp strip of cotton under his nose. When Jean-Luc Cartier had sniffed at my knickers in his office I had been mortified and imagined only a Frenchman would have such a sordid fascination with girls' underwear. I was wrong, obviously. Byron seemed transfixed by my soiled pants and looked as if he might stand there all night inspecting the pale yellow stain.

'Well, have you finished, mon?'

'I'm just checking.'

'So I see,' said the Laird, and turned to Binky.

In the same way that she had not been told to remove her bra before she did so, she hooked her thumbs in the elastic of her white panties and wriggled them delicately down her legs. The Laird held out his hand, and the triangle of cotton looked like the head of an orchid stretched across his palm. He gave her warm knickers to Byron, who again gazed lewdly in the gusset before running the fabric under his nose. The Laird watched impatiently.

'Well?' he asked.

'Ripe, I'd say, Hamish.'

The Laird nodded sagely before turning to Binky. 'You're a good girl,' he said, and glanced back at me.

He made me feel as if I were the bad girl. He had blamed me for breaking the padlock, for soiling his

fresh hay. I was utterly exposed, humiliated. I was
shaking, my breasts hurt, and I know hindsight is all
very well, but I had known when I had taken that first
sip of buck's fizz at the King's Head that Binky was
going to get me into trouble.

'Now, what do you think of this, Byron McBride?
Has a more pretty sight ever crossed those wretched
eyeballs of yours?'

'Not in this lifetime, Hamish. It's a rare and lovely
sight, a rare and lovely sight indeed.'

'Aye, and what are we going to do to punish these
defiant Jezebels?'

'It's not for me to say. It's for me to obey.'

'Ah, it must be the muse that's brought the poetry
out in you, laddie.'

They were gazing at us in wonder. At our pert
breasts and lush pussies, our tiny waists and thin
shoulders. I suppose we had never looked better and
there was some youthful arrogance in the way I kept
my back straight, my chin high. There was fear in me,
shame, too, but also a weird inexplicable excitement.

I glanced towards the uncurtained windows, as if
someone might be passing, not that anyone would
ever pass that house. The sky was black. The storm
had moved on and a sprinkling of stars had come out.
Orange flames floated across the grate like dancers
and the Laird's blue eyes were the eyes of a serpent,
drawing me back, holding me in their power. I was
naked, utterly exposed, my breasts tingling, my
tummy filled with butterflies. My breath came in hot
rushes and I realised I was panting.

Binky was staring at me. The Laird took her hand,
directing it to the base of my spine. Our hips crossed,
locking together, and I turned nervously as she began
to stroke the soft flesh of my bottom, over the sloping

43

hill to the undercurve and back again, her caress warming the moisture inside me, and I felt a dampness like dew on the lips of my vagina. The beautiful woman in the painting above the fire was staring down with a knowing expression, her dark eyes full of sadness and secrets.

In the darkness the two men had become shadows. It felt as if we were alone, two naked girls discovering something that had been hidden, our bodies drawn naturally, subconsciously together. Our breasts touched and my nipples burned like the fire in the grate. Binky's eyes flickered and closed. She had thrown back her head, presenting her long neck, which I kissed, softly biting the ivory skin, her hand on my bottom running up my back to the nape of my neck.

I circled her waist. I ran my tongue over her neck, her chin, into her mouth, her plump lips sucking at my lips, and I thought back to that first fleeting peck as we'd entered the barn. I had never kissed my sister before and it was exquisite, her soft tongue circling my tongue, our engorged lips sliding into new positions, pushing greedily as if we were devouring some rare gorgeous feast.

Our pubic mounts were touching and we swivelled our hips, grinding the bones together. I ran my hand over Binky's back. I had never appreciated how slight and fragile she was, her narrow waist widening over slender hips, her spine that I now traversed, up over the well-defined little nubs and down to the hollows in the small of her back. Her thin body relaxed as if it were a bowstring too tightly wound. Her bottom was soft, round, springy, and I felt a syrupy ooze between her cheeks. Binky's hand made the same journey, over my back, then through the crack in my bottom where she found the same oily wetness, the smell of our arousal so rich and shocking it took my breath away. We were the same height, the same size, and it was like touching yourself, like masturbating.

When the Laird's big hands rested in the middle of our shoulders, one on each side, the mood was disturbed, the passion drifting away like the swell of the tide retreating back to sea.

'Shush, now, shush. Be still.'

His voice was a chant and when we realised what was happening it was already too late. Byron was on his knees attaching leather straps to our ankles, binding us together. We struggled, but the Laird's hands pressed like the jaws of a vice and we were paralysed. Byron strapped our wrists, swiftly, with skilful fingers, right to left, and we had to widen our legs to keep balance.

The Laird still kept his hands on our backs. I looked up to plead with him but his eyes were glazed. He was staring across the room at the portrait of the lady and I imagined with a sick feeling the long history of debauchery that haunted this secluded manor house.

Byron dragged a heavy dining chair towards us and the Laird stepped up on the red upholstered seat. Immediately above on the beam were two hooks. Byron passed the Laird two lengths of leather which he attached. He reached down for our bound wrists, the swivel join between the straps allowing him to hoist our arms above our heads. He connected our wrists to the straps, first one side, then the other. We struggled, even though it was pointless. Byron was holding Binky because she looked as if she were ready to faint and, though I squirmed and screamed, I couldn't move, and there was no one to hear me. The

45

Laird tightened the straps in such a way that our feet only just touched the ground.

How did this happen? Did we bring it upon ourselves? We had taken our clothes off, not willingly, but we hadn't put up that much of a fight. I had stood there proud of my full breasts and firm pink nipples. Binky, too, she was just the same, her silky white body displayed so shamelessly in the firelight. While the Laird had been testing us, I'd thought I'd been testing him.

He stood down, stroking our damp flesh, a potter making a vase, over our backs and around the swell of our backsides. There is nothing more humiliating than to bind two girls in this way, and the Laird was aware of his masterwork as he paused to study us, our arms stretched above our heads, our stomachs pulled in, our bottoms thrust out. We were exposed and vulnerable in every way.

It was the most degrading thing that had ever happened to me and yet, and yet, there was a part of me that wanted to know what was going to happen next. What could happen next? I'm not sure why, but I kissed Binky. Not a snog like before, just a kiss to say it was all right. We would get through this. Tears rolled down her cheeks, one after the other, and I licked them away. Byron moved the chair back to its place at the table. The Laird circled us.

'Two wee sisters,' he said, a tone of awe in his voice. 'Now, girls, I want you to scream as loud and as long as you can. Do it for an old hill farmer, just to bring a bit of pleasure into my life.'

I lifted my head and stared at him, made him focus. 'What are you going to do?' I demanded.

'I'm going to give you want you need, girlie.'

He clicked his fingers and Byron went to the walnut dresser against the wall. He opened the top drawer, removed something, and closed the drawer again. He returned and placed across the Laird's two outstretched palms a leather riding crop with an ornamental tassel.

'I'm going to thrash you, lassie. That round bottom you keep pushing oot is going to be tanned until it's raw.'

I don't know where I got the courage from, but I spat in his face, an enormous mouthful of spittle that drooled down into his red beard. He grinned and chucked me tenderly under the chin. 'That's what I like to see, Byron. A bit of spunk.'

As he spoke, he slid the riding crop through the cheeks of my bottom and up, first between my legs, then Binky's legs, locked against my own. He bowed the crop as if playing a cello, slowly, gently, backwards and forwards, and the breath caught in my throat. I sucked at the air and felt a deep raging shame as the liquids leaked from me, wetting my thighs. He kept sliding the crop back and forth, back and forth, urging little gasps from my throat, the crop so soft and the sawing motion so mesmerising, without thinking, I dragged down on the straps and rolled my pelvis until the wings of my pussy opened.

When the Laird slid the crop out and showed it to Byron, I saw that it was sticky, slicked and shiny with juice. Why were we wet like this? We should have been dry with shame, but my sister's naked body pressed tightly to me was intensely erotic, the prurient gaze of the two men so decadent, my embarrassment was submerged by my arousal.

The Laird ran his finger along the length of the soggy crop, then leaned over me, tickling my bottom

47

playfully with the tassel. 'There, you see, lassie,' he said. 'You're going to enjoy this.'

He was close enough for me to spit again but I didn't. I'd made my point. I kept my dignity. He gave Byron the riding crop and the two men stood back, one on each side of us, our bodies in profile and, although I knew what was about to happen, it still seemed unreal, unbelievable.

'Are you ready, lad?'

'Aye, Hamish, as ready as I'll ever be.'

'Together then.'

There was no pause. Byron brought the crop down on my bottom, a swift, hard slash that cut across my pale skin, and the pain that roared through me was like no pain I had ever felt before, a sting, a burn with acid, a flash of fire. Yet even while I was absorbed by my pain, it was the sound of the Laird's big hand slapping Binky that resounded in my ears. She screamed so loudly, and was so close, it felt as if the scream came from my own lungs.

We rolled with the blow and as I watched the Laird draw back his hand, I knew that behind me, Byron McBride was lifting the riding crop. Down it came again, another flash of lightning, just above the first, cutting deep, searing my skin. Tears were gushing from my eyes. My back was drenched and Binky pressed against me felt as if she were on fire.

The next strike with the crop was lower, making a pattern, the line nearer to my sex. My vagina was shamefully engorged, pouting lasciviously between my thighs. Binky was sobbing against my neck, and I wanted to stroke her hair, comfort her, but our arms were pulled above our heads and the only comfort I could give was to kiss her ear.

The riding crop came down again like a whiplash,

48

the sound of the Laird's big hand spanking Binky's bottom like a clap of thunder that echoed and vibrated around the room. She didn't scream now. She just sobbed, her body trembling. Each new stroke of the riding crop was as painful as the last, but pain changes in character, and when you are familiar with pain, it doesn't seem quite so terrible.

Byron left six strokes on my backside, six red lines of burning agony, the fire in each stripe warming the whole area, up my back to my neck, down my thighs to my feet. My posterior was a furnace, my front was running with the sweat pouring from our two naked bodies and, as I stood there, arms suspended above my head, I felt like a diver at the end of the high-diving board, the void stretched out below me. Something had crossed over in me. I had changed. I had become under the beating a new person, more aware of my senses, more conscious of my own desires.

The Laird bent to inspect Binky's bottom. Now that it had become pitch black outside, the long windows were a wall of mirrors and I could see his reflection, this giant of a man bending over the thin elongated body of my sister, his big fingers pressing tentatively at her bottom as if it were a rare delicate fruit he was about to consume. Byron was inspecting my raw buttocks in the same way, then joined the Laird before they traded positions. Byron flexed his muscles, smiting the air with a test stroke, his eyes meeting mine.

'Now, are you ready, laddie?' the Laird asked.

Byron smiled. 'Aye, ready and willing,' he replied.

He raised the crop, and as he brought it down on Binky's hindquarters, I felt the terrible smack of the Laird's hand on my own. Binky was thrust against

49

me, our dank bodies slippery as fish, like two slimy creatures mysteriously mating. The pleasure and the pain were two threads woven together, making both stronger, more powerful. Before I could catch my breath, the second spank was scolding my flesh, the Laird's huge hand covering the entire surface of my bottom, the sting making the six stripes left by the crop blaze more brightly.

Binky was alternatively sobbing and screaming. I tried not to weep, but the Laird's will was stronger and I couldn't stop myself. It was what he expected, what he wanted. We had done everything he wanted. My body was numb. The fire in my raw bottom was growing calmer and, as the third smack found its mark, I hardly felt it at all. All I could feel was Binky pressed against me, our breasts so hot and wet, our pubic mounts slapping urgently together.

As the fourth smack made contact with my bottom, I didn't cry, and I didn't scream. I found Binky's lips and kissed her. She was surprised at first, but pushed back, sucking at my lips, running her tongue over my teeth, curling the trunk in little twirls down my throat. The two men pumped themselves up, readying themselves for the fifth stroke and, as I saw Byron's arm come down, I felt my stomach clench with contractions.

There was no breath in my body. I was a balloon emptied of gas. I gasped and panted. My mouth had fallen open. I pushed my bottom out to meet the Laird's hand, the muscles of my stomach tightened, and a spasm gripped my pussy. I was desperate with desire, aching with dirty, immodest needs. I could smell my fruity arousal. Or was it Binky's arousal? We were pressed so close I couldn't tell, and the air I breathed was charged on pure unadulterated sex.

50

Take me. Take me. Take me.

The words ran through my head and just thinking them made me feel carnal, defiled, promiscuous. I was eighteen. A virgin still. And I wanted the Laird to take me, take me now while the liquids were hot between my legs. I watched and I waited. Byron raised his arm one last time and I gazed at him, eyes wide, knowing that as the riding crop beat the small drum of Binky's bottom, the Laird's brutish palm would crash like a ringing cymbal across my bruised beaten flesh, the pain mingling with a crude pleasure that had begun to release the creamy juices brewing inside me.

He put more effort into that last grand wallop and I roared like a wounded beast as the Laird's hand tattooed its shape on my bottom. I was shaking, trembling, forcing my pubic bone into Binky's open legs, wailing frenziedly, and trying to reach for something just beyond my grasp. The chastisement was over but unfinished, incomplete.

The Laird was retrieving the chair. Byron was already unbuckling the straps around our ankles. I looked into Binky's eyes. They were glossed with tears and exhilaration. I could smell the piquant aromas wafting from her groin and soft white armpits. It made my head spin. The Laird untied the straps holding our arms.

'Get the carpet for the girlies, what are you waiting for, laddie?' he said, and Byron took the fleece from the fireside and placed it at our feet.

My arms hurt. We had been standing on our toes for so long, we collapsed on the soft pile of the fleece, our slippery soaked bodies coiling together. I reached for Binky's breast, popped the hard mount in my mouth, and bit down on the bud until she squealed.

She did the same to me, and the agony was excruciating, so intense fresh tears stung my eyes. I bit her neck. I licked the entire surface of her ear, and we kissed with some unimaginable yearning. I was grunting, sucking at the air, my body turning instinctively, driven by the pull of the moon, by some alien lust.

As I moved my tongue down between Binky's breasts, she did the same to me. I supped at the tiny cup of her belly button, and down into the sopping pink gash between her legs. Her puffy lips opened and her taste on my tongue was fresh and bittersweet. It was the taste of a girl, my own little sister, something new to me, divine, something to savour. Her clever tongue was exploring the cavern of my sex, pushing in and out, in and out, and I did the same, bathing my face in her smell, gorging on her lush creamy juice, oblivious to everything except Binky's hot oozing pussy.

I wasn't even aware of the two men standing above us, gazing down as if at animals in the zoo, two naked creatures with spanked bottoms slurping at each other's most intimate places. There had been knots inside my tummy ever since we had arrived at the manor house, but now those knots were undoing, smoothing out, caressing me like tiny hands, the feeling of relief spreading like nectar down my throat, through my breasts, my organs, my flaming insides. I gripped Binky's soft thighs in my palms and lapped at her, her thick creamy girl-juice sticky and warm on my face.

Binky's tongue was nursing the glowing nib of my clitoris. I did the same for her. We were *yin* and *yang*, blonde and dark, four emerald eyes. The spasms running through me were running through her. A sprinkle of pre-orgasm fluids soft as raindrops touched my tongue. Binky lifted her bottom up from the fleece and, as she started to come, my own orgasm broke from me like a fizzing firework, a beating pulse of pure energy that reverberated through my body. Never, never, had anything like this happened to me before, and I pressed my sex into Binky until I had emptied every last drop of hot fluid into her throat.

I gasped for air, then ran my tongue through the crack in her bottom, into the dark winking eyelet throbbing restlessly, wetly above, tasting her, wanting every part of her, giving every part of myself to her. Had we always wanted this? We had been together since we were babies, sisters more than step-sisters, but step-sisters nonetheless.

Stray thoughts fluttered through my mind. I felt Binky's little tongue wriggle into my bottom, the pressure reaching my swollen clitoris, and I started to come again, the pitch softer, the energy spent, a feeling like the last glow of the setting sun.

I was sopping and delirious, too exhausted to struggle as the Laird suddenly, unexpectedly lifted me from Binky in his big hands and carried me limply to the table. He placed me at the far end, away from the plates and silverware set for three, and I lay there exhausted.

'There, lassie, there,' he whispered.

Byron pulled at Binky's hand; she came unsteadily to her feet. He placed her opposite me across the width of the table, the expanse of polished walnut so wide between us, and when they again connected the bindings at our wrists, our arms were stretched out, my torso resting on the tabletop in such a way that my spanked bottom was forced up in the air.

'Together, then,' said the Laird.

I watched as Byron pushed his sporran to one side. He tucked the hem of his kilt in the waistband, and from out of the darkness revealed his erect penis. He eased Binky's legs apart, and at the same moment I felt my own legs being opened, the ricochet effect obscene and inexplicably carnal. As Byron slid his cock into Binky, the Laird's cock ran up my thighs until the head rested against the entrance to my vagina. It was huge and, as it pushed patiently through my drenched lips, the walls of my hot pussy were expanding and contracting, pushing back, the giant cock greased by my orgasm sliding slowly, inevitably, like a landslide up inside me, breaking my hymen. I'd finally lost my virginity and it was a little thrill that the Laird didn't even know.

My mouth fell open. I closed my eyes. I was a woman. I was making love, and it was like nothing I'd ever known before because I'd never done it before. My hips bucked and rolled. I pushed back, thrusting out my thrashed bottom, absorbing every inch of the monster. I was impaled, skewered, his big balls like church bells chiming mutely against my thighs, his coarse hair chafing my soft skin as he rammed into me harder and harder, faster and faster.

It grew more intense, more ferocious. He held me in one big hand and with the other started slapping my hips and sides as if urging a race horse to take a high fence, and I took the fence, and the next one, pushing back against the Laird and taking everything he had to give.

He started to groan, his voice emerging from far away, from deep down in the depths of his immense body. He was vanishing inside me, withdrawing almost entirely, then plunging back between the drenched walls of my pussy with great ardent thrusts, my thighs locked, my back arched in a bow, my arms stretched out until both Binky and I rose clean off the

54

table and I felt like a bird flying through the air. I was being split apart like a length of wood, the Laird's cock a sharpened axe, and then he exploded, roaring, pumping into me, and his semen was an endless gush like oil from a well, like lava from an erupting volcano, like a tidal wave, like a soft warm sea.

Byron was mutely wailing in the background. So was Binky. So was I. I was climaxing again, my body hollowed out. The contractions felt as if I were giving birth, and I was, to a new part of myself, to my future. The Laird kept pumping away, but already he was growing softer and already I sensed a woeful absence as his giant penis slipped from me on a torrent of steaming sperm. I could smell it, rich like fresh milk, thick as cream.

Now that it was over, I felt drained and, I had to admit, indecently satisfied. Binky was panting, her eyes staring without seeing, her cheek resting on the tabletop, the ridge of her bottom rising and falling. My ribs were bruised. My breasts hurt. The lips of my pussy were opening and closing, quivering like a sea anemone as the Laird's sperm oozed from me like syrup in bubbling slurps, vulgar and sensuous. The Laird caught his breath. He gave my backside a playful slap.

'You're a good girl, lassie,' he said and, absurdly, I felt proud.

Byron straightened his kilt, then released the bindings at our wrists. We slid apart and I came shakily to my feet. The Laird took me by the arms and stared into my eyes.

'Now, is that better?' he asked seriously, and I bit my lips and nodded.

Binky was still lying across the table, the tips of her toes just touching the floor. Byron was examining her and, when the Laird joined him, I followed, the sap and semen turning cold as it trickled down the insides of my legs.

Binky's swollen vulva was pressed between her thighs and Byron's emissions put a gloss over the inflamed pattern that covered the entire surface of her bottom. I stared and it was hard to turn my head away. I was transfixed, mesmerised. Binky's bottom was fiery red, glowing like the flames in the fire, the six livid stripes from the crop the same African violet as the trim on Binky's pink car: the same colour as the lines running down the Laird's kilt.

My mouth dropped open. My heart skipped. I stared at his kilt, then up into his eyes. He smiled, nodding his head warmly.

'Aye, lassie,' he said. 'You're a clever girl.'

I ran my palm softly over Binky's bottom, and looked back again at the Laird.

'It's my clan: the tartan plaid of the Black Watch.'

Binky had finally caught her breath. I put my arms around her waist as she slipped to her feet. The Laird crossed the room to the piano, grabbed the carved stool, and placed it at the end of the table facing the place settings at the far end.

'You can sit here, lassies, you must be famished,' the Laird said, and I felt grateful for his kindness. He turned to Byron, waving his hand towards the fire. 'Do you think we live in a barn, laddie, all this stuff hanging aboot. Put it away, for heaven's sake, mon.'

I watched without fully taking in what was happening as Byron gathered our damp clothing. My heart was pounding, and only slowly did I become conscious of us sitting there naked, my breasts throbbing, my nipples still erect, Binky holding my hand like a lost girl. My bottom stung, but all my senses were so

56

alive, the sting was more pleasure than pain. The Laird found a piece of cloth in the chest beside the fire. He gazed up at the portrait of the woman, turned momentarily to me, then turned his attention to the shiny wet discharges we'd deposited on the table.

'Here, lassie, look at the mess you've made,' he said, and obediently I polished the puddles of sperm from the table.

I had just finished the task when the door opened. Byron returned pushing an old-fashioned serving trolley, the wheels squeaking. Mrs McTavish carried two bowls and soupspoons; she was sucking at her gums and tutting to herself. She set the bowls down in front of us. Byron placed an enormous tureen in front of the Laird and Mrs McTavish served three plates of stew. She glanced in our direction as she sat opposite Byron. The Laird was between them at the head of the table.

'Come on then, eat if you're going to,' he said.

We ladled soup into our bowls, filling them to the brim. The steam was hot and the smell was delicious. We sat and ate like two little animals. Soup dribbled from my mouth, down my chin and fell, burning my breast. As I wiped the drips away with my hand, the Laird caught my eye and smiled.

'Tell me, Mrs McTavish, have you ever seen finer titties?'

'What are you talking about, mon?'

'Look at them, bright as wee buttons.'

'You're disgusting,' she said, and the Laird grinned as he ate his soup.

His eyes were flicking constantly from the bowl in front of him to the two of us, squeezed together on the stool like ornaments on a shelf. I tried to picture us both in the Laird's eyes, two naked girls like two little animals, our breasts perky, our cheeks and eyes bright, our bodies electric with life, with new sensations.

It was only as I filled my tummy and my heart began to beat more normally that I became aware that our clothes had been taken away. I gazed back along the table at the Laird.

He nodded.

'Aye, lassie,' he said. 'You can bed down in the woodshed. If you piddle in the straw like wee animals you cannae expect a bed to sleep in.'

'What about our clothes?'

'You won't be needing those. Not tonight.'

Binky looked at me for an explanation but there wasn't one. I looked back at the Laird and felt a warm dribble leak on his piano stool.

3

Primal Urge

I wasn't a girl any more. I was a woman. I had lost
my virginity. Did I look different? Did I smell
different? When I sashayed by in the street could men
sense that I had gone through some subtle transform-
ation? Subtle? Perhaps *total* is the right word. I think
I may have grown an inch taller! And as for the little
monkeys, they were just so *out there!*

I stared for hours at my face in the mirror. I looked
at my reflection in every shop window. I was even
studying my eyes in the shiny side of the butter knife
that day in the restaurant when we had lunch with
Mummy.

'Milly, you didn't used to be quite so vain,' she
remarked as she caught my eye.

'She's discovered the inner Camilla,' said Binky;
my little sister had a way with words.

Although I flushed, Mummy was rather too preoc-
cupied gazing at her own reflection in the mirror on
the wall facing our table to take much notice of me.
Someone once said the faults we condemn in others
we excuse in ourselves and I'm sure he must have had
my mother in mind when he said it.

The purpose of this lunch at the Jewel Royale was
for mama to tell us that she had to go away on

'urgent business' for the weekend and we mustn't invite the Chelsea riffraff back to the house for a party, which had happened before when we were younger and found ourselves deserted during school holidays by our parents. They were *so* spoiled.

'I know what you children are like,' she said.

As the waiter fussed around with bread rolls his eyes fell first on Binky's cleavage and then on my own. We didn't lunch together very often these days and dressed to kill when we did. Kill each other, that is. Mummy's eyes followed the waiter's eyes and if I could read her mind I am certain she was thinking just how much her daughters were like her, less children, more rivals. My step-mother was used to being the most beautiful woman in every room she entered and the expression on her face at that moment reminded me of the Wicked Queen when she inquired as to who was the fairest of them all and the mirror, inanimate thing that it is, gave the wrong reply.

'Do you really need quite so much bust on display, Binky?' she asked, and turned to me. 'And you, Milly.'

Binky glanced down at her breasts welling over the white lace trim of a bra pushing over the scooped neck of a sleeveless black dress. 'It's summer, Honey,' Binky said, and lit a cigarette with a golden tip.

Mummy had honey-coloured dark blonde hair and encouraged us to call her Honey which, except for reasons of irony, we never did. She sighed and as the air escaped from her scarlet lips it stirred the coils of blue smoke rising from Binky's cigarette. Mummy was one of those women who needed to be admired. She had always traded on her beauty and, at the unforgiving age of 39, I'm sure, like the Wicked

Queen's disillusionment with the looking glass, what mother saw in her own reflection was the cruel hand of gravity dragging her down. Her beauty was waning, fading, the freshness of youth was slipping, sliding, running away, and it occurred to me with my limited experience that what mattered to her most was her beauty. I don't think she was really interested in sex. What she wanted was to be desired.

A year ago during the last summer hols when I had gone one clammy hot day to look for something in the greenhouse, I found Mummy perched on the potting table with her knickers around the heel of a red Manolo Blahnik shoe, her legs spread and the Polish gardener with his tongue inserted in her like a key in a lock. Her back was arched and her head was thrown back, but what shocked me was that her pubic hair had been shorn like some porn star and the dome of her mount was as smooth and white as a porcelain vase.

My mother shaves her pubes! It was hard to believe, to comprehend, to appreciate.

I watched through the crack in the door, my hand over my mouth, my cheeks burning red with shame and embarrassment. I had still been a virgin then, of course, and was both repelled and drawn to this bizarre scene, this movie clip: my mother with her skirt rolled up around her waist, the gardener slurping over her wet parts like a dog lapping from a puddle, Mummy puffing away like a steam engine straining on a steep hill as she thrust her shiny mount into the gardener's mouth.

The gardener was about twenty, a sullen boy who spoke English without recourse to vowels. Neither Binky nor I had found him remotely fit with his stained teeth and overgrown Adam's apple, but he must have had a robust and energetic tongue. I watched it, long and pink and healthy as it moved in and out of Mother like the feeler of some enormous insect stabbing at ants or dipping for sap in the hollow of a tree. They kept going for ages, sighing and slurping, their bodies moving mechanically like a primitive machine. I was frozen like a statue in the park, my eyes glued to this terrible, extraordinary thing I was seeing.

The boy sank to his knees and pushed Mummy's thighs wider apart, his sweaty hands leaving muddy streaks on her ivory skin. Her bottom lifted from the potting table and when the red shoe clinging to her toes fell and clattered with a bang to the floor I involuntarily let out the breath I'd been holding in an anxious gasp. I'm quite certain Mummy heard me, but she was too far gone by this time and starting shrieking. It was the first time I'd heard a grown woman having an orgasm and it sounded like she was having a baby.

I crept away and never mentioned this shameful episode to my mother, although it came often into my mind. It was hard to believe I had seen her pristine white bottom on the dirty potting table surface, her £200-a-pair silk knickers hooked in the heel of her shoe, her pubic mount perfectly shaved and gaping over a thirsting mouth. I still find it hard to believe that she truly wanted to have sex with the gardener with the hot sun blazing through the greenhouse roof. What Mummy craved was the gardener, a boy of twenty, wanting to have sex with her. For Mother, being a great beauty was her *raison d'être*, an end in itself, and I suppose as she turned forty she would require a revolving door of East European handymen to confirm this axiom.

I glanced at Mummy across the table. Behind her was a tall graceful palm in a black ceramic pot, its fronds gently shadowing the side of her face. The waiter was still looming over Binky, peering through the cigarette smoke at the pale moons of her girlish breasts like an inquisitor analysing evidence of witchcraft. He was dressed as a bishop in a long white cassock and stood on a white square like a chameleon in camouflage. The Jewel Royale had a chequered floor and the staff were attired as chessmen, bishops, knights, the Maître D, an old queen, dressed as a king. Binky was enjoying the attention and as I studied her studying the menu I realised that my sister was just like Mummy. She wanted every man she met to fancy the pants off her but, in spite of our adventures on the Isle of Skye, she really wanted to keep her pants on.

I was different.

I was . . . ?

A complete tart, according to Binky.

A 'good girl' the Laird had said, as I had stood there absurdly proud with a tanned bottom and his sperm oozing from me.

Since my return from Scotland there had been a certain spring in my step, a twinkle in my eye, a vague new confidence. I had been a tourist. Now I had taken the journey. I felt serene, contented, in what the nuns at school would have called a state of grace. The world was my oyster. I was still waiting to hear whether I had got a place at Cambridge but, if I didn't, I would take this small failure philosophically. I would have a gap year and go and stay with Daddy so I could work on my French and ruin his love life.

It was so much easier being a grown-up. I had come to see that virginity wasn't so much a precious commodity, a prize a Geisha sells in order to pay for her education, but a terrible burden, a responsibility thrust on women, unasked for and unwanted, and one we are challenged to guard at risk of becoming outcasts of the clan. It was all so mediaeval. Virginity is like having a faint shadowy moustache, sort of sexy on certain Spanish women, but better not there at all. Virginity is for girls in storybooks, secret adventures and pony club.

I was a woman now.

I liked saying this to myself. I am a woman. I am the figurehead on my own ship. The master of my own destiny and desires. I am going to do *everything*.

They say you always remember your first and I know I certainly will! How could anyone forget the Laird of the Black Watch? When Hamish popped into my mind, as he often did, I had this terrible fear that I would never again meet anyone quite like him. That the first time would be the best time and my life would become an eternal quest in search of the next great orgasm. The next thorough spanking!

Spanking. It was still an absolute mystery to me. Two men had inveigled me into taking off my clothes and three men had spanked me until my bottom was a roaring fire and my pussy leaked liquid ecstasy. Spanking and orgasm. It was a surreal combination. What did this mean? What did it say about me? About men? Were all men obsessed by bottoms? Did they all want to put you over their knee and tan your buttocks? We had learned in Classics at school about Aristotle and he said the way to happiness is to be your 'authentic natural self'. It seems to me that it was perfectly natural that men would want to spank girls and, *ipso facto*, girls must all secretly dream of being spanked. They did and they just never got the opportunity to realise it. I was lucky.

When the girls had talked late at night in the dorms about their *first time*, no one ever mentioned spanking, corporal punishment, discipline, humiliation, sado-masochism, role play, words that whirled around my head like little birds on currents of air, flying for the chaste pleasure of flying. I had left school to take a journey with my sister. But the real journey I was taking without maps, without a route, with no sense of a destination. Confucius, or somebody else who was just as clever, said a journey of one thousand miles starts with the first step, and I thought a journey of one thousand orgasms would obviously start in the Isle of Skye. I was a wanderer in the dreamy dark realms of the senses and if being an explorer is my destiny, I suppose the best thing to do is pursue it with all the energy and conviction in my soul. Or in my knickers, anyway.

There, you see, I have become philosophical. I am the butterfly easing my wings from the prison of the chrysalis. I am a girl growing into the woman. When I lie in the bath running my palms over my nipples, they are a woman's hands enjoying the springy erectness of a woman's nipples. When I spread cream over my thighs, the dewy dampness around my natal cleft is the arousal of a woman who knows what it is to be a woman. I had enjoyed doing all the things that girls do, all that studying and gym and bitching and thinking about boys, but I had arrived back from Scotland with an intuition that the next bit of life is going to be much more fun.

When I was growing up, I had always thought of virginity as something sacred, mystical, a soap bubble, perfect and impermanent. When you reach the age of fourteen, you saunter along the high street on Saturday, the only time we were allowed out of the convent, and you are aware that men are analysing you, ogling you, sizing you up. When they catch your eye, you understand that what they are looking for is some outward revelation that the treasured little membrane stretched invisibly *up there* is still *up there*, and what they desire more than anything in the world, and would give ten years inside the walls of the chrysalis to bring that desire to fruition, is to go crashing through that cherished and ephemeral maidenhead.

It's heady stuff. Your little tits are exploding from your chest like anarchist bombs, your bum is growing pert and round, your hip bones are jutting out like scaffolding around the wall of a castle, a barricade you raise up to protect the prize while, conversely, and at the same time, you long for an errant knight to slash away your clothes and pierce the heart of your being with his comely sword. Like the butterfly stretching its wings and taking to the air for the first time, you are conscious quite suddenly of your girl power and you keep that power until your virginity has gone.

But then what happens? Do you become powerless? Or do you acquire a different sort of power?

I still wasn't entirely sure. Most girls lose their virginity at fifteen or sixteen in the summer holidays with the best friend of their brother in the garden, or on the living room sofa while parents are out at the theatre or at one of those irksome dinner parties my parents attend with dreary regularity and inflict on our own dining room when Daddy's home from his important work in Brussels.

That was the usual scenario with girls at Saint Sebastian's and those girls would appear in September with the braces removed from their teeth and a look of inner knowledge in their glossy eyes. They gazed dreamily out of the window, tossing their hair like startled ponies when the nuns in the classroom raised their voices to demand attention. I always had mixed feelings towards those girls, envy and superiority, and tried to imagine what it is like *doing it*, something, of course, you can't imagine, as baby birds can't imagine what it is to fly until they are shoved from the nest.

They say that girls at state schools are losing their virginities at thirteen and fourteen and half of them are pregnant before they even do their GCSEs. We loved reading about the underclass chavs in the tabloids left behind by the maintenance staff and gasped with wonder at the wayward morals the journalists described. *New Council Flat Given To 14 Year Old Girl With Twins!* Who's Going To Pay? Disgusting!!! Bring Back The Birch!!!

Yes please.

But it's true, though. I have seen with my own eyes girls pushing buggies who surely remember having been pushed in buggies just a few years before. From childhood to motherhood without passing GO. Mummy blames television and the fashion industry, television for its overt sex (and that's something she does know about!) and the fashion industry for dressing little girls still sucking dummies as starlets and models. Instead of ribbons and bows now it's chains and leather. By the time they take the dummies out of their mouths they are ready for the first cigarette and, as we were warned at Old Basher's, one thing leads to another.

If you were caught creeping into another girl's bed in the dorm for a kiss and a cuddle the nuns would turn a blind eye, unless they were perverts, but God help the girl caught puffing on a fag; one hundred laps of the top field, letters home to parents, an interview with Father McMurphy, the parish priest, with his slobbering lips and strange eyes: blue eyes that seemed to hover in a red sunset, the result, I imagine, of too much communion wine. Still, he didn't smoke, and the girls caught smoking redeemed themselves returning from their marathon wet with sweat and chanting a few Hail Mary's while Father McMurphy stroked their skinny knees.

Now here's something that I have been thinking about for a long time: back in Jesus's day, cigarettes hadn't been invented. There is absolutely no reference to tobacco in the Bible. So who decided smoking was a sin?

Anyway, I was not one of those girls with the new haircut and a twinkle in the 4th form and can only attribute this to the fact that I have no brothers, no male cousins and the Polish gardener clearly prefers older women. Perhaps being far from home he misses his mother?

During the long drought in my sexual growth, I had developed a romantic, 18th-century attitude to virginity. I was Emily Brontë drooling over Heathcliff; a Capulet chained to a Montague; Isolde burning with desire for Tristan; Honey Bunny with big eyes for Pumpkin in *Pulp Fiction*. Virginity was the pot of gold at the end of the rainbow, the Holy Grail, the answer to the riddle in *The Da Vinci Code*, something you wanted to share with the man you loved and, like most girls who managed to save their little pearl in the oyster until they were eighteen, I had grandiose dreams of sharing it with a knight in shining armour, some dashing Sir Lancelot who would whisk me away on his big white stallion to the world of make-believe. Instead I got naked, spanked and spangled by Hamish the Laird of the Black Watch and that was going to be a hard act to follow.

Since arriving back from Scotland, Binky and I had seen hardly anything of each other. The experience had woken me like Snow White from a dream, but Binky didn't want to talk about what had happened and was spending all her time with the mechanic boyfriend with dirty nails who had sold her the VW beetle with violet trim. I glanced at her across the table in the Jewel Royale. 'How's your boyfriend?' I asked, breaking the silence, and she shook her mop of yellow curls as if to shake away a migraine.

'Ready for the sack,' she said.

Mummy took a cigarette from Binky's packet, slipped it between her lips, sucked the startled flame from the lighter and looked like Lauren Bacall as she blew smoke over her shoulder.

'Now that you're back from wherever you've been, don't you think you should find some work?' she said.

'Work?' said Binky.

'I don't think you know the meaning of the word.'

'Like, you do, Honey?'

Mummy sighed with feigned exasperation, but except for being beautiful, our mother had never done anything in her life; horse riding, swimming from yachts in the Mediterranean, skiing at Cortina d'Ampezzo, tantric yoga, manicures, pedicures, colonic irrigation, sun beds, spreading her legs for the Polish gardener. But work? She had grown up with her two sisters and a brother in the country with stables and tutors in a big old house that was falling down around their ears and had been taken over by the National Trust when Pompa died to pay his debts.

'It won't kill you, either of you,' Mummy said without conviction, and when Binky lit another cigarette I was tempted to take up smoking it looked so cool.

'Actually, I've got an interview,' I said.

'Really?' said Binky. 'Where?'

'I'm not telling you.'

'You sound like a politician.'

'I'll tell you *when* I get the job.'

'When!'

'You're such a pessimist,' I said.

'A pessimist, Milly, is just a well-informed optimist,' said Binky, and turned to Mummy to add, 'I'm learning how to repair cars.'

'How lovely.'

Binky glanced up at the white bishop and added: 'A Chicken Cæsar Salad, please.'

Binky was good at changing the subject.

Like my sister, I had no intention of doing something brain deadening like stacking supermarket shelves or waiting tables and was rather pleased sitting in the restaurant that Mummy was about to bolt for the weekend. This little lunch wasn't so much about our finding jobs and not smashing up the house than the fact that if Daddy happened to call we shouldn't mention that she was away. Not that we would. Binky and I had met Daddy's 'friend'. She was about two years older than me, a Parisian *fashionista* with gamine hair, a little turned-up nose and the figure of a boy, which was Daddy's taste and, if truth be known, mine too.

'Milly?' said Mummy.

'Oh, just a green salad, I think,' I said.

'She's trying to lose five pounds of ugly fat,' said Binky with a sigh.

That wasn't true. Not exactly. But Binky was as thin as a blade of grass and if I wallowed in chocolate biscuits a little lip of fat would appear on my tummy and I'd have to eat more chocolate biscuits because I was depressed.

The waiter glanced at Mummy.

'Salad, please, and a glass of white wine.'

'Me, too,' said Binky.

'It's cheaper to get a bottle,' the bishop gravely intoned and we all nodded in agreement.

We pushed our food around our plates, picked at the bread that came with olive oil and a dish of garlicky olives and, what with the second bottle of wine and the Irish cream coffee, we were all a bit squiffy by the time Mummy called for the bill.

I tripped off downstairs to the loo and was sitting there peeing like mad and leafing through my address book in search of inspiration when the card given to me by Jean-Luc Cartier slipped out from between the pages and dropped into the crotch of my knickers. It was like an invitation to adventure. I had told Binky I had an interview to go to, now I would turn my white lie into the truth, the whole truth and nothing but the truth.

As I wiped my pussy, my clitoris started screaming for attention. I gave her a good hard pinch to keep her quiet. My knickers were round my knees and I really have no idea why, but I ran them down my legs, slipped them off and pushed them into the bottom of my bag. I was wearing an immodestly short skirt and it wouldn't take very much for *everything* to be on show.

I climbed back up the stairs wiggling, my bottom enjoying the sense of freedom, and it struck me that

71

bottoms really do want to be out there, free and exposed. Your bottom is a part of you, but special and separate, the gateway to your soul. It's almost religious. Or was that the white wine doing the talking? Anyway, Mummy was wearing a white suit and standing on a white square in the restaurant foyer. Binky was in a black dress unsuitable for daytime on the black square beside her, swaying slightly from side to side. For some reason, an uncontrollable wave of happiness passed through me as I joined them. Mummy seemed happy to have Binky drive her home, even drunk, but I was almost on top of Leicester Square and left them to it.

I tripped along Piccadilly and it was nice to feel the air around my thighs and between my legs. A man washing windows gave me a hard stare and I was tempted to pull up my little skirt a couple more inches and give him a flash. I didn't but probably should have done. It's important if you have urges to act on them, I think. People hold back much too much. If everyone would just give in to their fantasies I'm sure the world would be a much better place.

An open-top car slowed beside me in the traffic and the driver said 'Great legs,' as I trotted by.

I ignored him, of course.

I wound my way through the narrow streets of Soho, pressed the buzzer on the only door I knew and ran two at a time up the narrow staircase.

Now this is very weird. Jean-Luc Cartier didn't seem at all surprised to see me; quite pleased, I must say, but I had the distinct impression that he was almost expecting me. He was the first man to have persuaded me to take off my clothes, the first man to have spanked my bottom, the first man who had rolled back the stone from the mouth of the cave and

72

released all the pent-up power of my first orgasm. A virgin orgasm, and as rare as ambergris, I had come to realise. It had been special to me, a wake-up call, but there had no doubt been zillions of girls who had offered up their backside to his hand and mine was just one of a gallery of mooning bottoms belonging to girls who had scurried in looking for work. *Please, Monsieur, spank my bottom and give me a job!*

'You're back,' he said, and beckoned with his finger.

I followed Mr Cartier down the spiral staircase. There was a girl about my age sitting at the computer and looking intense as she scrolled through photos of actresses, doing it so quickly it looked like a speeded-up film. My head was swimming with those lunchtime drinks and my mind was spinning as I watched the smiling faces come and go as if on a roulette wheel and when the wheel stopped the lucky actress would be a star. Perhaps all of life is like that. Just chance. One fluky thing happens and it leads to the next, success is just a spin of the wheel.

I wondered whatever happened to Virginia Ward, my old school chum who had beaten both me and Binky to the job, but now wasn't the time to ask.

The girl swung round on her swivel chair and her full lips broke into a smile that made me wonder if she knew something I didn't know. She was wearing a tight-waisted blouse with a hint of tanned flesh that peeped provocatively over the top button and pulsed faintly with her breath.

'This is Tara Scott-Wallace,' said Mr Cartier. 'Tara, this is . . .'

He'd forgotten my name.

'Milly,' I said. 'Camilla Petacci.'

Tara smiled and turned back to the computer where the spinning wheel had come to a stop at a well-known TV star who had just walked out of one of the soaps. She had made her point, confessed her 'substance abuse' to the tabloids, and now she was smiling seductively from the screen looking for a job.

Like me.

Jean-Luc Cartier looked me up and down, at my white mini and kitten heels, at the T-shirt two sizes too small that I'd stolen from Binky's room. My step-sister was right: I was a complete tart.

While the old seducer was studying me, I gave him a good once-over at the same time. Jean-Luc was much younger than I'd first thought. Everyone over thirty looked positively ancient. Daddy was about 45 or something and I suppose Jean-Luc was a few years younger with a lush sweep of hair going faintly silver at the temples, an open shirt with a few sexy coils of dark hair peeking over the buttons and beautifully creased trousers.

'I won't be a minute,' he said.

He turned away and looked over the girl's shoulder at the screen.

The office was just as I remembered it, the same blinking blue lights on the computers, the same low table where I had discovered there was more to life than A levels. I had laid back on that table with my breasts exposed and lifted my bottom from the glass with barely a moment's hesitation when Mr Cartier had pulled at my knicker elastic.

I'd been dying to take my knickers off. I don't know why. Being naked under the gaze of a stranger is a special sensation that's so hard to describe I think girls should just take a deep breath, clench their teeth and do it. It's liberating. It's fun – illicit pleasure and that's the best. It's life on the high wire and everything after is just waiting to get back up there and strip off again. There is no greater pleasure than being naked. Well, except being spanked, of course.

It occurred to me as the water fountain gurgled rudely in the corner that had Jean-Luc Cartier not initiated me into the mysteries of discipline I would never have been ready for the Laird and his knicker-sniffing companion Byron McBride. *Sooo embarrassing!*

I had come away from the encounter feeling eager to learn more about myself and my unknown desires. And I had come to the conclusion in the last few days, during those long afternoons in the bath, that Binky was more the orgy type. I don't think she was really cut out for S&M, although she is nearly a year younger than me and has plenty of time to learn its odd delights.

I giggled. I was in a silly mood. I was becoming decidedly wet thinking about our trip to Scotland and that wasn't what I was doing in Jean-Luc Cartier's office. I was on a mission.

Mr Cartier glanced at his watch and gave Tara her instructions. 'Choose six from this file and print out the details for me,' he said, and glanced at his watch again. 'Bring them up to me in about ten minutes.'

Her green eyes sparkled as she turned in her seat. 'Oui, Monsieur,' she said.

I followed *Monsieur* back upstairs to another office where he sat in a big leather chair. I sat opposite him in a smaller chair set back a few feet from the desk, the glass top reflecting the lights sunk into the ceiling. I was crossing and uncrossing my legs like Sharon Stone in *Basic Instinct*, and he leaned forward with his elbows on the desk, staring up my skirt.

'To what do I owe this pleasure?' he asked, and I opened my legs a little wider to applaud his double entendre.

'Are you casting any films?'

'You want to be an actress now?'

'Nooo.'

He smiled. 'What then?'

'You didn't answer my question.'

'I am casting films and television shows every day. That is what I do.'

'Then there must be some work for me, as an extra, or a runner. Isn't that what you call those people who run around on a film set?'

'Do you have any experience?'

'I was in just about every play at school ever. You should have seen my Lady Macbeth.'

He smiled. '*Très bien*,' he said. 'Now, what is it, you want to be in a film crew or you want to see yourself in a movie?'

I pulled at my bottom lip while I thought about it. What did I want? What did I really want? After taking off my clothes for Monsieur Cartier and, rather more reluctantly, for the Laird of the Black Watch, what I really wanted was to be exposed, to be on show. To be seen. I was, at eighteen, at my very best. I was Aphrodite, the daughter of Zeus, born from the swell of the sea, mysterious and mythological, the goddess of love, beauty and sexual rapture. Binky had come along less than a year after me. She had always been the baby. She had always got all the attention. Now, it was my turn.

'Either,' I said after a long silence.

'You seem to be filling out rather nicely,' he remarked.

He was gazing at the skimpy T-shirt stretched across my breasts. As I looked up into his eyes I had a strong feeling he was going to ask me to take it off, you know, just for old time's sake, and of course that's exactly what he did.

'Slip it off, Milly, let's have a look.'

'I beg your pardon?'

I was pretending to play hard to get. Well, I mean, you have to. It's part of the fun.

'You do want me to represent you?'

'Oh, yes.'

'I haven't seen you in performance. I can't sell the goods if I haven't had a feel in the pig bag.'

'A pig in a poke I think you mean.'

'A pig in a poke! You English are really very funny.'

'Thank you.'

'Don't mention it.'

He clapped his palms softly together then swept his hand through his hair as if to enjoy its lushness. 'Come along now, off, off. I am getting old waiting.'

'That's not why I'm here . . .'

'Of course you are,' he said.

'I'm *not*.' I giggled and the white wine turned red as it burnt into my cheeks.

'Milly!'

'Oh, all right, then.'

I stopped crossing my legs and crossed my arms to pull my T-shirt over my head in one smooth movement. I was wearing a white cotton bra and the little monkeys were jouncing freely with each beat of my heart. So wanton.

'No under-padding?'

'Sorry?'

'In the brassière?'

Such a funny word brassière, but so sexy when it's said in French.

'Absolutely not.'

'I don't believe you.'

'What?'

'Let's not, how do you say: beat about the bush!'

'Very funny.'

He smiled. I think Jean-Luc Cartier really liked me. I liked him, anyway. He was fun. I unclasped the hook at the front of the bra and peeled back the two cups like I was opening two halves of a coconut. What is it about Jean-Luc Cartier that makes me want to do this? Those velvety brown eyes, that velvety soft voice like a mantra, like a chant . . . take it off, take them off, take everything off. My pussy was sticky and my breasts swelled out above my ribcage like slowly inflating balloons. It felt good to be sitting there in nothing but my white mini and high heels.

Mr Cartier stood to get a proper look and sat on the corner of the desk looking down at my pert nipples and willing me to fondle them. I tried fairly hard not to. This was a business meeting, wasn't it? But, as Oscar said, I can resist anything except temptation, and my itchy fingers were soon rolling the plump pink buds of my nipples between the pads of my fingers, squeezing and pinching until a delectable flush ran up over my neck and cheeks. The damp feeling between my legs was beginning to haemorrhage and warm juice smelling of the girls' dorm at Saint Sebastian's was coating my thighs.

I was dying to take off my skirt. Why? Where did these impulses come from? It was all new to me, new and fun and exciting. I didn't know where these feelings came from or where they might lead me, but I knew it was best to follow your instincts, wherever they led you. I adored being a girl. A woman. I wanted to be ogled and fondled. On show. I wanted to be spanked until my bottom sang, spanked and licked and *buggered*. Before I had set off with Binky for Scotland I hadn't been exactly sure what buggered even meant. Now? Now, just thinking about it made the breath catch in my throat. I had three openings and when they were filled I felt fulfilled. I remember Sister Theresa saying she felt complete when she was on her knees and I suddenly understood what she meant.

A million questions were flying about inside my head and while I was searching for answers it came as a relief when Mr Cartier took my hand and eased me to my feet. Without giving it a thought, let alone a second thought, I pulled down the zip at the back of my skirt and let it fall to the floor.

There, naked at last!

'You're not wearing any knickers.'

'No.'

'C'est colossal! Excellent!'

'It was just . . .'

'A lady never explains.'

Jean-Luc Cartier ran his finger like a saw between my legs and when he took his finger away it was shiny and slicked with my sticky discharge. We stood there for ages like a *tableau vivant*, frozen in that solitary moment, both looking at that glistening wet finger. He took a deep breath through his nose like a wine connoisseur and then popped the finger in his mouth.

'Delicious,' he said.

I had come to ask him for a job and here we were, five minutes into the meeting, and I was starkers, wet dribbles leaking from my pussy, my poor little breasts tingling like electric fuses.

'You are so wet, Milly.'

'Am I?'

'You mean you didn't realise?' he said.

He put his finger back in my pussy, ran it in and out, in and out, then popped it back into his mouth again. He had a perplexed look about his features, two lines crossing his brow. He looked me up and down for a long time, he stroked my shoulder and hair, then stared into my eyes.

'It's gone, hasn't it, Milly?' he asked.

'What?'

'Come on. You know.'

I felt the colour rise once more over my cheeks.

'Was it . . . glorious.'

I nodded.

'Good. You are just beginning. You have a special gift,' he said. 'You will be marvellous.'

I felt my heart thumping, my breasts taut and quivering. 'I don't know what you mean,' I said.

'Well, you'll learn soon enough, come on now, close your eyes and open your legs.'

I did as I was told. I'm always a good girl and like to do as I am told. He stroked my bush like you would stroke a cat; it was lush, the hair soft and silky, a shade darker than the hair on my head. My pussy parted like water when a swimmer takes the plunge. He slid two fingers up inside me and remained still for several seconds. He then worked his fingers back and forth, in and out of the ooze. I pushed against his hand, rocking slightly, and a luscious feeling of pure debauchery swept through me. I could have stood there all day, rocking on my white heels, his fingers like the head of a drill pumping out a steady stream of oily gunk that trickled into my pubes and rose smelling like the stable into the air. I arched my back, I rose on my heels and dropped down again, screwing his finger into me, his eyes on my eyes and like a cat I shamelessly purred from the attention.

There was a tap on the door that I didn't so much

hear as feel, like someone tickling your nose when you're asleep.

'Come in, Tara,' he called.

I awoke from my somnambulant state when I heard Tara's voice.

'Sorry . . .'

'Come in, I said.'

I opened my eyes and Tara was peeking through a crack in the door, just as I had peeked into the greenhouse at Mummy and the Polish gardener that summer's day a year ago.

'Come, come, come,' he added and I wasn't sure if he was talking to me or Tara.

She remained outside. 'What shall I do next?' she asked.

'Do you remember our little talk about discipline?'

'Yes.'

'Then, when I say come in, what I mean is come in.'

He carried on running his fingers up into me as Tara entered clutching an assortment of photographs and papers. She closed the door softly behind her. I wondered what she must be thinking. I was totally ashamed standing there with Mr Cartier's finger stuck in me like a doctor doing an internal and modestly lifted my hands to cover my breasts.

Ashamed? Yes, and fascinated, too. It was like being in a strange play and it was exciting making it all up as we went along.

'I've got the . . .'

Tara had lowered her eyes and wasn't sure what to say. I just carried on tightening my thighs and bottom, my pussy muscles sucking at Jean-Luc's hand, my neck turning from pink to crimson.

'Photographs?' he asked.

81

'Yes,' she murmured.

'Put them on the desk, then.'

I was standing against the side of the desk. Tara placed the photographs on the other side and, as she did so, he bent my back forwards like he was closing the lid of a suitcase and I rested my arms on the glass top. I automatically pushed my bottom out and spread my legs to get more comfortable.

'What is the first rule of acting, Tara?' he asked the girl.

'I'm not . . .'

'Timing,' he said before she had finished speaking. 'What's the second rule?'

'I'm . . .'

'Discipline,' he said, and with that he brought his hand down on my bum with an enormous thwack that brought tears to my eyes and an aromatic spray of misty sap from the lips of my pussy.

'How was that, Miss Petacci?'

'OK.'

'That's not very good, now is it?'

Thwack.

Down it came again. I could feel a warm glow seep over my posterior like a slowly moving tide of agony and ecstasy, those conjoined twins of desire, those extremes of all pleasure and sensation. What was a girl like me doing with my bare bottom being spanked by a virtual stranger with a complete stranger watching? It was a mystery, but I felt oddly complete. This was my role, my mission, my purpose. You are just beginning, he had said, but beginning what? Would I, aged 39 like my step-mama, have the gardener's tongue up my pussy?

The questions sprinted through my mind like a little mouse running on a treadmill. It made no sense.

They were questions without answers. I hadn't come to the office intending to take off my clothes, but it had taken so little for it to happen. I had taken off my knickers in the lavs at the Jewel Royale for heaven's sake. I had been getting dressed for the show, or undressed to be on show. I knew there was a good chance that I was going to get another spanking and another spanking was what I really, really wanted.

Was spanking an obsession? An addiction? I had gone straight from the authoritarian regime of the nuns at convent school to the disciplinarian antics of Jean-Luc Cartier, from puberty to depravity! It was still all new to me. There was so much I didn't understand. I'd lost my virginity to Hamish, the Laird of the Black Watch, and he didn't even know it. He thought I was some naughty girl up from London looking for trouble and that wasn't really me at all.

And again.

Smack No 3. His big hand was signing the plump cheeks of my bottom with a pattern of palm leaves. I was all wet sticking to the glass top of the desk. There was sweat on my back. My hair was hanging down over the far side of the desk, my toes were stretched and my pretty little bottom was just where it wanted to be: the centre of attention.

'Now, how does that feel?'

'Better,' I murmured.

'You see, Tara,' he added, addressing his assistant. 'This girl says she needs to find a job but what she really needs is to be spanked. Do you understand?'

'Yes, I think so.'

'She wants to work in the movies and what she doesn't yet appreciate is that to do so she needs ... what does she need?'

83

'Discipline.'

'*Voilà*,' he said, and he hit me again, much harder, and a sizzling jolt of electricity ran up my spine and down my thighs.

'Is this your first time, Tara?' he asked.

'I'm not sure what you mean,' she said timidly.

'Come, come, come. Don't be shy. You are among friends here. Is this the first time you've seen a girl spanked?'

'Well, I've never seen a girl being spanked before. Not exactly . . .'

Ah! I wondered. There is more to Tara Scott-Wallace than meets the eye.

'And?'

He spanked me again while she thought about it.

'It's quite nice.'

'Mmm,' he said thoughtfully. Then he addressed me again. 'How many is that?'

'Five, Monsieur Cartier.'

Thwack.

'That's six,' he said and took a deep breath. 'Tara, come here. Stand here, where I am, that's right. *Très bien.*'

I heard them shuffling about behind me. I felt a soft girlie hand resting on the small of my back.

'Here,' I heard him say.

I had a very firm notion that what he had placed into her hand was the wooden ruler I'd seen earlier on the desk. I had thought at the time how out of place it had been in that high-tech office, but now it all made perfect sense as a sharp snap from the ruler cut a path across the soft flesh Jean-Luc had carefully tanned.

'Come. Come. Put some feeling into it.'

Tara beat my bottom once more with the ruler and it really hurt. She was beginning to enjoy herself. No

3 came down just above the last one and the sound ricocheted off the walls with an abrupt retort that brought a little round of applause from Mr Cartier.

'That's better, Tara. You're getting warmed up. Take your blouse off now.'

'Sorry?'

'Your blouse. Take it off.'

'But . . .'

'Remember what I said about discipline? Come along, now, we don't want to keep Milly waiting, do we?'

Jean-Luc Cartier was a genius. It was that accent, soft as silk, yet so commanding. Men on the battle-field would charge enemy cannon if he gave the order and girls like me wanted to obey, wanted to please, wanted to be disciplined. You spend your whole life waiting for something special to happen, and when something special happens you have to recognise it, know that it's happening and go with it, wherever it takes you. The first time I stepped into that office and Jean-Luc Cartier told me to take off my school blouse it was like a call to shed my old skin and become myself, shed the constraints of the chrysalis and become the butterfly. Inside us all is a desire to change, to be all we can be, in my case to be free and outrageous. A sort of animal instinct, a primal urge, the deepest expression of our humanity. I had wanted to take off my clothes for him and I had a feeling that Tara wanted to as well. We were the same age. I was exploring my potential and she surely was doing just the same.

'Monsieur Cartier . . .' Her voice trailed off.

'Yes, Tara.'

'I've never . . .'

'Then now is as good a time as any.'

85

There was a long pause. She had more resolve than me. But not that much.

'It's not something I want to do,' she finally said.

'Are you feeling all hot and sticky?' he asked her.

'Yes . . .'

'Do you like spanking Milly?'

'Yes . . .'

'And you don't want to take your top off?'

'Not really.'

'And why is that exactly?'

'I don't know.'

'You can't dismiss something you've never tried, Tara.'

'Yes, but . . .'

'No buts. It's warm in here. Take off your blouse.'

She stamped her foot. 'I won't,' she said and of course that means I will.

'Come along now, let's get on with it.'

'But Monsieur Cartier . . .'

'TAKE OFF YOUR BLOUSE.'

His voice had a different tone, stricter, more demanding. The air was charged with a sense of waiting, of anticipation. I could smell pheromones and fear. There was a brief silence. Then I heard a button snap open and a smile crossed my lips. Once that first button is released you are on a shiny silver chute. There is nowhere to go but down, down to the next button. You have made a decision to expose yourself and, once you start, you want to go sliding down, faster and faster, your head in a topsy-turvy of unfamiliar desires and new emotions. I heard the ruffle of material, the cotton blouse slipping from her skinny arms. She was on the slippery slide and I knew where she was going even if she didn't.

'And that, if you don't mind.'

Again the pause.

The same thing had happened to me. Jean-Luc had created a special set of conditions and taking off your top seemed logical, normal, natural; it is a reasonable thing to ask, a reasonable thing to accept. You could justify it in your mind. But exposing your breasts was a step into the unknown. I knew as the pause extended that Tara had every intention of removing her bra but needed to imagine for a few moments that this wasn't her intention at all. It is a mind game, a game you play to lose.

I stood up straight and nursed my poor bum with my palms. Tara avoided looking at me. She was looking at the floor and her voice was just a whisper.

'I can't see why,' she said.

'I think you can, Tara,' he said, and he raised his voice, just slightly. 'Now, don't let me have to ask you again.'

The pause was shorter than before.

She ran her arms up her back and the elastic made a little ping as the clasp parted. She took the straps down one at a time. Did she know this looked really cool, really sexy? She held the bra clutched like a white dove between her palms.

'There,' he then said. 'Excellent. Bring it here, give it to me. Now, Tara, tell me honestly, doesn't that feel better?'

'Yes, Monsieur Cartier.'

He smiled at me. 'What do you think, Milly?' he asked.

'Pardon?' I said.

'She's quite delectable, no?'

I nodded. 'Yes, yes she is.'

We were standing close. I could hear the electric lights humming, hear the faint beat of my breath. My

87

breasts were fizzing and I had a terrible urge to ignite Tara's nipples with my own. I bent forwards and, the moment our flesh touched, all her fears and reservations evaporated. Her arms went round me like the coils of an octopus and her lips were immediately jammed against my own, her tongue probing my mouth like a little fish. I slid my hand down her jeans and the moment my finger found its way through the ring of her bottom all the air left her body in one great exhalation and I thought for a moment she was going to collapse.

She was panting for breath as if she had just done those 100 laps around the top field. She whipped down the zip on her jeans and I thought how silly it was for a girl to wear jeans, they are so awkward, so hard to get off, and you just never know when you might want to get naked in a hurry.

I held her shoulders as she pulled down her jeans and knickers in one movement. She was sopping wet and I pushed my fingers straight up inside her cleft, drawn as if by some force outside my control. We were doing what nature intended us to do, two teenaged girls with healthy bodies, ripe and juicy and eager to be touched. We kissed and fingered each other until Tara came in a long rumbling orgasm and I had a feeling that it was just what she needed.

'Over the desk now, Tara,' Mr Cartier said. 'Over the desk.'

His voice was soft, so soft, almost a whisper, a chant, a spell. He glanced at me and the faint nod of his head, the shrug of his shoulders, made it clear that it was my turn to spank Tara and it was something I had never done before. I had never done it but now, as she did as she was told and bent over the desk, I understood the attraction.

Her bottom peered up at me, round, tight, quite perfect, the slit down the middle like the entrance to some wonderful place, an unexplored continent. And inside me was a feeling that this pert white bottom needed the caress of my hand, it needed to be applauded with a good hard slap and automatically, almost unconsciously, I brought my palm down upon Tara's bum as hard as I possibly could, so hard it stung my own hand, so hard the sound of the slap almost burst my eardrums. I had concentrated on the little cheek furthest from me and left a perfect white imprint outlined in baby pink where the blood rushed protectively to the surface.

'Yeooi,' she screamed.

'Good girl, Tara, don't move,' said Jean-Luc.

I brought my hand down again on the other cheek and the feeling of Tara's soft flesh as it gave way under my palm sent a feeling through my whole body like jumping on a trampoline. The higher you jump the more the trampoline springs you back into the air; the higher you go the harder you come down again. There were two white prints now, a perfect match, a perfect pattern which I slowly obliterated as I spanked her again and again, harder and faster, and she screamed in pain and then she screamed with pleasure as another orgasm burst like an erupting geyser from her drenched pussy. Her bottom was bright red like the flames of a fire with blue tinges around the edge and although it lacked the surreal colouring of the tartan plaid of the Black Watch, I had signed my first abstract and couldn't help being pleased with the result.

After coming so copiously Tara seemed drained. She pulled herself up from the desk and clung to me, pressing her lips to mine, and I soothed the ache in her raw bottom, stroking and gently squeezing as she rammed her pubic bone into my wet crotch. She slipped as if exhausted to her knees, took my thighs in her two hands and her warm tongue wriggled up inside me, nursing the sharp little nub of my clitoris and draining the last liquids still stored in my body.

When we were both satiated we seemed to awake as if from a dream. I wasn't sure where I was. My head was still slowly spinning from the lunchtime wine and I had the absurd notion that I wanted to rush home and show Mummy my spanked bottom. Tara held on to my thighs and a big contented smile of pleasure played over her lips.

I'd spanked my first girl and it was great.

'Happy?' Jean-Luc asked, and we both nodded. 'Was it fun?' he continued and we both nodded more vigorously.

'Divine,' I said. I loved that word.

'Good. Stay there, and don't move.'

Monsieur Cartier unbuttoned his shirt and slipped it over the back of his leather chair. He removed his shoes and socks, folded his creased trousers and when he removed his boxers his cock sprang out and bobbed up and down like a little boy arriving at a party. It was pink and sweet, not huge like Hamish but playful and it was fun when he stepped forward and slipped it casually into my waiting palm.

Tara was still on her knees and he placed his hand gently on top of her head to keep her in that position. I started to roll the soft outer skin up and down the shaft of his cock.

'Slowly,' he whispered. 'Always slowly.'

I felt like a conductor directing a piece of music, Bach, obviously, slowly, slowly, the notes climbing and building, and it was such a joy to be there in that office on a warm summer's day, two spanked girls and a naked man with wisps of silver in the brown mat of hair on his chest. Slowly, slowly, up and down, up and down, the skin growing warmer, more solid, more alive with each stroke, up and down, up and down.

'That's very good, Milly. I think I might have just the right thing for you.'

'Really?'

'A short film,' he said thoughtfully. 'It's a bit flat at the moment. You might be able to give it a bit of oo la la.'

'Oo la la?'

'Mmm,' he said. 'Mmmmm.'

I was so excited I started going faster, my hand moving like a piston, up and down, squeezing as hard as I could, squeezing, releasing the squeeze, and squeezing again. I'd never done this before but it's really quite easy, like swimming or playing the piano, you don't need to think, it's all instinct, all feeling, all so sensual and wanton with Tara on her knees gazing up like a worshipper in a temple. Up and down. Up and down.

Jean-Luc was caressing the back of her head and she wriggled forward. She smiled in such a way that her pink lips opened a tiny distance from the swollen head of his cock. Like me, she didn't need to be told what to do. These things you know without having to be told. Everything that's natural comes naturally, I thought, and this was probably quite profound and I would try to remember to write it down.

I kept a firm grip on Jean-Luc's cock. I could feel it pulsing like something alive in my palm. Tara Scott-Wallace kept her mouth open and her eyes open and suddenly, quite unexpectedly, a great stream of frothy sperm jetted over her face and into her mouth, over her hair and into her eyes and she leaned forward to take the head of his cock deep into her throat to suck out the last juicy warm drop. Jean-Luc kept his hand on the back of her head and rocked backwards and forwards, in and out, the whole length of his cock vanishing down her throat, and at the same time I nursed his balls in my hand, squeezing gently. He ran his hand down my back, between my cheeks and a finger found its way into my wet bottom.

'A short film?' I asked.

'Mmm,' he replied.

He kept Tara's mouth running up and down the length of his cock, his fist gripping a clump of her hair. Her eyes were closed, her head was thrown back and there was a look of deep satisfaction on her finely etched features. I thought he was probably spent by now but Tara made such a good job sucking him off, when he finally slipped his cock from her mouth it was like taking a baguette from an oven, hot, crusty, stiff and hard, totally gorgeous and ready to be devoured. He still had his finger in my bum and when he pulled it out with a saucy little pop I didn't need to ask what was going to happen next. I bent over the glass-topped desk, spread my legs and made myself comfortable.

'You have an incredible mouth, Tara. *C'est colossal*. Here, here.'

Tara was still on her knees, still praying in the temple, and now she leaned forward to pay her respects to the holy orifice. Her little tongue all wet with Jean-Luc's semen snaked up my bottom and after the spanking it took the heat from my fiery back passage. She parted my bottom, got a good grip on my cheeks and pushed her tongue in and out, in and

92

out. It was the reverse of taking Jean-Luc's cock down her throat, the same but the other way round, and everything was a pattern, our bodies shaped to enter each other and become one.

'*C'est colossal.*'

Jean-Luc eased Tara aside and she clung on to my leg as his cock pressed at the fragile ring of my bottom. The sphincter, that timid little muscle at the lip of the anus, is designed for pushing outwards, but by careful manoeuvring, with patience and practice, the sphincter reverses and will entice a lubricated cock deep into the sensitive tissue where a million nerve endings wait to be ignited. It is pure ecstasy. Pure fulfilment. You are flooded with feelings of joy and contentment. Our maidenly chalice, the Holy Grail itself some say, is a *yonic* V designed to be pierced by the *phallic* Λ, the male blade, it's all there in the Tarot cards, all so geometric, so symbolic, so precise, the back door to the castle keep holding its own special delights and triumphs. Girls want to get their clothes off, get down to some good healthy sex. They really, really do. Girls will take it any way they can get it, but given the chance, given the opportunity, given the education, girls will take it in the bottom and write poetry in the moonlight.

Men may think of anal sex as some masculine rite of passage but what they don't understand, what most girls don't understand, is that it is a girl's rite of passage, too. It is the pinnacle, the main course, the high point of human relations. When a warm cock slides in and out of your backside you are totally in touch with your inner self. If we have a soul, that's where we will find it, I'm sure.

I pushed up on my kitten heels to try to take more of him, all of him. I wanted Jean-Luc Cartier to vanish inside me. My bottom was an underground cavern with untold secrets, unknown places. His cock was swelling against buried treasure and, like a finger stroking the trigger on a gun, his cock hit the right combination and the key to the treasure trove turned in the lock. He exploded in another orgasm and I felt my insides turn to liquid.

'Agh. Agh. Agh. Agh!'

'Agh. Agh. Agh. Agh!'

My back arched. My knees were shaking. I was coming, I was coming. I was reaching down somewhere deep, somewhere unknown. If before I had been base metal, at that moment I transformed into molten gold. I have been designed to be buggered. Spanked first, of course, but then thoroughly and deliciously sodomised. It's important that a girl knows these things and with this in mind I would set off the following day to meet the director of *Cheats* with new confidence.

4

Cheats

Part I

This is the story.

RICKY SIMMONS is forty, a copywriter who dreams of being an author or a scriptwriter. Something romantic. He's growing plump around the belly and feels that life is passing him by. What he really wants is to find a young girl for a night of wild sex so he can feel young again. Ricky lives with Amanda.

AMANDA is an actress, also forty, slender and gamine, feminine in a boyish sort of way. Amanda is not famous, but gets regular parts on TV and in the theatre. Amanda and Ricky have been together for more than ten years and things are dull, dull, dull.

Amanda has a three-day job in Paris appearing in a TV commercial where she plays the English wife of a Frenchman who must learn from her French neighbour that the way to keep her husband frisky over the cooking pots is to buy the correct brand of floor cleaner; an old idea with a French twist.

After dropping Amanda at the Eurostar terminal, Ricky drives to Greens, a Soho wine bar, and hang-out for starlets and media people. He's drinking a beer when a stunning GIRL appears at an interior doorway looking agitated.

By coincidence, the Girl is also named Amanda.

THE GIRL *glances at the clock behind the bar, then down at her watch. She stares directly and angrily at* RICKY SIMMONS.

I was reading the script in a clammy office thick with the exotic blend of scent wafting from eight fretful girls looking agitated and suicidal as they mumbled their lines to themselves. They stopped and glanced up with passing pleasure as a girl with hennaed streaks in her hair left the casting suite with gritted teeth and a tear in her eye. A second later Dudley, the cameraman, poked his head out and grinned like an executioner.

'Next,' he called, and closed the door again.

As I came to my feet, the weepy girl slid from the building and the rest of the hopefuls studied me with frosty smiles and daggers in their eyes. The film was a good chance for an actress to show her range and they all wanted it so badly the tension was chipping away their self-confidence. I had no long-term plans to make movies, Cambridge was calling, but I do like to accomplish my goals and I had every intention of playing Young Amanda.

From what I had gathered listening to the girls chatting in the office, this was a regular ordeal, a test of stamina as much as talent. They had all been to drama school and since leaving had spent weeks and months visiting photographers for head shots which they duly sent to theatrical agents before setting out on the eternal pilgrimage to auditions for parts on stage, in short films, feature films, TV soaps and corporate videos, the cattle market they called it, and it occurred to me that the way to get film roles, the way to get what you want, is to go about it in any way except the normal way, that you are more likely to get it right if you get it wrong.

Does that make sense?

Like wearing blue shoes with a green dress: blue and green should never be seen. So, get it wrong and you get noticed. Better than going to drama school, get your bottom tanned by a casting agent. Arrive early. Arrive late. But don't get there on time. Be contrary. But be open. Jean-Luc Cartier had opened my mind as well as spanked my bottom. I didn't know these things at school and I'm sure if I had done I would have been the head girl.

We had learned in Art History that when Salvador Dali went to New York with his paintings for the first time he had the baker on board ship bake a twenty-foot loaf of bread with a hat-sized hole in the centre. When the boat docked, Dali walked down the gangplank wearing the largest baguette in the world and everyone said he was a genius. He had a weird sex life, but that's another story. Dali knew how to get noticed. The eight girls waiting in that stuffy room with their breasts on display could have been gingerbread girls all stamped out from the same cookie cutter, a dance troupe, not the star; they were all at least twenty, a few of them must have been edging towards twenty-five, and all had the same desperate darting eyes as the teary girl with hennaed hair.

I was the odd one out, an unknown quantity, too young for the part, at least as far as the other girls were concerned, and I wasn't looking sexy. Quite the reverse. I was wearing a high-collared maroon velvet suit with trousers tight at the knees and black patent shoes more suitable for a funeral or an interview at the library. I also happened to be carrying my script in a pink folder with the name *Agence Jean-Luc Cartier* printed on the front.

'Good luck,' one of the girls said.

'Oh, thank you,' I replied.

Sister Theresa at school had a habit of rapping her knuckles on the desk and saying: Knock and the door shall be opened.

I knocked.

I waited.

And Dudley opened the door.

David Trevellick, the writer/director, came to his feet and smiled.

'Camilla?'

'Milly.'

'David.'

'How do you do?'

I put out my hand and glanced away as he shook it. He smiled. I didn't. He bobbed about for a couple of seconds looking bashful and then we both sat. While Dudley was adjusting the camera focus and Daniel, the soundman, fiddled about with the dials on a machine with blinking green lights, David explained the story, which I didn't really think needed to be explained. I had picked up the script from Monsieur Cartier's office and learned it by heart. It was pretty clever, with some neat twists and quite sexy, although not quite sexy enough. A ten-minute short film gives a director the opportunity to show his range, his skills, his vision, and *Cheats* still lacked, as Jean-Luc had said, a certain oo la la!

Well-known actors had been cast in the roles of Ricky and Older Amanda, lending their time for the noble but poorly paid cause of the short film. David was looking for a 'fresh young face' for the part of

Young Amanda – the Girl. He had already done castings with 'dozens' of contenders but only I had come recommended by a famous casting agent.

'He said you have a special gift,' he added, and I turned positively pink with embarrassment.

'Did he say what?' I asked.

He shrugged. 'No, he said I'd find out soon enough,' he replied.

Oh, yes, I forgot to mention, David was about 23 and totally dishy. He read all the parts, except mine, of course. The sessions were filmed for David to show the producer – 'Hermann Mann from the Film Council,' he said in awe, not that it meant a thing to me.

His brow fluted.

'OK. Rain beats against the bar windows. The Girl enters from an interior door wearing a pink satin jacket and a low-cut white dress. Cool and sexy. Take One. The Bar.'

> THE GIRL *glances at the clock behind the bar, then down at her watch. She stares directly and angrily at* RICKY SIMMONS.

I stared into David's eyes and kept staring until he felt uncomfortable. I took a breath through my nose and hissed loudly through my teeth.

GIRL: Do you have the time?

RICKY: It's a . . . just gone ten.

GIRL: I've been in the other bar for an hour. I wasn't aware there were two.

> THE GIRL *drops her bag on the bar and lights a cigarette.*

GIRL: Shit!

> *She stares again at Ricky and shakes her head.*

RICKY: Do you want a drink, now you're here?

She rolls her eyes below arched eyebrows. She's heard it all before.

GIRL: No.

She glances again at her watch. Flicks her ash.

GIRL: Red wine.

RICKY *orders a bottle of Rioja. The* BARMAN *fills two glasses; he sporadically refills them.* RICKY *leans forward to tap the rim of the* GIRL'S *glass.*

RICKY: Ricky Simmons.

GIRL: Amanda . . .

RICKY: . . . Amanda?

GIRL *(now*

AMANDA): Is it so weird?

RICKY: No, no, no. Not at all.

AMANDA: Amanda Marshall.

RICKY *recomposes himself. He's a man of the world.*

RICKY: Let me guess, you read the weather for Sky News?

AMANDA: I'm an actress.

FLASHBACK:

OLDER AMANDA *is looking with nostalgia around the living room in a London flat. There is a framed photograph of herself and* RICKY. *Also a publicity shot of a long-legged girl running through the streets clutching a bottle with the heading: You Get A Good Rum For Your Money!*

RICKY *is out in the street, double-parked, looking agitated. He runs up the path and screams from the front door.*

RICKY: Amanda, for heaven's sake, you're going to miss your train.

RICKY *realises the girl is speaking.*

AMANDA: And you?

100

RICKY: I just had a brain wave and switched
            from copywriting to PR. (*beat*) You
            had a date?

AMANDA: A date? Yes. With a producer. *She's*
            normally reliable. We did some erotica
            stuff.

RICKY: Really!

AMANDA: For the dyke market.

   RICKY *watches the* GIRL *cross and recross her long
   legs.*

   A MAN *and a tough* WOMAN *scantily dressed
   bondage style are leaving. They are* SPIKE NEAL,
   the screenwriter, and IMOGEN BLACK, *nominated
   best director at Cannes! They pause as they pass*
   RICKY.

SPIKE: Early start tomorrow.

RICKY: You're working Sunday?

IMOGEN: You don't get ahead by getting behind.

   The door closes. RICKY *refills the glasses.*

AMANDA: That's Imogen Black?

RICKY: In the flesh.

AMANDA: I'd love to work with her . . .

RICKY: Maybe you will. (*beat*) What have I
            seen you in? Or is that gauche to ask?

AMANDA: Don't they say it's not what you've
            done but what you're doing? I've just
            finished a costume piece for the Broken
            Biscuit Company, you know, all
            smouldering glances and heaving
            bosoms . . . *it's not as if I'm built for it.*

   RICKY *gazes at her ample breasts.*

AMANDA: Apart from some stage and the lesbo
            films, that's about it. (*beat*) And you?

RICKY: I've done a few ads. I wrote *You Get A
            Good Rum For Your Money.*

101

AMANDA: You did that? (*beat*) It was totally
           brilliant!
RICKY: I'm just setting up on my own. I need a
           couple of good accounts. Industry. Or
           politics.
AMANDA: Politics?
RICKY: PR is the administration and
           management of dissemination,
           distortion and lies. Politics is the big lie.
           It's where the money is.
AMANDA: Right. I don't want to spend my life
           with my boobs hanging out for the
           BBC. (*beat*) You know Imogen Black?
RICKY: I do her PR.

AMANDA *gives her body a little shake. The bar is
empting. The famous writer* CHRISTIAN THOMAS
passes.

CHRISTIAN: Night.
RICKY: Have a good one.
AMANDA: (*whispering*) That's Christian Thomas
           . . .
RICKY: That's him.
AMANDA: He looks older in real life.
RICKY: He's even older in real life.

AMANDA *moves so close to* RICKY *he can't help but
stare down at her cleavage. The mood has grown
more erotic.*

AMANDA: Did you read his last book?
RICKY: Yeah, it was good, but . . .
AMANDA: Not that good.

They laugh. The BARMAN *pours the last of the
wine.* AMANDA *speaks flippantly.*

AMANDA: I suppose you'd better go home. Back
           to . . . whoever.
RICKY: And if there isn't a . . . whoever?

AMANDA: Isn't there?

RICKY: We broke up. We had a few good years . . .

AMANDA: I'm sorry.

RICKY: It's one of those things. She's in LA now. (*beat*) She's doing Kevin Spacey's new film.

AMANDA *gives another involuntary shiver and stares adoringly into* RICKY'S *eyes. There's a long beat. The clock behind the bar strikes eleven.*

RICKY: Let's go.

AMANDA *hesitates for the briefest moment, then slides from the bar stool.*

It was quite well written. The Girl was super sexy with her talk of lesbian films and Ricky Simmons was confidently seductive with his name-dropping and sly humour: *She's doing Kevin Spacey's new film. He's even older in real life.*

We recorded the second reading, then I was put on the spot having to read that scene from *Magnolia* where Julianne Moore is buying drugs in the pharmacy and goes *ape*. That was it. Someone would call me. When I left the office the hopefuls with their little tits and short skirts glared at me.

'How was it?' one of them asked.

'A nightmare,' I replied. 'I was awful. I'll never get the part.'

It's nice to make people happy, I thought, and went straight to Jean-Luc's office. He admired my suit, I kept my clothes on, and came away with David's mobile phone number. Although I believe in discipline, it's fun, there comes a time when a girl has to take the initiative. I called David later that day. I told him I thought his script was *totally brilliant* and was thrilled *my agent* had sent me to the audition.

'I have some ideas for the last scene, something . . . sexy,' I said.

'Sounds interesting.'

'Are you free?' I asked.

'I have a meeting with Hermann . . .'

'The man from the Film Council?'

'Yes,' he said breathlessly. 'Then I have to look at today's auditions . . . you were really good, by the way.'

'Do you do that at home?'

'Yeah . . .'

'Shall I pop round? About nine, or something?'

'. . . er, yeah, OK, why not?'

'Divine,' I said. 'Where are you?'

There was a pause as he realised he'd been manipulated but he gave me the address.

I dropped the clothes I was wearing among the clothes already carpeting the floor and ran into the shower. I washed my hair, perfumed my parts and showed great resolve not playing naughty games with the shampoo bottle. I was ambling naked around the bedroom taking big sighs and considering the sorry state of my wardrobe when Binky appeared in a matelot shirt and white bell bottoms. Her mouth dropped open and she stared with big eyes.

'Milly, now what?' she said.

'What?'

She pointed at my bottom. 'That?'

I shrugged and rolled my shoulders. It was barely pink now. The tanning only lasts a few days and the hot shower had brought the colour back.

'I've got a job,' I told her.

'Where? At Rent-a-Bum? Bums are Us?'

'Bums are Arse,' I replied and was rewarded with a rare Binky smile.

She came up and turned me around so she could have a closer look. She pressed a finger into one of my round cheeks and the pink fled away and left a white patch. 'You like all that stuff, don't you?' she said.

'I think all girls do if you give them the chance.'

She shook her head. 'You've always been weird,' she said. She bent and planted kisses on each of my cheeks, which was sweet. 'But why?' she then asked.

'Why what?'

'Why do you like being spanked?'

'It's hard to explain. It's like asking a bird why it likes singing. Or why fish like to swim.'

'Fish just swim because that's what they do. It's natural.'

'So's this,' I said, and spanked her bottom with the flat of my hand.

'Ouch. You bitch . . .'

'Come on, Binky, that didn't hurt.'

'Yes it did.'

'Binky . . .'

'It did. Sort of.'

We stared at each other. Binky's green eyes were shiny with that look girls have before a party or a pop concert, excitement and expectation. The sun was going down, bathing the room through the tall windows in a pastel glow. Everything was feminine, sensuous, seductive, the pink walls, my pink bottom, Binky all coy and smouldering like Brigitte Bardot in *Et Dieu Créa la Femme*, Daddy's favourite film. Binky's eyes flickered about my features, my shoulders, my breasts, wantonly erect and throbbing. In the orange light on a summer's day, anything might happen . . .

I spoke softly but forcefully.

'Binky, take your top off.'

'What?'

'Take your top off.'

'Milly, are you crazy?'

'Roberta, take your top off. Don't argue, just do it.'

She looked back at me as if I had lost my mind. She was dressed and I was stark naked but, oddly, being naked gave me a sense of authority, of empowerment. I stared into her eyes and kept staring until she blinked and her chin dropped. Her delicate features wore a puzzled look, but then slowly she pulled her blue and white sailor's shirt over her head and dropped it on the bed.

'Satisfied?' she demanded.

'No, Binky, that too.'

She was wearing a sexy little white bra that held her breasts like cocoons, like fresh fruit ripened from sunbathing in the garden. She went topless, just to upset the Polish gardener, or Mummy, should I say, who thought of the boy as her own personal property.

'Milly . . .'

'Now!'

'God, you are such a bitch,' she said but, as she spoke, she unclasped her bra, held it out at arm's length by her fingertips and dropped it on top of her matelot shirt.

My sister had perfect breasts, two precise domes with small hard nipples the colour of pink champagne, the same colour as her engorged lips that she was nervously biting. I'm sure the Polish gardener must have found them totally gorgeous. Binky certainly did. Mummy, too, aesthetically, of course. I stared at her breasts and she impulsively started to stroke the enflamed tips with the pads of her fingers. I heard the breath catch in her throat. The top button on her bell bottoms was undone. I waggled my finger up and down and she responded instinctively, her long fingers snapping open the rest of the buttons one by one. She wriggled her hips and slid the white material down her long creamy legs.

She stood defiantly before me. I had used Jean-Luc's power, Jean-Luc's technique. She was in my hands. I was certain I could do anything and there was something I was dying to do. I often pictured in my mind that day when Monsieur Cartier pulled at my knicker elastic and stared greedily down at my pubes. And that's what I did. I pulled at the thin band of white elastic, just gently, and gazed over Binky's flat stomach at the nest of copper-coloured hair like filigree on a statue. We both looked up at the same time and, at that moment, without being told, Binky pulled at the sides of her knickers and eased them over her round bottom.

Binky likes to be admired and I admired her. I turned her round like an antique, like a sculpture, running my palms over her precise curves. She writhed and wriggled, rolling her shoulders, pushing out her breasts.

'You're beautiful,' I said.

'Do you really mean that?'

'Yes, Binky, I do,' I said as I reached for the leather belt discarded on the floor.

She watched my movements like a kitten, frightened but fascinated. The thing with beauty is that it expects *everything*, to be admired and chastised, adored and abused, worshipped and whipped. I slipped the tongue of the belt through the buckle, made a loop and tightened it over her wrist. Binky stared into my eyes. This was a new game, new territory. She didn't know where it might lead her, and where it led her was across the length of my bed. I tied the end of the belt to the bedpost, reached for the long Gucci scarf thrown over the key to the wardrobe and secured her other arm to the bed.

She turned, looking up at me. 'What are you going to do?' she asked.

I kissed her bottom. 'I'm just making you comfy,' I replied.

Binky likes to be in control. She didn't necessarily want to be tied to my bed but she had found me pretty and perfumed and completely starkers and if there is one word that describes my sister that word is competitive: the eye is drawn to nudity; go into a room with a thousand women and one of them is naked and every gaze will be on her, young or old, shapely or shapeless, she will be the centre of attention. Binky's motto since the age of three has been anything you can do I can do better. Just like me that first time in Jean-Luc's office, Binky had not taken off her clothes because she had been told to. She had taken them off because that was what she wanted to do.

In the wardrobe I found two more scarves which I tied around each of her ankles. Each ankle I tied to the end of the bed. Binky was prone, stretched like a starfish, her white bottom peering up at me like the moon, pert and seductive, the lips of her vulva pushed through her thighs. I ran my hands between her legs. She was sticky and sopping wet.

'You didn't answer me,' Binky said.

'What am I going to do? I'm going to thrash you, lassie. That round bottom you keep pushing oot is going to be tanned until it's raw.'

I spoke with a Scottish accent, naturally, and Binky yelped as I brought my hand down across the pouting cheeks of her bottom.

'Right, that's enough. Untie me you bitch . . .'

Smack. Down came my hand again.

'I'll kill you, Camilla . . .'

Smack. She was twisting and turning, but I had done a good job binding her to the bedposts and it didn't matter how much she turned, I found the target. I smacked her again and again, and her bottom turned pink and red and crimson. She sobbed and she spat and then she pushed herself up on to her knees, stretching the scarves to offer up her little bottom to be more thoroughly and efficiently disciplined. I counted, six, seven, eight, nine, and she pushed her bottom higher and I smacked her harder.

Her pussy had opened like an oyster shell between her legs and the puffy lips were slicked and shiny, oily jism leaking down the inside of her thighs. This was what Binky needed, what she secretly craved. And ten, I counted. My palm was sore, but I had a job to do and wouldn't stop until I'd finished. Her cries of pain had become sighs of pleasure. Eleven. 'Agh, agh, agh.' She was biting the bedclothes, tossing her golden curls, wriggling like a fish, her back arched. Twelve. 'Yes, yes,' she screamed, and I tasted the oyster on my tongue as I slipped into her wet pouting cleft.

'Milly, Milly, Milly, Milly . . .' She took a deep breath. 'Yes, yes, yes, yes, yes.'

She collapsed back across the bed and as I licked the sting from her red bottom she purred contentedly. I felt inordinately proud. I had spanked Tara Scott-Wallace in Jean-Luc's office, but Tara I'm sure knew more about discipline than she was letting on, and I was pleased to have taken my little sister in hand and led her into the magic kingdom. She wouldn't have to waste her time with that awful car mechanic with the petroly breath and dirty nails. She could go out into the world and really find herself.

I untied her. She reached down with her hands and nursed her bottom in her palms. Her hair was stuck to her cheeks and her eyes were glowing like coals.

'Your turn,' she said.

'No time, darling, I told you, I've got a job. Almost.'

From my exertions I was covered in perspiration and had to step back into the shower. When I came out, Binky was curled in a ball on the bed. She watched sleepily as I spread my clothes all over the bedroom. One thing we had learned from Mummy and that is that you should dress for the occasion and with that in mind I tried one thing after another. Sometimes Binky nodded with approval. Sometimes she shook her head and pointed her thumb down like Cæsar. I really didn't have a thing to wear and only after rejecting everything did I remember that in the seduction scene in *Cheats* Amanda wears a red kimono over red underwear.

I found just the thing in Mother's closet. She has more clothes than the designer floor at Harrod's and more shoes than Imelda Marcos. Binky and I were getting into the habit of stealing her things and she never even noticed. I dressed in front of the mirror and, turning to my sister, I did Mummy's Lauren Bacall look over one shoulder.

'We did some erotica stuff. For the dyke market.'

'Wow!'

I glanced at the clock. It was the right time to leave but I thought it was important to be late, keep David waiting, let him think I wasn't coming. Binky was rolling around on the bed, bending into all sorts of funny shapes trying to get a good look at her bottom. It was bright red, as red as the kimono, and I could feel the heat from across the room.

'I'm going to tell Mummy what you did,' she said, playing at being a little girl.

'If you do, I shall spank you again.'

'Then I'm definitely going to tell her.'

She grinned and then stretched out her arms as she clambered up on her knees. We kissed and although I was sure I would in my life kiss hundreds of girls, I was sure none would ever quite feel the same as Binky. It was like kissing yourself, erotic and auto-erotic at the same time, her lips like my lips, a mirror image, a perfect fit, plump and delectable. Now she had found the Bardot look she was going to be unstoppable. She ran her hand up my leg.

'It's not the time but the hour,' I said and skipped from the room as the sun slipped over the rooftops.

Part II

I was tempted to get a taxi, but walked all the way to Gloucester Road. I had to ask directions at the Indian newsagents and a man with a turban and big shiny teeth directed me to the adjoining street with its Victorian lampposts and red brick buildings. I climbed three steps to a blue door with the number 36 in brass numerals. I hit the bell beside David's name and he buzzed me into a darkened hallway of black and white tiles that reminded me of the floor at the Jewel Royale.

He was standing in the doorway of the ground-floor flat and ushered me into his living room, a typical boy's flat with screens and keyboards on every

111

surface, cream walls and a fire of false logs that made the room so hot I had an immediate desire to take all my clothes off. The fire was in front of a long black leather sofa – the casting couch, I thought, and it occurred to me that David Trevellick had probably brought loads of girls to his flat and now it was my chance I really had to make the most of it. Girls want to get into erotic situations, but it's up to them to make sure they do.

'Red wine?' he asked.

'You read my mind.'

'I wrote the script.'

I laughed. He had been studying the day's castings on his laptop and one of the girls I'd left in the outer office was frozen with her mouth open. As he poured the wine the computer went into stand-by and the girl faded to black. I sat on the corner of the sofa with the split in the kimono displaying a peachy slice of thigh and we got straight down to business. Script business, that is.

In the story, Ricky and Young Amanda leave Greens and it takes ages to find a taxi. In that time, they get soaked to the skin. Amanda suggests going back to his place, but Ricky tells her he has the builders in (a lie, of course, as the viewer will know from the flashback with Older Amanda staring around the living room). Young Amanda agrees to take Ricky back to her flat. They are now in the back of a minicab.

I glanced down and read the instructions in the script.

AMANDA *shivers.* RICKY *puts his arm around her and she cuddles into his side. Then his mobile phone rings. He doesn't answer.*

AMANDA: It might be important.
RICKY: Nothing's that important.
   RICKY *is squeezing his thighs together. He clearly needs to use the loo. He speaks to the Asian driver.*
RICKY: Can't you go any faster?
DRIVER: Sorry, filthy night.
AMANDA: (*whispering*) Hope so.

This, I thought, was where the script started to go off course. Amanda is a shrewd and sensual woman. She would not make it so obvious that she wants to be seduced. I thought it cleverer if after the Driver says: Sorry, filthy night, it cuts to Ricky trying to control his elation, as well as his bladder: here is this gorgeous 20-year-old girl (well, 18) and she's just gagging for it.

The taxi arrives at a big old house where Amanda shares an apartment. Her mates are away, of course. They go in, and Ricky rushes to the loo. While he's peeing, his mobile phone rings again and as he takes the machine from his pocket, he drops it down the lavatory pan. This slightly comical turn is to make Ricky endearing, David explained, even though he is about to betray Older Amanda and sleep with the young girl.

'Brilliant,' I said.

Ricky fishes the phone out of the loo and it is Older Amanda telling him she had a safe trip to Paris and the production company has put her up in a swish hotel. He speaks softly and hurriedly and, after drying his phone on Young Amanda's towel, he turns the mobile off and goes to join her.

   AMANDA *has changed into a short red kimono.*
David nodded appreciatively as I read the line. I was in character.

AMANDA: You're not in a hurry?

RICKY: Not at all.

She gives RICKY a bottle of champagne which he opens. She takes the bottle to fill two glasses – the glasses have been in the refrigerator and he doesn't notice the faint trace of white powder in the bottom of one of them. He raises his glass.

RICKY: To . . . to what? To beauty.

AMANDA: Beauty?

RICKY: To you.

AMANDA: To me? Or to beauty?

RICKY: To you both.

AMANDA: Beauty's not always what it seems.

RICKY: But it's always beautiful. You're beautiful.

AMANDA: I suppose the casting directors must think the same. I've been gang raped, beaten up, locked up and cut up by a dominatrix in a leather mask. But there's a moral backlash, don't you think?

RICKY: I guess . . .

AMANDA: Not in the going to church sense. But in the important things. The only thing we have is relationships. That's what matters to me. If I had a boyfriend and he cheated on me, I'd pay him back. I mean *really* pay him back.

RICKY: Hell hath no fury.

AMANDA: You bet.

RICKY: *(raises glass)* To relationships.

AMANDA: Relationships. *(beat)* I won't be a minute.

AMANDA refills the glasses.

FLASHBACK:

114

RICKY *waves to* OLDER AMANDA *as she enters the train terminal at Victoria.*

RICKY: Bye, Amanda.

OLDER

AMANDA: Goodbye, Ricky.

RICKY *watches* YOUNG AMANDA *sashay across the room and out the door.*

His head spins. It's the wine, the champagne, the hour. *I mean really pay him back.* What did she mean by that? Little bitch! He swallows hard. Drains his glass. He should go home. Text Amanda. *His* Amanda. But the girl is a gift, fresh as the dew, all legs and breasts, pink pouting lips, neat little ankles in pointy red shoes. She is Eve and he is the first man, Adam at the gate of temptation. He just wants to carve another notch on the gun. Put another deposit in the memory banks. Just be there. It has nothing to do with sex, betrayal, lust. He wants to be himself. Be the old Ricky Simmons vanishing under the weight of time and disappointment. And what does that bitch Imogen Black mean by *You don't get ahead by getting behind?* He's not getting behind. He's getting there. He's making it. *You Get A Good Rum For Your Money!* Just one more good fuck.

He goes to look for the Girl and finds her in the bedroom. Young Amanda has removed the kimono and stands motionless in a red bra and knickers. She glances at the bed and says 'wait for me', then disappears into the bathroom. Ricky undresses and climbs into bed. There is a satisfied smile on his face. Then we cut to the denouement. The twist.

I flicked through the script, reading the end, then looked into David's eyes.

'Why is she wearing underwear?' I asked.

'How do you mean?'

'Well, she is seducing him, isn't she?'

'Yes.'

'But then she'd be naked, wouldn't she?'

'I don't know.'

I glanced around the flat. 'David, let's try it,' I said. 'See how it works.'

His doubtful expression showed that he was going along with something he wasn't sure about. David had set out to write a revenge story, but Jean-Luc must have seen the themes of sexual supremacy and frustration coiling like snakes beneath the surface. Writers don't always know what they have written until after they have written it, and readers interpret things according to their own experience. A month before while I was doing my A levels, I would have seen the story in the way David saw it. But Mr Cartier had opened my eyes to new vistas and it was clear to me now waltzing through David's flat in Mummy's Agent Provocateur underwear that *Cheats* was not about Ricky trying to pull a young girl, it was about Amanda Marshall destroying Older Amanda's relationship with Ricky thoroughly and forever. She was not a sweet girl who had been corrupted. She was the corrupter, a complete and absolute bitch. It was a great role.

David may have thought he had been in command of the situation up until this point, but there was a definite lift in his director's baritone as we played out the scene. I did the *I won't be a minute* line and wound my way through the hall to the bedroom. The bed was at the far end of the room, a four-poster veiled in sweeps of material like a sailing ship in the dim light. I lit the bedside lamp and doused the glare with the red silk knickers. David took ages to come and,

116

when he did, my clothes were tossed about the floor. I was naked.

'Wow,' he said.

'It's a surprise?'

'Yes . . .'

'Then it will be a surprise for the audience.'

'That's true, but . . . would she really do that? I mean, be so brazen?'

'I wouldn't. But Amanda Marshall would,' I replied. 'She's like a snake mesmerising her prey. She is punishing Ricky. She wants him to see and desire what he will never have.'

'Character drives plot,' he said, as if quoting from a book.

'The story seems to be about Ricky, but it's not. It's about the girl. Everything that happens, she makes happen.'

He stood there nodding his head and I stood there all bashful in my girlie nakedness.

David's eyes drifted down to my breasts, my rib cage, the indentation of my tummy button, the curly little creature nestling between my legs.

I let my head fall to one side as he approached. He put his arms around me as if he were hugging a tree and I wilted, the air escaping in a long sigh from my body. David wasn't Jean-Luc Cartier. He would need help. His arms circled my waist and his palms strayed cautiously down to cup my bottom. I pushed against his hands, just slightly, rocking my pussy against the swelling in his jeans. I sighed and trembled. David sucked at my lips, he kissed my chin and I thrust back my neck like a kitten waiting to be stroked.

He stood back and dragged off his T-shirt. He was fit without being too muscular and had soft skin with no hair on his chest. His hands moved away from my

117

proffered bottom and, as he circled my waist in his arms, he looked at me more closely, at my eyes and nose, my pink lips.

Had he found his leading lady?

I felt like a virgin and I was in a way. David was a real boy. I felt feverish, so hot and nervous it was like a flame was burning inside me. All the things the girls said about boys at convent school skipped through my mind like the pages of an encyclopaedia, a manual, a novel by Anaïs Nin. My heart was beating like a drum. I ran my tongue over his collar bone and bit his neck.

'You're not a vampire?'

'Different genre,' I replied, and he smiled.

As he unbuckled his belt I had a sudden vision of the shiny black leather uncoiling across my backside and the thought released a loose bead of liquid that leaked into my pubic hair. Was David a spanker? I'm sure he wasn't. But I was sure he would learn. He unbuttoned his jeans, stripped them off and stood there shyly in his boxers. I took the wide band in two fingers and pulled back the elastic to peep inside. It was stirring restlessly in the folds of cotton like a snake waking in the desert.

'He's getting up,' I said.

He pulled his shorts down and his cock jumped out playfully and poked me in the belly. It was straight and smooth with a shiny pink cap and I knelt automatically to kiss its little nose. I ran my tongue around the eye and looked up at him as it slid into my open mouth. Up and down, up and down. His skin was as soft as velvet. The head of his cock swelled in my throat. I looked up at him as if he were a god on a plinth. His eyes were goggling . . .

Then: disaster.

He came immediately, a gush of foamy sperm that filled my throat and ran out from the corners of my lips, dripping on my shoulders, forming little pools in the hollow of my collar bones, warm and sticky like melted ice cream.

'I'm sorry, I'm so sorry,' he said, and I sucked out every drop as his cock shrank into a little marshmallow in my mouth. I rose from my haunches and as we kissed it was so romantic sharing his bittersweet milkshake on our lips.

'That's never happened before,' he said.

'It's all Amanda's fault.'

'You must hate me.'

'Not yet,' I said playfully, and he smiled.

As we looked down at his shrivelled penis, I noticed the leather belt threaded through the loops of his jeans and a shiver of adrenaline ran like an ice cube up my spine. I unthreaded the belt and wrapped the buckle around my hand. I gave a practice swing and, as I brought the belt down on the bed, it made a nice crisp snap like a yacht sail in a stiff wind. I tried again, a bit harder, and his limp cock quivered with anticipation, with new life. His eyes were glowing.

'Here.' I gave him the belt and looked deep into his eyes. 'Hard, but not too hard,' I said.

His Adam's apple bobbed as he swallowed. 'You mean . . .' he asked, and his voice trailed off.

I raised my shoulders in an innocent shrug. We remained still for several seconds. I could hear the beat of his alarm clock on the bedside table. His bottom lip was trembling. I reached up and took his bottom lip between my teeth and bit down until he flinched with pain. I then pulled back the curtain swags from the end of the bed and made myself

119

comfortable, spreading my legs, leaning forward over the mattress and pushing out my bum. It seemed as if an entire lifetime had gone by since Jean-Luc and Tara Scott-Wallace had disciplined my bottom and in the shadowy light the pink stripes were invisible.

'Are you ready?' he asked.

'And willing,' I replied.

There was *another* pause. 'I've never done this before,' he added and I looked back at him over my shoulder.

'Neither have I.'

He waited a few moments, revving himself up. I closed my eyes. I heard a swish of air and took a big breath through gritted teeth. The belt crackled like lightning as it uncoiled over my protruding bottom and I realised that dead leather had more of a bite than a live hand, a sting like a branding iron as it scolded across the mounds of soft yielding flesh. I gripped the bedcover in my fists, I went up on my toes and pushed out my bum, waiting for the second.

'Again?' he asked.

'Yes please.'

Crack. Down it came again in an overlapping stitch, the belt like a saw biting into my soft parts and I thought next time I have Binky tied to the bed I'm going to use the belt to beat her. She deserves it. I screamed and buried my head in the bedclothes, pushing out my backside still further, spreading my thighs and opening myself up in the most intimate way possible.

Binky had asked me why I liked being beaten. It had been hard to find the right words at that moment and now it came to me like a revelation: when you're naked and sweaty and your bum is receiving attention you feel utterly and overpoweringly alive. You are living that moment before it drifts away. There is just you, stripped to your essence, naked as Eve, sharp as a razor, every nerve end sparkling with verve and feeling. Your bottom is the sun around which the universe turns.

Crack. It was delicious. Delectable. I could feel all the liquids in my body boiling and bubbling, seeping from my wet pussy, rising from my scalding flesh in showers of sweet-smelling perspiration. The pain was like no pain I had ever felt before. I adored corporal punishment. I needed a master and even though David Trevellick was a mere novice he clearly had a feeling for the role.

Down the belt came again, the leather biting into my bottom. My knees were shaking, but I held myself steady and absorbed the pain, bringing it into me, up through my stomach and chest, my breasts quivered and my nipples felt as if they were burning. That was four. Two more, I thought. That should wake him up. I gritted my teeth and raised my chin, my back was arched in a bow, flexed and ready, and down the leather came once more, uncurling like a tongue of flame, searing my bottom and sending a wave of heat up my spine, across my shoulders and down to my tingling fingertips.

'God, that must hurt,' he said, his voice escaping from him in a whisper.

'One more,' I said.

'Okay . . .'

He put his soul into it. David had never beaten a girl before and didn't know when he might get another chance. The leather cracked like a shaft of lightning, slicing into my flesh. My legs trembled, my body was running with sweat and my pussy gurgled as the oils gushed to the surface and reached David's nostrils like an invitation to the feast. I didn't move. I rocked on my toes, waving my red bottom towards him like a little monkey in the zoo, and finally he got the message.

His cock slid into me and it wasn't soft any more. It was a rod of steel stoking me like I was a boiler needing to be recharged. I pushed back against him, each slap of our flesh sending ripples of pain over the six belt wheals etched across my white flesh. I thought about his come filling my mouth, my bottom waiting for his belt, the look of fear and desire in his eyes when he first saw me standing there naked in his bedroom. This was new territory for David and I had a feeling that now I had shown him the secret path across the frontier he would make it his home.

Once you have been spanked there is no way back. You want to be spanked again and again, spanked and whipped and beaten and humiliated. It's an essential part of the pleasure, more than that, it *is* the pleasure. It's just the same for the spanker, they are the reverse poles of magnets drawn charismatically together: *yin* and *yang*, identical yet opposites, a perfect fit, the seed of their opposite like an all-seeing eye in the very heart of the other, the soul of the other. No man is wholly man, no woman wholly woman. You have inside you the potential to be everything, to be anything you want to be, and I would never have reached this understanding without stripping away the silly and frivolous and submitting my bottom to chastisement. How easy it is for the *yin* to become *yang* and the *yang* to become *yin*, I realised, and with that thought I pushed back harder as David released another little squirt of spunk up inside me. A month ago I'd been a virgin. It was hard to believe.

I crawled up on to the bed and lay there quivering like an eel out of water, my body wet and slippery, trembling slightly. David kissed my bottom, then licked the lines branded over its surface, his salty tongue drawing out the sting. He couldn't get enough of my bottom and I couldn't get enough of his tongue soothing the plum-red skin, over the hills and into the dark valley. I pushed up on my knees and waggled my bottom, tempting him to enter the starry opening to my secret place.

This was new to David, a new experience, a new taste to savour. He licked gingerly around the entrance to my anus before delving experimentally further in, then further still. He took a grip of my hip bones, perfect handles, and pulled me back on to the extended wet tentacle of his tongue. I pushed into his face. He pushed into my bum. Squelching noises drowned the sound of the beating alarm and I cooed with unutterable pleasure. My pussy was leaking constantly, oiling my parts. My body was throbbing, a giant erogenous zone, all feelings and vibrations. This was the first time I'd had a man's tongue in my bottom and men's tongues are big and juicy, they reach new heights, new depths, new places. After a spanking there can surely be no greater pleasure than having the spanker's tongue buried inside you. The master imagines he is the hunter but he is also the prey.

'Yes, yes, yes,' I mumbled, 'yes, yes, yes.'

He kept going, in and out, in and out, and I was overcome by feelings of completion and empowerment. Women have through history been made to cover up, shut up, speak when spoken to. They have been repressed and made to feel guilty by men because men lack female spontaneity and intuition, the ability to find pure pleasure in natural things. How often do you see a man walking barefoot on the grass or along the water's edge, shoes in hand? Girls can't wait to take off their shoes, loosen their buttons, their hair from ribbons. We go out with bare legs, bare shoulders, we sunbathe in the park, we submit our breasts and our bodies to the breath of the wind, the eye of the sky, the chill ghostly light of the moon. We have been kept in chains and now those chains are our joy and our freedom. Men for centuries have had all the fun. It's a new century now, I thought. It's our turn.

David's meaty tongue pulsed through all my channels and passageways and sent shock waves of pleasure to the burning heart of my clitoris. I was coming. I was coming. *Don't stop. Don't stop. Don't ever stop.* I screamed and yelled and shook and he held my thighs and stayed glued to my bottom as the orgasm exploded through me in waves like a tsunami and ricocheted around the walls and across the ceiling and over the oak strips of the polished wooden floor.

The numbers on the digital clock clicked to 10 and we collapsed on the bed, wet and spent.

'You're amazing . . .'

'Amanda is so inspiring,' I said. 'I think she would have to sleep with Ricky, to justify what they do to him.'

David's eyes were spinning round inside his head. He was trying to focus but he wasn't sure what he should be thinking about, focusing on.

'That was like . . . like the best ever,' he said.

'Me too,' I replied.

He smiled and I smiled. It was great being a girl. David Trevellick was the first boy I'd done it with, the first boy to do it all. Not that I was going to tell him that, it would be far too embarrassing. Sex with Binky and Tara Scott-Wallace was all very nice, but you can't really count girls. They're soft and they smell nice. But they don't penetrate. With girls it's just fun. I would never forget Hamish of the Black Watch, of course, or Monsieur Cartier for that matter. But David was a proper boy and I just loved his silky smooth body, his little cock coiled like a seashell against my thigh, his sweet breath against my neck. Boys have a nice smell, too, grass and earthy sweat and walnuts and ambition.

We lay in each other's arms, the alarm clock ticking, the lamp shining through my silk knickers making a red moon on the ceiling. I closed my eyes and all the little problems in the script became clear to me. That's what a good beating does. It makes you think clearly. Should I tell him my ideas? Would it make him angry? Or would he be pleased? You have to go on tiptoes when you approach film directors, they're so touchy.

'Tell me the rest of the story,' I said.

'What?'

'Let's go through the end of *Cheats*.'

He looked at me now as if he wasn't sure whether what had happened had happened because, well, those things happen, or whether I had only stripped off for him in order to get to play Amanda in his film. He shrugged and I suppose it didn't really matter.

'Well, Amanda has put something in Ricky's drink and, in the bedroom, he falls into a deep sleep.'

'Like Snow White?'

'He wakes up with a pain in his chest. He's not sure where he is at first. Then he realises he is back in his own flat, in his own bed. There's a picture of Older Amanda in a frame beside him. The Girl is nowhere to be seen. He pulls back the bedclothes and discovers that his chest is bandaged. There are spots of blood on the bandages. It's a total shock. It doesn't make sense.'

'It's like Amanda's a doctor and she's stolen his organs or something,' I ventured.

'That makes the surprise even better,' he replied. His eyes were glowing. 'Ricky slips out of bed and in the bathroom, when he unwinds the bandages, there are big blue letters tattooed on his chest. It says the word TEACH. He keeps saying it. He studies the mirror for a long time before realising the C and the H are transposed in the reflection. He looks down and becomes aware that tattooed across his chest is the word CHEAT.'

'Wow,' I said and exhaled a gasp of breath. 'It's really a great story. Amanda is such a bitch.'

'That's what makes her interesting.'

'But how does she know about tattoos?'

He thought for a long time. 'She just does,' he said.

'And she's a lesbian?'

'Yeah . . .'

'Then maybe . . .'

He sat there quietly playing catch-up. I'd had my derrière flogged. I was shooting ahead, thinking clearly. Finally he grinned.

'She should have a tattoo,' he said. He was sitting cross-legged, his hands pressed together in a spire, the diffusion of red light on his face giving him an impish appearance.

'Brilliant,' I said. I was staring into his eyes, mesmerising my prey. 'She's like a snake . . .'

'That's just what I was thinking.'

'If she had a snake on her leg,' I said, thinking through the sequence, 'in the bar he would see the tail below her skirt . . .'

'. . . and when she changes into the red kimono,' he added, 'he'd see it climbing up her thigh . . .'

'Yes, yes, yes.'

'And when she's naked in the bedroom it would be . . .'

'Wherever,' I said.

'I can see it all now, of course,' he continued. 'Amanda does have to sleep with Ricky.'

'While the drug is taking effect,' I said.

'Absolutely.'

'If she doesn't, then Ricky's being punished with that awful tattoo when he hasn't really done anything to deserve it.'

'Cause and effect,' he remarked.

'It also gives the girl power in her relationship with the other Amanda.'

'Really?' he said. The creases were back on his brow.

'Yes, I think so,' I replied. 'If she's a lesbian, then sleeping with Ricky will be a sacrifice, not a pleasure. She is doing it for the other Amanda, to show her that she really loves her. It's like Euripides, or something.'

'Wow, yes,' he said, and gripped my shoulders. 'Would you do it? I mean, nude scenes, pretending to have sex with Roddy Wise . . .'

'Only if I get the part.'

He grinned. 'Roddy will be up for it.'

We both laughed, and I thought it's nice when people laugh together, when lovers laugh together.

'Amazing!' I said.

And it was. Just think, little Camilla Petacci from Saint Sebastian's was going to do it, or at least pretend to do it, with Roddy Wise. *The* Roddy Wise. A real celeb. I couldn't wait to tell Binky.

David rushed off and made coffee and we sat in the kitchen under a neon light, our heads pressed together as we read through the rest of the script.

'Okay,' said David, 'after he's found the tattoo on his chest . . .'

RICKY *hears music playing. He tightens a towel around his waist and when he goes into the living room, he finds both* AMANDAS. *They are dressed alike, very butch in tank tops and camouflage trousers.* OLDER AMANDA *holds a CD.*

AMANDA: Is the flamenco yours or mine?

RICKY: What have you done to me?

AMANDA: I think you bought it for me?

RICKY: What have you done?

YOUNG
AMANDA: Leave it. We'll get another one.

AMANDA *glances back at* YOUNG AMANDA. *They are in love. She puts the CD in one of the two piles she is making.* RICKY *notices gaps in the bookshelves, paintings missing from the walls.*

RICKY: Why, Amanda, why?

AMANDA: You know why.

RICKY: I don't.

AMANDA: Yes you do.

RICKY: Why this?

He indicates the tattoo. The towel around his waist nearly falls and he has to grab it tight.

YOUNG
AMANDA: That was my idea.

RICKY: You, you fucking set me up. You fucking bitch. You fucking slag.

YOUNG
AMANDA: (*to* AMANDA) You see?

128

There is a box beside the door containing books and picture frames. YOUNG AMANDA *scoops the box under her arm.*

YOUNG
AMANDA: I'll wait in the car, Sweets.
RICKY: Sweets!
AMANDA: You can keep the flamenco. I always hated it.

AMANDA *finishes sorting the CDs and places one of the piles in a bag. The flamenco she puts in its case and throws to* RICKY. *As he catches it the towel drops to the floor.*

Camera rises to RICKY'S *chest and closes on the word CHEAT.*

'Fade to black,' David said.

'It's so good.'

'It can be, it can be now,' he added.

In his eyes as he stared at me across the table was trust and uncertainty, a bit like a puppy dog and, although I'd always suspected, I now knew for sure that with boys you have to let them believe they have the best ideas, pretend they know all the answers, ask subtle questions that make subtle suggestions, mould them like wet clay on a potter's wheel until they are ready for the oven. I gave him my big schoolgirl smile and we went back to the bedroom with the sweet musty smell of sperm in the air and the navy-blue sheets stained in patterns like an archipelago of islands on a dark sea, the red moon motionless on the ceiling.

I lay on my back with the pillow under my bottom. Like a thirsty creature at a salt lick, David spent hours drinking from my pussy and the thing about sex is it's a drug. The more you have the more you want. The more you need. Like a drug, or so I'm told, except for a sip of wine and the occasional flute of shampoo, it's not something I really know anything about, but apparently, like a drug, when you're high on sex you have more energy. You see things differently. Colours are brighter. Jokes are funnier. Life is glorious. Look at the girl walking dreamily down the street, wide-eyed, tossing her mane, taking long slow strides, and you know she's fresh from carnal knowledge, her face radiant with promise, and a little anxious, too. Anxious for the next time.

We drifted into a lazy sleep curled in each other's arms like baby birds in a nest and I awoke in the triangle of dusty light that angled through a gap in the curtains. It was the first time I had spent the night with somebody and it was sort of weird waking up with a man in a strange bed.

Part III

Of course, I had to shave off my pubic hair and it's not as easy as you might think. It's easy enough with a lady razor removing the furry coating over the Mount of Venus (such a silly term!) but then you have to use the nail scissors to snip off the stray curly hairs around your labia (another silly word!) and it takes like forever.

I did wonder if I should ask Mummy for some advice. She was actually quite pleased that I'd found a job. I was being paid £200 for four days (that's how much Mummy pays for her knickers), but it was a low-budget short and the point was for the actors to be seen, the crew to hone their skills, as David put it, and the director to show everyone how clever he is.

When I'd finished shaving, I stood in front of the mirror and admired my shiny mount. I looked like a little girl, like a child again, although not really. I adored being a girl but I was a woman. I was fully grown, fully grown and at my very best. My breasts since going to Scotland had swelled up to a sensual C cup 36 and I had been so busy with rehearsals, my waist had shrunk to 24 inches. I measured myself three times a day.

Binky was positively green, not about my figure, she knew she was cute, but about everything else, my chance to prance around naked on a movie set, a real live director my boyfriend, sort of, and Roddy Wise's name listed on my mobile phone. Binky spent her days reading books by Michel Houellebecq and sunbathing in the garden.

On the only occasion when I had time to join her she said I had tabloid tits just perfect for builders to ogle but *hardly* refined. 'I expect I'll be seeing you on Page 3 next,' she said.

'That's a thought,' I replied.

She lay there looking sad, running her small hands over her narrow hips. Binky was feeling sorry for herself. She had sacked the mechanic. The Polish gardener really did prefer older women, and one night when Binky went back to some grotty flat in Camden with a boy she'd met in a pub playing pool, his three mates appeared out of the woodwork for a gang bang and then they all pissed over her.

'What was it like?'

'Like really embarrassing in the taxi coming home,' she replied.

'I mean, you know, when it's happening. When the boys were pissing on you?'

'You are such a pervert, Milly, I'm sure you'll find out.'

'I can't wait . . .'

Binky is such an attention seeker, I wasn't entirely sure whether she was telling the truth about her ordeal but, before I could stop her, she rolled back on her shoulders, whipped down her bikini bottoms as she rolled forward and straddled me in one amazingly gymnastic movement. She had been dying to get revenge for the smacking I'd given her and, as she shuffled forwards along my trunk, a golden stream of Binky pee rained over my tummy, between my breasts, over my chin, my face and into my mouth that had dropped open in shock. She jiggled her thighs up and down, shaking out the last little drop, and as I sat forward I caught a glimpse of the Polish gardener watching us through the greenhouse windows.

'Roberta, you've been sussed,' I said. 'He's watching.'

'He's always watching. I saw him taking notes once.'

'Perhaps he's writing a book.'

'*Lady Chatterley's Lover* redubbed,' she said and when I laughed, Binky looked happy for the first time in weeks. That's all it takes. Revenge!

I wriggled away from her knees and raced off to the bathroom. I was already late and in the movies everyone makes a point of being punctual, even the stars.

We had three days for rehearsals and, naturally, Roddy Wise was perfectly content to spend hours pretending to have sex with a girl of eighteen lying on top of him. 'It's a tough job but somebody's got to do it,' he kept saying. We kept our clothes on during rehearsals and would take them off when it came to filming. Roddy was on a strict diet and every spare second he did press-ups, building himself up for his nude scene.

132

I think Stephanie Jones, Older Amanda, was quite jealous. Her part was a lot smaller than mine for one thing and, for another, it wasn't really sexy. 'I mean, there's nothing for me to get my tongue round,' she said to me one day while we were out with the costume director, a girl a bit older than me named Maja, very serious, tall and totally gorgeous. There was money in the budget for me to buy the red underwear and I was standing in Harvey Nichols with the curtain open for Maja and Stephanie to see.

'That looks very nice,' said Maja in her lispy European way.

'Very,' said Stephanie despondently.

Stephanie Jones was a star, I mean, she'd made loads of movies and was always on TV. She was a household name. And she wasn't happy. I told David that night that her part had to be built up or he was going to lose her. The problem for David was that now we had made all the changes, the film would run for about 9 minutes and 15 seconds, it's all *very* precise, and once the credits were added, it would bring it to about 9 minutes and 45 seconds: the ideal length for a 10-minute short film.

'Why do they have to be ten minutes?' I asked. It seemed silly to me.

'That's the preferred length at festivals,' he replied.

'So you have about fifteen seconds to play with?'

'Mmm,' he mumbled.

He was running his tongue around my aureolae, sucking and slurping. He adored my breasts and I adored his big tongue. He gripped my nipple in his teeth and pulled it out as he raised his head. 'Maybe twenty,' he said, and as he spoke with his mouth closed it sounded like *baby benty*.

As I stroked his hair I pushed his head down over

133

the grille of my rib cage to the pearly plain of my shaved pussy. He got the message, kissed and licked his way across my soft skin and my legs parted like a bridge opening to allow a tall ship to pass. He peeled back the outer lips of my vulva with his cupped hands and the tip of his tongue nudged its way under the gossamer cowling of pink flesh to the little nubble of my clitoris. I let out a long sigh and pushed my bottom up from the mattress.

Welcoming David's tongue inside me was like welcoming an old friend back from a long journey overseas, making me wet, searching for new nerve endings to arouse and stimulate. After working together all day we spent our nights in his four-poster, but it was sort of strange that after that first night when I had encouraged him to beat me with his belt, we had got into a routine of what I believe they call vanilla sex, all pleasure without the scorching spice of a little pain.

David liked to come in my mouth and then watch as I gulped down his sperm. His cock would slowly shrink and I would keep sucking until it slowly hardened again. Then he liked me flat on my back in the missionary position, legs up, shoulders flat, and I imagined this was what it must be like for old married couples and I was glad I was eighteen and everything was still new and exciting. I had a feeling that if I kept searching, kept experimenting, there was out there in the world the ultimate pleasure, the ultimate climax, a magical fusion of bodies and souls that would bear you as if on a flying carpet to a place beyond the daily concerns of making films and going to university and trying to make Mother happy.

His tongue was moving like a piston, in and out, a little twist one way, a little twirl the other, polishing my clit like it was a brass handle on a door. I was an IED, an improvised explosive device, the mounting spasms warning of an impending detonation and I wriggled away from his tongue to save it till later, sacrificing pleasure with the expectation of greater pleasure, something I'm sure Sister Theresa at school once said, although not in exactly the same context.

David looked disappointed for a second and I kissed him. We kissed like people in the movies. We were in the movies. All sloshing and slurping like we were devouring ripe mangoes, the juice running from our mouths. Except for kissing girls, I had never really kissed a boy until I met David and wanted to make the most of it. I paused for breath and ran my tongue down his neck.

There is a point where vampires bite their victims and he adored it when I nibbled at that magical spot. Perhaps that's where he kept his clitoris? David threw back his head and it was so tempting to really sink my teeth into his flesh. His skin tasted of ice cream. I wanted to eat him. I licked his shoulder blades, I chewed his nipple. It was pink like a girl's and I sucked and bit that little rosebud until it popped up, first one then the other, and an eccentric thought entered my head: I would just love to have seen David made-up as a girl. Shave his legs, cut his hair in the same gamine way as Daddy's girlfriend, dress him in a long evening gown and pointy shoes. I'm sure he'd enjoy being a girl.

There was a small indentation in his chest which was sweet and I kissed it, and fine fur, soft as baby's hair, running in a slowly widening line down from his belly button to the thick downy cushion of pubes. I pulled at the hair with my teeth and he winced with pleasure. His cock was huge now like . . . like

135

Goliath. David and Goliath, I thought, and in one movement I swivelled across his thighs, took the giant down my throat and lowered my wet pussy over his mouth, plugging us together like two halves of a Chinese puzzle. We were locked in, my old friends *yin* and *yang*, rocking backwards and forwards and I thought I should get hold of a copy of the *Kama Sutra* because apparently there are hundreds of positions and this one was merely 69. In fact, 69 looked like *yin* and *yang*, I realised and, if I ever had a real tattoo, that's what I'd have, somewhere discreet, the pit of my back between the two dimples David so adored.

The spasms started almost immediately but I was learning one of life's most important lessons: self-control. I held back selflessly and waited, and I waited, and I waited, until David's body grew tense with the pressure and, as he let go, jamming Goliath down to my tonsils, a hammer striking a bell, I pushed up into his tongue and our bodies went electric as they exploded in one universal orgasm. His come filled my throat and I nearly gagged, but I didn't. I swallowed it down, savouring the flavour, and kept pumping out little sprays of girlie juice that David lapped up greedily like a thirsty man sucking dew from a flower in the desert.

Is there anything better than sex? I don't think so. It is what we are here for, what we are designed for. Yes, of course, I wanted to go to Cambridge and get a First and work in the media and be awfully clever, write books on the history of art and say catty things on Radio 4. You can't spend your whole life in bed, I suppose, but it seems like everything we do is just filling in the time between love and lovers, between sex and anticipating more sex, between getting up from bed and going back to bed. My body was coated in perspiration and the smell of our bodily fluids was like a narcotic filling the air and making me want more.

David lay back with his eyes closed and his mouth open, spent and satisfied, the lion in his own jungle. I was lying flat on my stomach and tickled his nose with my tongue.

'Twenty seconds?' I said.

'Aghhhhhhh!'

'Amanda is a lesbian,' I continued, 'and Older Amanda is, well, sort of learning the ropes . . .'

I spoke pensively. He opened his eyes slowly. He was nodding his head up and down, but then his brow creased with the same two creases it always did when he was thinking about his film.

'She'll never agree,' he said.

'Are you sure?'

'She's a family actress. She's always on the box. She's married as well.' He paused and sat up. 'What about you, Milly, would you, you know . . . ?'

'For the film I would.'

David and I seemed to have a different view on sex. To me, it is the most natural thing in the world, like breathing, or eating. Every stranger I passed in the street made me wonder what it would be like to have his cock up inside me or her pussy clamped to my mouth. Would the man who looked a bit like David not make love like David? I am sure the tall slender girl with flashing eyes who studied me on the 22 bus this morning would adore being tied to my bed. Now Binky had peed over me I could imagine peeing over the girl on the bus. Every stranger is a potential lover, an echo of other lovers that awakens memories of past pleasures and anticipates the pleasure to come.

His eyes were wide now. The creases on his brow had gone. I was still lying on my tummy, my head twisted at an odd angle. He stroked my back, inserted his fingertips into the two dimples just above my bottom as if he were pressing the buttons on a lift. 'Going up,' I said, and in turn I drew my knees up and presented the round orbs of my perfect posterior for his careful consideration.

'Your bottom is so, so . . .'

'Spankable?' I said.

He paused like a man at the end of a diving board. He took a breath. His arm went up, drawn by a magnetic force, and like the diver launching himself into the pool his hand came down, a cymbal ringing out melodically against my yielding skin. I breathed a long slow sigh of relief. I wriggled as if to say more, not that my bum needed to ask. The sound of one hand clapping a bottom creates an instant retort, an echo that can only be answered by another clap. Zen monks have spent aeons pondering the sound of one hand clapping and surely the mystery isn't as profound as they imagine. Get a life. Get a girlfriend!

David drew himself up on to his knees to make himself more comfortable and brought his hand down again. 'Two,' I said, and he was just getting warmed up. I heard David spit into his palm and number three had a different tone, a different texture, more a slap than a smack.

'Three,' I said, and a frisson of warmth ran up my spine and down my thighs like code, messages of old memories and new feelings flashing through my nervous system.

'Four,' I counted in a steady voice.

I squirmed and writhed, I wriggled and pressed my head into the pillow. And again. 'Five.' A full, lovely hard smack, the sound like wet fish dropped in the fryer, sizzling, sparkling. I had tried the belt, but preferred the intimacy of a hand, it's familiar, human, and it occurred to me that the further you went along the road of discipline the more the beatings may thrill but the more they may do lasting damage. I wasn't into that. It was getting oily and girlie that I liked. I couldn't imagine a hand smacking your backside would ever be more than a passing moment of tenderness on the way to ecstasy. Being smacked was like being a virgin. It's painful opening the doors of perception but once inside the magic garden an endless array of gifts were there for you to explore.

'Six.'

I rolled over with open arms. I was in control. David kissed my lips, he slipped his tongue into the hollow of my collar bones, salt cellars, as Nanny used to say. He milked my breasts, running his tongue around the tips, biting and sucking, and down he drifted to the shiny shell of my naked pussy, shorn of fur for his film, for him, a lustrous jewel of tender flesh that opened like a cream meringue and coated his tongue in my buttery essence. We had learned in science at school that we are 99% fluids. It always seemed silly, but now it made sense. I was a reservoir, a honey pot, an oil well, a bottomless ocean of sticky liquids and it didn't seem to matter how much leaked from me, there was always more. I held David's ears. I drew his tongue up inside me and another little ripple of climaxes like waves pressed my lids tight over my eyes and I slept in his arms like a baby.

We sat in *Starbucks* drinking espressos. Stephanie had an almond croissant in front of her and was about to take a bite when David told her he thought there was a scene missing from the screenplay.

'Which one?' she said and we smiled.

David's neck began to colour, he was so nervous, and I took over.

'In the story the two girls are lovers,' I said and she put the croissant down to listen. 'Amanda, the young one, me, she hates men and wants to show the other Amanda, you, that Ricky is a bastard, that all men are bastards . . .'

'They usually are, darling! Present company excepted,' Stephanie said and patted the back of David's hand.

I smiled across the table. I thought she was really great. 'When Amanda sleeps with Ricky, to prove her point, she's not thinking about Ricky . . .'

'She's thinking about me, darling.'

'Exactly.'

We sat in silence. Stephanie looked closely at David. She looked closely back at me. Then she pushed the croissant across the table. 'One does suffer for one's art,' she said in a theatrical tone and we all raised our espresso cups to celebrate.

David decided to shoot the lesbian scene without rehearsals and decided to shoot it first in case Stephanie changed her mind. It's obvious to me now that I know a bit more about filmmaking, but it hadn't occurred to me at the time, that you don't make a film chronologically, but shoot all the sequences and then put them together like a puzzle in the editing suite.

'The editor is God,' David whispered, and that made me wonder where Hermann Mann, the man from the Film Council, fitted in the pantheon.

The scene was going to be a flashback dropped in at that moment when Young Amanda says to Ricky: 'The only thing we have is relationships. That's what matters to me. If I had a boyfriend and he cheated on me, I'd pay him back. I mean *really* pay him back.' Then Ricky replies glibly: 'Hell hath no fury.' And Amanda says: 'You bet.'

The exchange warns the audience that Ricky is on the brink of the abyss and that Young Amanda is not an innocent lured by Ricky's apparent glamour, but a spy in the house of seduction. It was powerful stuff and I had practised my lines in front of the mirror so many times Binky had threatened, well, visualise rain falling on a tin roof and you can imagine!

The build-up before shooting a film is called pre-production and although it seems to take forever, after all the costume fittings and location checks, the run-throughs and read-throughs, after that last restless night sliding through David's navy-blue sheets like two fish in the ocean, the day arrived, my début, and I was frightened out of my life. My tummy was knotted like a cat's cradle. Nervous sweat prickled my underarms. I could taste something awful like cold pizza at the back of my throat. I thought I was going to be sick. Break a leg, said David, and I thought that sounded like a jolly good alternative.

Cars and taxis were criss-crossing the city with the cast and crew. A van with the camera kit appeared at the house loaned to us for the shoot and the electricians set about chipping the furniture as they unloaded metal stands, big lights with metal flaps, and spools of cables that wriggled like eels across the floorboards.

An old girlfriend of David's who looked as if she

had swallowed a live toad before leaving home that morning had been drafted in to do the catering and she eyed me resentfully as she whipped up plates of eggs and bacon with thick slices of white bread Nanny would have called doorsteps. Like an army, a movie crew marches on its stomach, I was told by Murray McVite, an older man like a sergeant major with creamy white hair in a ponytail. Murray was the assistant director and his job was to shout at everyone.

I sipped black coffee, butterflies in clogs dancing in my stomach, and was grateful for Stephanie's hand holding mine under the table. I don't know who was the more anxious, more apprehensive, Steph with her reputation on the line, or me, with nothing to lose. We pecked on the lips and I went off to get ready first as it was going to take more time.

In the shower I freshened up my pussy with the lady razor, patted myself dry and climbed into a big white bathrobe. If I was tense, Adam Green, the gay boy in make-up, was a nervous wreck. His bottom lip was trembling, his hands were trembling, and he had the job of painting the snake on my leg. He gritted his chattering teeth.

'You're so brave,' he said.

'So are you,' I replied, and he smiled weakly like a brave man about to be tortured.

He had done loads of drawings and had practised on a prosthetic leg that stood on the table like a bizarre work of art by the Chapman Brothers. I removed the bathrobe and stood before Adam like a blank canvas, like the Duchess of Alba before Goya, I thought, and recalled for some reason a terribly risqué poem Sister Nuria had told us in the Art class.

The Duchess of Alba once said to Goya
Remember I am your employer
So he's painted her clothed to please her
And he painted her nude to annoy her

I'm not sure why, but remembering this silly poem brought a smile to my lips and the knots in my tummy began to untangle. I had begun to appreciate the weird pleasures of being naked, the little monkeys were perky and my tummy had grown as flat as an ice rink, so flat it was hollow when I lay flat and David simply adored resting his head there while he thought about his script. Adam looked away as he took my hand and I stepped up on to a plastic box. He sat on a stool, spread his pots of acrylic around him and took a big breath as he looked up at me like a child looking up at a parent.

'Here goes,' he said.

'Don't be frightened.'

'I'm not frightened, Milly, I'm terrified.'

I laughed and that seemed to calm him. We were making a movie. We were in this together. Adam first used a green felt-tip pen and his hand grew steady the moment he began to draw the outline of the snake. We were in the bathroom, a minimalist place of black tiles and shiny chrome which Adam had contrived to make into his boudoir with the boxes of make-up, the photos of reptiles blu-tacked to the mirror, a pink Teddy with *I Love New York* on his tummy and little ornaments that revealed his fondness for silk and satin, feathers and fur. Radio 1 was playing a Kylie Minogue song.

Adam worked quickly, sliding the point of the pen over my flesh in bold movements. Once the outline was completed, he dipped the tip of the brush in the

143

paint and began with the tail, the place where I always seemed to end up when I used to play Snakes and Ladders with Binky who, as the baby, was expected to cheat and was forgiven the moment she did so. Adam worked more slowly now, like he was painting the ceiling of a chapel, the brush gliding over the soft flesh at the back of my knee. I started wriggling.

'Don't move,' he said sharply.

'It tickles,' I said.

'Just imagine it's David's tongue.'

'What?'

'There are no secrets on film sets, Sweets.'

'Sweets! That comes from the script, you plagiarist!' I looked down at Adam over my shoulder and he was grinning from ear to ear.

His nerves had gone. He worked faster, teasing the brush from the space at the back of my knee in a sweep across my thigh, the body of the snake coiling up to just below my hip bone before plunging down to my pubic bone, the V of my pubis forming the head of the creature and it's quite amazing because the Creator in His wisdom has designed the snake's head to be exactly the same shape as the pubic mount.

Adam switched from green to blue, making a pattern. He added streaks of silver and I watched in the three-way mirror as the beast came to life. I could feel it slithering motionlessly about my thigh, really creepy, but oddly sensual. Adam with great decorum painted two maroon eyes just above the lips of my pussy. He went to stand back, but then leaned forward again and ran the tip of his finger between the open flaps on my vulva.

When he removed his finger it was glossy and wet.

'Milly, you're oozing,' he said.

I was mortified but like his finger Adam's blue eyes were glistening with intimations of forbidden fruits and unknown pleasures. It was terribly Biblical. I should have been named Eve.

'I'm just trying to tempt you.'

'Jezebel,' he said. He pulled a tissue from a pink box covered in tulips and delicately ran it between the lips of my pussy. He took a second tissue and stuffed it inside me. 'You girls,' he mumbled. 'Now, don't move.'

He sprayed the snake with a sealant stored in a scent atomiser and then took loads of shots with his digital camera. Adam would have to re-paint the snake every day for the four-day shoot. 'If it's not perfect, the continuity girl'll kill me,' he said, and slit his throat with his finger.

I removed the sodden tissue from my pussy, stepped down from the box and pressed my breasts into his chest as I kissed him.

He shook himself free. 'Milly, you're incorrigible,' he said. 'Girls are getting so, so predatory.'

'Not before time,' I replied, and he took up his hair brush in a threatening gesture.

'Right . . .'

'Oh, no, are you going to spank me?' I said playfully, turning and bending my bottom to him. My cute bum must have been so tempting he couldn't resist bringing the back of the brush down on my extended cheeks.

'Now sit down and behave, or you really will get a smack.'

'Promises promises,' I said and sat grinning, my bottom all warm, and Adam was shaking his head as he worked on my face and hair.

I adored the attention and thought given the right circumstances I was sure Adam Green would succumb to my feminine wiles. He tutted away as he worked and had just about finished when Stephanie arrived eating an apple.

'Is he behaving himself?' she asked.

Adam looked at the apple, looked at me, and pushed his fists against his sides.

'Is this a plot?' he demanded.

Stephanie looked nonplussed and I burst out laughing. 'Adam was just talking about Adam and Eve,' I said reassuringly, and left them to it.

I walked on set wearing the bathrobe and I was shocked to see so many people. David was speaking in whispers to Dudley, the cameraman, who in turn spoke with shrugging gestures to Pete, the gaffer, the man in charge of the lights. Dudley had an assistant known as the focus puller, an Oriental girl named May Fuk, which I thought highly suspicious, and I had no idea what she did but she was walking about with a long tape measure and scribbling figures on a pad. Pete also had an assistant, also named Pete, and they were continually fiddling with the lights.

'Stop fiddling with those bleedin' lights,' shouted Murray McVite.

'I haven't even started fiddling yet,' said Pete.

'Yeah,' said the other Pete.

'Bleedin' sparks,' said Murray and lit a cheroot.

Daniel, the soundman, who I had met during the castings, was sitting at a machine that reminded me of the deck of the Tardis, headphones clamped to his big red ears, his long fingers turning dials, raising levers. His assistant was named Owen, the boom op, and what he did was stand motionless like a tree to one side of the action, away from the eye of the

146

camera, holding a long pole with a mike on the end. The mike was covered in grey fur and looked like a cat clinging to the end of a fishing rod. Owen was wearing a sleeveless shirt and had the biggest muscles I had ever seen.

Well, the second biggest. There was a man named Dirk who was called the grip, I've no idea why, and he was about as big as a house. He was laying tracks like a railway line. The camera was bolted to a dolly and settled on the tracks so that it could move without jerking towards and away from a large black leather sofa that gleamed in the pool of lights set up by the two Petes. The dolly was very elaborate with a seat for the cameraman and a sort of jib that raised the camera so that the lens could get an aerial view of the action. David had told me that crane shots were very important and showed that the director knew what he was doing.

There was a continuity girl named Amy, a stills photographer named Alex and a gaggle of runners with names like Max and Garth and Jake. Everyone was smoking and shouting, but when Stephanie stepped on set accompanied by Adam and Maja, the banter ceased, the cables stopped wriggling and the crew acknowledged that they were in the presence of a star by stubbing out their cigarettes and setting about the last-minute preparations. Stephanie had beads of moisture on her top lip which Adam mopped away before redrawing her lips with a brush. 'You look fabulous,' he whispered, and she smiled and dropped her bathrobe into Maja's waiting arms.

Everyone switched from being quiet to being totally silent as Stephanie stood before us stark naked, arms slightly apart, her bush thick and curly and it occurred to me that when David had suggested

I shave off my silky fleece it had been for his fun, not for his film. That's what happens when men learn how to spank girls. They learn how to take liberties.

Stephanie pulled at the belt securing my robe and Maja slid the garment from my shoulders. The crew had already had a good look at Stephanie Jones and now as all eyes fell on me a wave of colour ran over my neck and cheeks. It's quite strange being naked in front of so many people. I had imagined it often enough, but it was a curious pleasure to finally experience it.

'Where do you want us, darling?' said Stephanie in her plummy voice and I noticed David's Adam's apple wobble as he swallowed.

He wanted us on the sofa, petting and touching, kissing and caressing, doing what comes naturally. It's not something you can describe in a script, and although David only wanted twenty seconds of film, we wriggled about under the hot lights for sufficient time to give the editor plenty of material to cut and the crew a full-on lesbian show with the queen of family television in the starring role.

I'm not sure how it happens, or why it happens, but with the camera eye watching all other eyes disappear. Your nerves disappear. Your inhibitions disappear. The sofa was a black planet spinning in the white universe of the tiers of lights. I had acted before in a million school plays, but acting for the camera is different, inanimate but intimate, you feel real, your feelings are real, authentic. I felt love, desire, an aching tenderness. I was wet, my back was wet on the leather sofa, my armpits were wet, my pussy was open like a wet exotic flower, warmed by the lights. My body I realised was a magnetic force, a personality in its own right. People wanted to touch me, kiss me, pet me, suck me. A sheen of dew coated my thighs. I was a lake of desire and pleasure. I had never been so wet before, never felt such stimulation before, and I was suddenly terrified that I would always need an audience to reach true satisfaction, the ultimate orgasm.

Stephanie kissed my breasts, she kissed my lips, and I opened myself like the gates of paradise as she abandoned my wet mouth to sew kisses like rain spots over my neck, my collar bones, the dimpled cavern of my throat. She traced a trail of saliva down between my breasts, my diaphragm, vibrating like the skin of a drum. She spread my thighs and began to climb the snake from behind my knee, across my hip bone and down, down to the open cleft of my clean-shaven pussy. Her long tongue like the probing tongue of a snake explored the honey-strewn lips of my vulva and as her tongue slipped inside me I was aware of the grey boom lowering above my head to capture my sighs, the juicy ripples of Stephanie's steady motions between my thighs, the soft slap of our damp flesh under the hot lights.

When David whispered 'And Cut,' his voice seemed to come from a great distance and it took me a few moments to remember we were on a film set, that we were making a movie, this was art, not sex. Adam wrapped Stephanie in her robe. Maja did the same for me. And we walked slowly, proudly, chins high like Oscar nominees across the trip wires of the wriggling black cables and upstairs to the costume department.

Stephanie was aglow, eyes like fireflies, her lips gripped in the way of people trying not to smile. She was Christopher Columbus on the deck of his galleon staring out at America; what would become America. Maja and Adam seemed to realise that we wanted to

149

be left on our own and when they closed the door, Stephanie put her arms around my waist.

'Hope you didn't mind, you know . . .' she began.

'It was lovely,' I replied.

'I didn't know,' she said, and paused. 'I didn't know it was so . . . so nice. I've never, you know, never experimented.'

'Then you should,' I told her. 'I certainly am. I want to do *everything*.'

David had been really rather clever starting with the lesbian scene. It settled everyone's nerves and, apart from being an hour or two over schedule each day, the shoot ran like clockwork. We did the long seduction scene at a bar in Soho owned by a friend of Hermann Mann. He had told David that the rushes had made him 'truly excited'.

The editor had played around with the lesbian scene and the twenty seconds he'd cut from the twenty minutes was all rather pretty and innocent, a girlie kiss, a pan over my swollen lips, a shot of the little monkeys, then a close-up of me looking like the cat that got the cream as Stephanie slides from frame to lap up the liquids gurgling between my thighs. One sip and you are addicted.

Cheats had taken a serpentine course from the original concept and now contained more of the indefinable oo la la Jean-Luc Cartier had said it needed. It had grown complex, more *nouvelle vague*, David explained, although being a first-time director, he remained angst-ridden as we sat below the neon strips in his kitchen shaping the dénouement to keep the sexual tension as taut as a bow string.

It was just what they did when they were shooting *Casablanca*, the best film ever made, said David, write the script at night and go out and shoot it next morning. That was David's dream, to remake *Casablanca*, which I thought rather silly. If *Casablanca* was the tour-de-force everyone said it was, if no one could match the stature of Humphrey Bogart and Ingrid Bergman, what was the point in making an insipid colour version of a black and white masterpiece?

There wasn't a point, none at all, not that I said as much. I grinned and agreed. That's what girls are expected to do. We play roles. We are obedient. We become what we are expected to be ... although I could see a time coming when I rebelled. When I met the right man, I would be the perfect woman.

Anyway, we gave the script the final tweak and I was feeling feisty when we climbed into bed. I laid David down in the missionary position, straddled him like a jockey and worked my knees into his flanks as I rode him across the finishing line to an ecstatic climax.

It was late. We were drained, literally, and the last day of shooting was the longest, a full twelve hours from eight until eight. I could hardly open my eyes when I rolled out of bed all damp and sticky, but a film set is like a drug, as soon as you get a whiff of eggs and bacon frying the fatigue flows from your body and you feel completely alive.

We returned to the house of those kindly people the electricians were tirelessly chipping. Murray McVite exploded every five minutes and the runners named Max and Garth and Jake were running around with polish and marker pens concealing the scratches and scuffs.

'It's like being a virgin letting your house be used by a film crew,' said Murray. 'It only happens once.'

The gaffer shone the spotlight in Murray's eyes.

'Just testing,' said Pete.

'Bleedin' sparks,' Murray muttered, and I realised that all the yelling and complaining was just movie ritual, that the crew, like members of a family, like the actors themselves, had roles to play. Assistant directors would always be ill-tempered, the sparks would always be grumbling, and the runners were destined to run around like headless chickens never entirely sure what they were supposed to be doing.

The two Petes, ably assisted by the runners, were now chipping the paint on the stair stays as they lugged the light stands upstairs. David would be shooting two scenes in the bathroom, the one where Ricky drops his mobile phone down the loo, then the space would have to be 're-dressed' to look like a different bathroom for the scene where he peels off the bloody bandages and reveals the tattoo on his chest. First though, in natural light, we would be shooting the scene where the girls are clearing the shelves and Ricky appears with a towel around his waist.

Roddy Wise was already in make-up with Adam. I managed to squeeze by the commotion on the stairs with a cup of coffee and was leaning on the windowsill in the back bedroom watching the sun polish the glass sides of the buildings at Chelsea Harbour when Stephanie Jones arrived in a little white dress and a straw hat.

I hadn't seen Steph since we'd done our lesbian scene and she had gone through a complete metamorphosis. She was 42 and looked suddenly like a girl, her hair mussed when she removed her hat, her eyes aglow, her lips painted scarlet. Just as I'd suspected, my girlie juice was an elixir. I had between my legs the fount of eternal youth, the philosopher's stone, the white shell from which Venus emerged in a painting by Salvador Dalí, sublime and surreal. Steph looked marvellous and I was certain I was responsible. I had awoken the inner Miss Jones and it was something to be proud of.

Maja delivered our camouflage pants and tank tops and Stephanie asked me to lower the zip on the back of her dress. She stepped from the material and my mouth dropped open. She was naked, not a stitch, just a pair of white killer heels that bowed her back and made her breasts all perky.

'Well, it is hot,' she said, 'and I feel so sexy walking along the street exposed.'

I remembered that day when I'd gone for lunch at the Jewel Royale with Mummy and Binky, and after lunch for no apparent reason I'd whipped off my knickers and marched through Soho to see Jean-Luc Cartier. It confirmed my theory, girls just want to be seen in the altogether, bare as new-born babies, they want to be free of macho posturing and enjoy the gift of their beautiful bodies. I stared at Stephanie's fiery-tipped breasts and a curious thing happened, my own breasts started to buzz and tingle as if the sparks had joined us with invisible wires.

There was a rap on the door. 'Ten minutes to make-up.'

Steph opened the door and found Jake still standing there. 'Tell Adam we need fifteen,' she said, and closed the door again.

I peeled off my clothes and the electrical charge zipped across the room and drew us together with a force that took my breath away. Stephanie had tasted the elixir and was thirsting for more. I dropped into the leather chair under the window, stretched my legs over the arms and she kneeled to the holy orifice. Now girls' tongues are not like boys' tongues, but I was soon a river of oily goo that Steph supped from my clean-shaven pussy and I thought how brilliant, we needed a high degree of sexual tension in the living-room scene and what could be better preparation?

When we finally got to make-up, Roddy Wise was just leaving. He looked closely at me, he looked closely at Steph, and his lips pressed together in a knowing smile.

'Well, well, well,' he said.

Adam leaned out the door. 'This isn't a conveyor belt, you know,' he said. 'I can't do two at once.'

'Tyrant,' hissed Steph and he grinned.

Roddy strolled off along the corridor, his shoulders rising and falling as he chuckled to himself.

We managed to get the morning schedule done by the middle of the afternoon. We were two hours late already but everyone seemed to think the three morning set-ups had gone well and after lunch, Adam carefully painted the snake tattoo on my leg. I dressed and stood in the bath so that he could spray my clothes; in the film we'd been caught in a downpour leaving the wine bar; girls in wet clothes look sexy and it gives them an excuse to change into something more comfortable, like nothing at all.

I had put on one of Mummy's dresses, a reproduction chiffon ensemble from the thirties with a bow like the bow on a chocolate box on my shoulder. To hold the bow in place, Maja had found a silver snake pin in the Portobello Road; it was perfect: the snake was the film's leitmotiv and my bare leg with the fake tattoo would one day grace the case of a DVD. We had written out Amanda's change into the red kimono. It was redundant. Girls like Amanda Marshall wouldn't waste the effort.

Maja and Adam followed me downstairs. The crew was waiting. Murray shouted for everyone to be quiet and one of the runners gave me a bottle of champagne; it had already been opened so it would be easy for Ricky to open. The sound people would put the pop in later in the edit.

'And, action.'

Max snapped the clapper board. 'Amanda's Flat. Take one,' he said.

'Mark it,' said Dudley, and the cameras were turning.

I stood there in the damp dress, hair sticking to my forehead.

'You're not in a hurry?'

'Not at all.'

The camera stays on Ricky as I leave the room and return with a bottle of champagne and two cold glasses, one containing the sleeping draught. I give the bottle to Ricky. I smile girlishly as the cork pops. Some champagne spills over his hand. I smile again. I take the bottle and the camera follows me on the dolly as I go to fill the two waiting glasses. Amanda is such a bitch and I feel like a bitch as I turn with a look of adoration pasted on my sweet features.

'To . . . to what? To beauty,' he begins, and I say my lines as I watch him drink the champagne. I talk about being gang raped, being locked up and beaten up, the dominatrix in a leather mask, the backlash. I am a siren singing from the rocks, Eve the snake woman, a girl of eighteen, the ultimate object of desire. What man could resist betraying his lover?

We drink. I refill the glasses and the camera follows as I leave the room, the lens tracking my high heels. I unclip the snake pin as I go. I pause and let the dress fall to the floor. You see the dress, my legs, the

155

snake. I continue, the camera always on my heels, my calf, my thigh. I let my bra drop like a white cloud behind me. I pause again and delicately, oh so sexily, slip off my knickers, one leg at a time. Now I am naked. The camera pans slowly up my legs, over the snake circling my thigh, over my bottom, my back. I glance over my shoulder for a fraction of a second and toss my hair as I leave the room.

The reverse shot reveals Ricky wearing the expression of the man about to be given the biggest box of chocolates in the world.

We do four takes. Between every take Adam sprays my dress with water and the runners scurry around polishing the damp spots from the floor.

Next comes the scene with me waiting for Ricky in the bedroom. It is the first time that the head of the snake is fully revealed and, while the crew took absolutely hours shifting the camera gear, I lay back on the table in the make-up room, my legs gaping and Adam working with a fine brush trying to achieve a lifelike appearance about the snake's head, the gleam in those maroon eyes, the expression on its thin lips. Adam had stopped being embarrassed by my nudity, in fact he seemed to enjoy it, and what with all the attention, and what with my pussy wide open, I was positively oozing.

'You smell like you're in heat,' he said.

'I thought you were gay?'

He looked up across my tummy. 'You have to be flexible,' he replied, and he kept his eyes on mine as he lowered his head and licked the warm juice from my fragrant lips. I was pleased to have made a convert.

Maja accompanied me to the bedroom for the scene where I am standing naked waiting for Ricky.

Roddy Wise was already there, looking dishevelled and excited, the glass of champagne in his hand. Our eyes meet when he appears on the threshold. Again I tell him I won't be a second. As I slide from the room, he undresses and climbs into bed.

Ricky is supposed to be getting sleepy and, when I saw the rushes later, I thought Roddy was brilliant the way he was fighting to keep his eyes open. I re-enter the room looking shy and slide between the sheets. Although we had rehearsed the scene dozens of times, this time it was different. There was an extra element. Two in fact. We weren't wearing any clothes for one thing and, for another, Ricky had stopped being Ricky and had become Roddy. He didn't say anything. I didn't say anything. But a look passed between us, a pulse, a message, a frisson. The camera lifted on the jib high above the bed and as Roddy Wise slipped into my wet warm place it was a thrill knowing that David was watching.

5

Erotique Diabolique

Even short films cost a fortune and they take *forever*. In pre-production you rehearse, tweak the script, drink endless cups of cappuccino and go out looking for costumes and locations. During production you shoot the film. The days are long but it's lots of fun. The hard work begins in post-production.

Francis Ford Coppola said a film is made three times, first by the writer, then the director, then the editor, which was terribly clever and absolutely true. When we first entered the editing suite the scenes on the monitor seemed fragmentary, like overheard snatches of conversation or views glimpsed from a passing train. But Sacha Vance, the editor, could see in his silvery-blue eyes the best in every expression, in every gesture.

When I saw the raw footage of Stephanie Jones bringing me to an irrepressible orgasm in front of the director and crew I was so embarrassed I went red to the roots of my hair. But Sacha had cut the mildly pornographic into something charming and sensual. He did the same with the last scene when Roddy Wise eased my knees apart and slid his celebrity member into the jaws of the snake.

'You're a very dedicated actress,' Sacha whispered,

and I didn't like to tell him I was about to go up to university and I wasn't really an actress at all.

David needed constant reassurance as Sacha brought the emotional heart of his film to life, snipping out a few seconds from one take and combining it with another, moving from a close-up of a clock showing ten o'clock to the rain-lashed streets to Amanda Marshall striding into the bar, the femme fatale and de rigueur for ciné noir. Excuse my French!

According to Sister Theresa, the role of the writer is to put into words universal truths that will be understood intuitively and, as the writer's work goes through its metamorphosis to film, the editor is the director's conscience. The director has to get the shots in the can, but those gripping moments that send icy fingers running up our spine and bring a tear to our eye are all in the editor's hands.

After the edit, David had the soundtrack to worry about, and Hermann Mann came through by persuading George Trevor to take a sabbatical from his work on a West End musical to compose an original score. He began by asking David to name his favourite film and the velvety piano filling the bare spaces in the background was reminiscent of *Casablanca* and transformed the little movie once again. It had become a morality tale rooted in the zeitgeist, compelling, with something of the titivating, something of the tragic, and good enough, according to Mr Mann, to enter for the Cannes Film Festival, an honour indeed.

David was elated but I was growing bored and a little anxious. I'm sure I even saw a line on my brow one morning and it had never been there before. It was still hot, but as the leaves died on the trees and we entered an Indian summer the turning of the seasons was a reminder that for me it was time to turn the page.

I had never really had any doubts that I would be going up to Cambridge but still it was a relief when the letter arrived; there's only one place for every forty students who apply, and my parents in their undemonstrative way were terribly proud. Binky, if I knew Binky, would be working hard through her last year to keep up with me. It is the younger sister's plight to be competitive, as well as spoiled, and now that I was growing up I could see these things more clearly. All she had ever really needed was a good spanking, and now that her bottom had received some attention we had become the best of friends.

My life was on course except for one problem: by the time I got to King's at the end of September, there was no space in halls. I was the Virgin Mary without a manger and gratefully accepted a sofa in a flat occupied by Tamara Tucker, who had gone up to university from Saint Sebastian's the year before me and, as an Old Basher, was obliged to play the Good Samaritan.

I had never really liked Tamara's hockey-playing set at school, and now I couldn't bear those cacophonous nights with the headboard in the next room banging out Beethoven's *Fifth* on the dividing wall. Tamara was a fleshy, big-boned girl with a penchant for rugby players and was busy working her way through the college First XV.

Dark rings were forming under my eyes, and when Professor Martin asked me if everything was all right, I felt such a child as tears started rolling down my cheeks. When I told him I was homeless, he produced a big white handkerchief and made me blow my nose.

'You'll never get ahead sleeping on someone's

sofa,' he said, and I sniffed as he wrote down a telephone number. 'Give Dr Goetz a call, Milly,' he added, pulling the page from his notebook. 'He has a very nice attic that's ideal for a girl like you.'

I dried my tears, returned the damp handkerchief, and keyed the number into my mobile the moment I left the room. I told Dr Goetz I had been given his number by Professor Martin and raced through the cobbled streets of the old town when he asked me to call on him immediately. By the time I reached the house and gave a tap on the daunting lion's head knocker, I was hot and sticky, my breasts heaving in the tiny white blouse I had put on that morning not knowing that I was to meet the great Luther Goetz in person. He opened the door and studied me like I was a laboratory specimen.

'Camilla Petacci, I presume,' he said, and I nodded as I caught my breath.

'Please call me Milly.'

'I would be charmed.' He paused. 'Professor Martin's your tutor?'

'Yes.'

'And your school . . . ?'

'Saint Sebastian's,' I replied, although I couldn't see how this could possibly be relevant.

He stroked his beard as he stood to one side to let me in.

The hallway was big and airy with diffused pastel light falling through the stained-glass panels beside the entrance door. Dr Goetz closed the door and, having given me a close examination while I was waiting on the threshold, did so again while I stood on the shiny black and white tiles of the hall, my gaze drawn as if against my will to the haunting portrait on the wall beside the hat stand.

161

'Donatien Alphonse François, comte de Sade,' he said. 'It's a William Masterson copy of the portrait by Charles-Amédée-Philippe van Loo.'

I turned from the painting and the black eyes seemed to follow me. I smiled and felt silly.

'Any message from Dr Martin?' Dr Goetz now asked.

'No, he just said to give you a call. You have an attic.'

'I do indeed.' He leaned forward and our noses were almost touching. 'Let's go and take a look, shall we?'

I followed Dr Goetz upstairs to a room with a slanting roof. A big dormer window had a view over the River Cam that ran sparkling with sunshine at the foot of the garden. There was an iron bed with white cushions and an empty bookshelf waiting to receive my tomes of art history and Italian culture. My heart was thumping and I'm sure a faint smile was turning the corners of my lips. As my step-mother had learned from the Polish gardener, when you transfer plants from one place to another some wither and die and others take to the new soil and flourish. This room was the rich pasture I needed and I could see myself sitting there in the glow of a table lamp leafing through my books.

I looked out of the window, at the trees, at the river beyond, at the spires of unknown churches piercing the horizon. The attic was like a room in a fairy tale. I would take it whatever the price, even if I had to go hungry, and was completely taken aback when Dr Goetz explained that he did not charge rent, but I would be expected to serve drinks when he had 'little soirées', and 'it would be awfully kind' if I were to give the study a weekly dust because he didn't like the maid disturbing his papers.

162

'Would that be suitable, Milly?'

'Yes, of course, Dr Goetz.'

'I'm sure you're going to be very happy here,' he added.

I was on a strict budget imposed by my stingy mother and couldn't believe my luck as we descended the wide oak staircase to his study at the back of the house. It was a large, sunny room with French doors and ochre walls studded with sepia photographs. When I realised those photographs were of naked girls a crimson flush moved in a tide over my cheeks and neck.

'Do you know Man Ray?' the doctor asked, and I shook my head.

'No,' I said.

'Wonderful photographer. Such light. Such attention to negative space. The devil, Milly,' he whispered, pausing for effect, 'is always in the detail.'

As I drew closer to the photograph, I could see that the girl bent over a table being spanked by a bearded man had short curling horns that appeared to be growing from her skull and between the cheeks of her protruding bottom a long tail extended to the floor.

We both turned and I looked into Dr Goetz's deep-set eyes. They were green like pale chips of marble and seemed to shine with an inner light. His precisely-trimmed beard grew lush over the lower half of his face and gave him a distinct resemblance to the gentleman spanking the girl in the photograph. My palms had grown damp and my nipples for some frightful reason had hardened, pushing against the fabric of my thin blouse.

'You're not embarrassed, Milly?' he asked, and again I shook my head.

'No, of course not.'

163

'It's only art, my dear. Man Ray was the consummate photographer,' he added, 'really the forerunner of the new nude.'

We continued the tour. There were whips and canes in patterns adorning the walls between polished bookcases and stone sculptures of Indian deities in positions that made me blush once more. We paused at his desk on which there was an open book with a photograph of a faded painting of a naked girl with her arms suspended by a length of rope from the branches of a tree. On each side of the girl were two men with bare legs, each holding a long cane. Alongside the men, like an audience, were two animals.

'As you probably know, the tiger and rhinoceros have long been revered for the aphrodisiac qualities of their tusks and teeth,' the doctor said, and he reached for another book which he opened at a page containing a black and white photograph of a nude girl tied in similar circumstances.

'The original painting comes from the walls of the Ellora caves in India,' he explained. 'Buddhists, Hindus and Jains have been carving temples into the mountainside from as early as the 6th century, but what's intriguing is that their sculptures have an eroticism clearly influenced by the mystical religions from before anno domini.' His eyes moved from one picture to the other. 'But here's what's interesting,' he added, his voice intense with passion. 'The plate from circa 1860 restages in close detail the fresco from India. Why and who made that plate we can only hypothesise but, for my money, I'd say it is the work of a missionary who dabbled in photography and made a pilgrimage, as many did, to the Ellora caves.'

'Extraordinary,' I said.

'If you look closer, you'll see that the girl in the photograph is practically identical to the girl painted on the cave wall,' he continued. 'What this means, Milly, at least to me, is that man's idea of beauty and man's aspiration to beat the object of his desire has remained unchanged throughout time.'

I couldn't at that moment see why man wanted to beat the object of his desire, but I didn't think Dr Goetz would have appreciated the question. Instead I asked, 'Are you writing a paper?' and he stroked his beard as he glanced back at me.

'I am, yes. I'm in the midst of my research and would dearly like to learn more about the photographer before I publish.' He paused. 'Perhaps you'll find time to help, my dear.'

As he fixed me with his marble eyes, my mouth was suddenly dry and I could only nod my head in response. The sun was pouring through the open doors and it was so warm in the study, the gusset on my panties was growing damp. The material had worked its way into the lips of my vagina and, what with the array of naked girls and the whips on the wall, I grew shamefully aware of the whiff of arousal filling the room.

I hurried out to the garden feeling humiliated, but Dr Goetz, as if lured by the scent, came up behind me and we stood gazing at the flowerbeds around the edge of the lawn. 'Ah, don't you just adore that sweet aroma,' he said, and as he spoke a warm dribble leaked from my pants and slid down my thigh.

He glanced at me, eyes twinkling. 'Saint Sebastian's, that's the convent school out near Harrow, isn't it?' he asked.

'Yes. Quite close,' I answered, and his gaze ran from my lips, which I was biting, down to the strip of bare tummy below my blouse, and down to my knees which were trembling faintly below my white skirt.

He pointed then at the stack of turfs on the far side of the garden. 'We'll have to get those laid before winter sets in,' he said, and we turned to study the patches of bare earth. The garden was totally secluded behind mature trees and a lattice fence.

'There is one more thing, Milly, just a little fetish, really,' he added. 'You'll find a maid's uniform in the cupboard in your room. Please wear it when you do your jobs in my study.'

'Yes, of course, Dr Goetz,' I blurted out. 'Now I must go and get my things.'

I fled from the garden and ran all the way back to the flat. The way Dr Goetz had sized me up with those shrewd luminous eyes may have tempted me to remain in the sanctuary of Tamara's uncomfortable sofa, but it wasn't even lunchtime and already the headboard was beating against the wall. A number 11 rugger shirt hung like the flag of a conquering army from the standard lamp and, as the drumming grew louder, I packed my bags and set out with the double-edged sword of anxiety and elation stirring my insides. A taxi dropped me and my books outside the house and the Marquis de Sade was watching from the portrait on the wall as Dr Goetz helped carry my things upstairs.

When he opened the cupboard, the maid's uniform shimmied from the sudden gush of air.

'Here,' he said, and turned, stroking his beard. 'Just my little fetish,' he added, and of course he had told me that already.

I listened to his footsteps echo down the stairs and reached for the uniform. I slipped out of my clothes and my breasts tingled as I wriggled into the black

166

frock. The fabric was silky soft, so sensuous against my bare skin I couldn't help wondering what arcane secrets Luther Goetz had uncovered researching *Mediaeval Sorcery & Debauchery*, his classic work on the subject.

The frock was high-fronted with a white collar, a white apron that tied in a bow at the back, and was so short you could see the frilly white knickers that completed the outfit. There was a pair of black heels, uncannily my size, and so high that in order to stand straight my legs grew long and tapering, my breasts were thrust enticingly forward and my bottom pushed out as if willing passing hands to give it a smack. As I fixed the little white hat in place, I remembered from school plays that the moment you put on a costume, you become the character; I was the waitress from a saucy postcard, the ingénue from French farce. I painted my lips red, slapped my cheeks to give them colour, then stood back to get a full-length view in the mirror.

'Oo la la,' I said and wiggled my bottom like a parlour maid. *If only Jean-Luc Cartier could see me now!*

I didn't put the uniform on again until Sunday morning. Dr Goetz was in the garden preparing lectures and that feeling that I was on stage came back to me as I drifted through the gallery of naked girls, flicking the feather duster over the canes and whips on the wall.

The panelled room was like a museum with perverse implements ranged on shelves under the bejewelled watchful eyes of the Indian deities. I paused to examine a long phallus and, while I had no experience of such things, I knew it was odd having, not one, but two penises joined end to end, and couldn't imagine what purpose it served. It was faintly yellow and had the look of old piano keys, the surface veined and warm to the touch. The body of the object was connected to straps and the ends of those long penises were finished as leering snake heads with glinting emerald eyes.

'It is made from the tusk of a white rhinoceros,' said Dr Goetz as he entered. 'All these things are rare and precious, the symbols of our innermost secrets and desires.' He paused and fixed me with a mischievous expression. 'Do be careful, won't you? Like a sailing ship, a good house is driven by the winds of discipline.'

My cheeks flushed as I put the monster back on the shelf. The doctor was amused by my reaction, and studied the maid's uniform as I stood with my hands submissively at my sides. Dr Goetz was wearing black espadrilles tied at the ankles and his bare legs below khaki shorts seemed oddly out of place belonging, as they did, to a famous scholar.

'Very nice, my dear. Very nice,' he said finally, and I curtsied, keeping in character, as he turned to go back to the garden.

A day or two later, I was sweating over an essay when there was a polite tap on the door.

'Come in.'

Dr Goetz entered with a large white box. He had invited his coven, as he put it, for drinks on Saturday, and would like me to dress appropriately to serve hors d'oeuvres. He placed the parcel solemnly among the books and papers strewn over the bed.

'An essay?' he asked.

'On the role of castratos in Renaissance opera,' I replied.

'Let me read it when it's done,' he said. 'We all want you to do your best, Milly.'

He left the room and I felt like a child at Christmas when I pulled the lid off the box. I peeled back the tissue paper. 'Oh, my God, I can't wear this!' I gasped, but even as I spoke I was popping open the buttons on my jeans and pulling my blouse over my head. I slipped out of my underwear and watched my reflection in the dark window. I had spent so much time stepping out of my clothes on the set of *Cheats* there hadn't been time for eating, and now I rather liked being all angular and shapely, a geometric figure like the sign for infinity, rounded at the top and bottom, wasp thin in the middle, my hip bones like the handles on a school trophy.

Inside the white box was a costume, a pair of green tights with a long tail attached to the crotch, green stilettos, again an oddly good fit, and a silk top that scarcely concealed my flagrantly pert nipples. Perhaps I should see the doctor, I thought? The little rosebuds were tingling painfully, aroused at the least provocation. I gave them a pinch and felt a contraction in my pussy. I was wet all of a sudden and stuffed a Kleenex between my legs so I didn't leak into the green tights. I once asked Binky if she got wet *down there* all the time.

'Only in the shower, Cammy,' she replied. It was her baby name for me and she used it on those occasions when she felt a need to be disapproving.

At the bottom of the box there was a rubber mask that fitted over the back of my head and covered the top half of my face, the swirling eye-slits in the same shape as the curling horns. I went to the bathroom and standing there before me in the full-length mirror was an emerald demon that reminded me of the photograph by Man Ray on the study wall, the girl with the tail bent over a table about to be spanked.

169

The costume was curiously, coldly erotic. With your face half covered I imagined it would be easy to believe you were someone else and once you were someone else there was no telling what that someone might be capable of. I thought about something Dr Goetz had said: *We all want you to do your best.* I'm sure he had not been talking about my studies. On the contrary, I had a feeling that I was being prepared for something and dressed as a green demon I felt ready for it, whatever it was.

It was getting late. I folded the costume back in the box and placed my books on the shelf. My essay would have to wait for another day. I cleaned my teeth, thought about wearing my pyjamas, but didn't, and stepped naked between the white cotton sheets. I was sopping wet and feeling so revved up I knew I wouldn't get to sleep without resorting to the discreet charms of the hand cream bottle, a perfectly shaped phallus, even the top was like the head of a penis, but I suppose that's the point. Everything made for women makes you think of sex. I slid the bottle up inside me.

Agh, that's better.

I like to do it slowly, churning the goo like whipping butter for a cake, my free hand screwing my nipples until they sting, first one then the other, the dear little monkeys. Mmm, it's so wonderful being a girl. You're never bored. There's always something to do, something to play with. When I feel myself coming I make myself stop. I caress my breasts, my hip bones, the flat of my tummy, delaying the moment of pleasure to extract more pleasure, then back to the hand cream bottle, in and out, slowly, slowly, until my hips lose all sense of gravity, my toes curl and out it comes, a great gush of oily juice that

170

stains the sheets and has the bittersweet smell of deep dreams and faraway places. I feel tempted to insert the tube in my bum but I feel so relaxed I roll over, close my eyes and doze off thinking about David's smart little soldier.

At the gathering that Saturday were several men, feudal academics attired in the eccentric manner of their calling, and a sprinkling of women with wan features, carmine lipstick and a weakness for gypsy dresses. Professor Martin was constantly brushing his hair from his eyes and studying me as if he were my mentor, rather than my tutor, and was proud of some girlish achievement.

The last person to appear was a younger woman in a leather catsuit with a long zip open to her navel to reveal two perfectly round breasts in cups of scarlet satin.

The other guests seemed relieved that she had arrived and were orbiting her like space dust drawn to a heavenly body. I felt the same pull and could hardly take my eyes from her ivory-white breasts as I passed the crackers and guacamole dip. I was aware subconsciously that while I was captivated by the woman, the rest of the group was intrigued by my reaction to her.

I left with the empty tray and opened a fresh bottle of cava sent privately from the mediaeval convent in Peralada in Spain and celebrated, Dr Goetz had said, 'for its primordial flavours and the bitter taste of tears'.

When I filled the woman's champagne flute we were introduced by Professor Martin.

'Milly Petacci, my student,' he said, and paused, 'Dr Alba Iliescu . . .'

I was juggling the icy bottle and as I tried to shake hands, she put her arm around my waist, my mouth fell open in surprise, and she inserted her tongue halfway down my throat.

'. . . Ethics,' added my tutor, and the others smiled.

'It is the custom of my country,' Dr Iliescu explained.

The cava was frothing over my hand. She ran her fingers down my spine, playing me like a flute, and the feeling was both eerie and erotic in that room of spanked girls and contorted deities.

'There is a man in the Carpathians who reads the future from the back bone and in these little hills and valleys I sense good fortune.'

I didn't know whose, hers or mine, and as I didn't like to ask, I popped my tongue back in my mouth. She drank the cava in one long gulp and held out the glass for it to be refilled.

'You have heard of Count Dracula, I presume?'

'Yes.'

'I share his blood.'

Dr Iliescu raised her glass and turned to Dr Martin.

'Young but perfectly charming,' I heard her say, although I wasn't sure if she were referring to me or the Peralada cava.

I toured the room, filling glasses, feeling light-headed, my spine like jelly, the ghost of her fingertips still waltzing to some faraway music. In the kitchen, I peeled the foil from another bottle of cava and poured a glass for myself. I sat to catch my breath, the bubbles making me feel light-headed as they went up my nose.

More time than I had realised must have gone by and, when I returned to the study, the guests were already leaving and Dr Goetz was furiously making notes at his desk.

From the entrance I watched Professor Martin looming over Dr Iliescu like a deferential shadow as they made their way into the gathering darkness. I took the empty plates and glasses back to the kitchen. Dr Goetz was staring at the open page of a book showing a pentangle surrounded by the signs of the Zodiac and, when I said good night, he didn't look up. It was a shame to waste the cava and I drank two more big glasses before tipping the rest down the sink.

It was a relief to scurry upstairs back to my room and when I pulled off the devil mask my eyes were red, my ears hurt and my head was spinning. I climbed into bed and fell into a deep sleep where I saw myself running in a diaphanous negligee with footsteps pursuing me along the endless stone corridors of a castle. Every corner I turned led to another corridor and when I fell exhausted to the floor the black nuns of Peralada surrounded me like a flock of cackling ravens.

I awoke in a sweat, stood for ages under the shower and as I got dressed in my uniform it occurred to me that nuns and parlourmaids wear the same colours.

It was housework day and I had a whine like a radio stuck between stations playing in my head. I polished the sculptures and phalluses, the canes and whips, the leather spines of weighty books. I was running a duster over the glass protecting the prints when I noticed that one of the antique frames had opened at the join. I took it down from the wall and, like I was snapping a wishbone, I pulled the frame apart.

Now you've done it!

Dr Goetz was a perfectionist. He enjoyed beauty and ritual. He demanded order and obedience. I knew all that, you didn't have to be a psychologist to work it out, but somewhere between my throbbing head and a sudden sense of Sunday madness, I wanted to see what would happen. Like a cat bringing home its kill to be admired, I wandered out into the garden to show Dr Goetz the damaged frame.

He was sitting in the shade of a green canopy writing with a fountain pen and looked at me for a long time without saying anything.

'It's broken,' I said finally.

'So I see.'

He screwed the top back on his pen. My heart was pounding. It was the first days of October, the Indian summer had lasted and the sun was so hot I was running with sweat inside the maid's dress.

'A civilised house runs on discipline, don't you agree?'

'Yes, Dr Goetz.'

'The canes on the wall like the books on the shelf are not merely for decoration. A good cane, like a good Stradivarius, needs to be played,' he said, and a shudder ran through me.

I was afraid of what he might do, afraid but excited, an adventurer at the beginning of a journey. Studying can become awfully tedious. You have to get out of yourself sometimes. Dr Goetz was drumming his fingers on the arm of his chair, weighing me up.

'Perhaps later, my dear,' he finally said, and I felt oddly disappointed as he stood and pointed at the bare patches of grass below the trees. 'The ground

174

has been prepared,' he added. 'What I would like you to do is lay the turfs, lay them as close together as you can, then we'll give them a thorough dousing.'

'Yes, of course, Dr Goetz,' I gushed.

I gave a little curtsy before turning and making my way towards the stacks of turfs.

'Milly,' he called, and I stopped. 'You're not thinking of gardening in that nice clean uniform, are you?'

My heart started pounding even more. I stood there, frozen like a rabbit in the headlights of his marble eyes.

'Come along then, girl. Put the uniform over the back of the chair here.'

'But, doctor . . .'

'Do it now, Milly.'

There was something in his voice that made me want to obey. I was dripping inside the black dress and the very notion of taking it off was oddly appealing. I slowly approached the vacant chair and he made a twirling motion with his fingers. I turned and, as he pulled the tails of the white bow on the back of the apron, I had the sense that I was a gift being unwrapped.

I bent my arms up my back to lower the zip and placed the dress on the chair. I removed the little maid's hat and stopped for a moment. His eyes were on me, willing me to continue and, when I unsnapped my bra, releasing my breasts, my nipples seemed to grow pinker and sparkled in the autumn sunlight. I lowered the frilly knickers. I was wearing cotton briefs under all those frills and when I stood straight with the briefs still in place, Dr Goetz made a stern downward motion with his forefinger.

'Everything?' I asked.

'Everything,' he replied.

175

I bit my lip. We looked at each other and his marble eyes glowed.

I tucked my thumbs in the elastic and paused like Cæsar on the banks of the Rubicon. I ran my knickers down my legs, and as I stepped away from them they could have been a white rose blooming on the grass. I went to pick them up, but the doctor's hand was quicker and he scooped the damp triangle of cotton into his palm.

'There, now, isn't that better?' he asked and as he ran my knickers under his nose I was back with the clan of the Black Watch in bonny Scotland. *Why do they do that? Men are just too weird!*

I stepped out of my heels and wandered back across the garden, the dry grass tickling my toes, my breasts bobbing and swaying with the centrifugal force of my steady gait, my bottom like two moons, my pubic hair cropped like a boy's haircut. I had known the moment I had seen the maid's uniform in the cupboard that the time would come when I took it off for Dr Goetz, and now that I had done so I felt a sense of liberation, a sense that I had obeyed my own instincts. I had not taken the uniform off for him. I had taken it off for me. With the right words, the right conditions, girls want to obey. We are programmed to obey, and those men who understand that can take girls with the right attitude to the extremes of their true potential. I looked back at Dr Goetz and our eyes met.

'One at a time, Milly, otherwise they break.'

'Yes, Dr Goetz.'

I could barely reach the top of the pile of turfs and as soon as I lowered the first one I was sprayed with a shower of dust that went into my eyes and mouth and up my nose. I sneezed.

'Bless you,' he said, and sat back to watch, his bare legs crossed, his hands folded in his lap.

I carried the roll of earth across the garden and set it down in the turned soil below the trees. As I went down on my hands and knees to push the turf in place, I was aware that in that position my breasts hung heavily below me like swollen udders. My bottom would be gaping open in such a way that it would give Dr Goetz a bird's eye view of my most intimate places as well as recreating another of the sepia prints on the study wall, a girl on all fours, her back bowed in a downward arc, her face turned to the camera with the bewildered but contented look of a gazelle coming across a vacant salt lick.

Of course, I should have started laying the turfs in such a way that I was facing the doctor, but it was obvious to start at the furthest point and, now that I'd started, like skydiving from an aeroplane, I was freefalling through the void and could do nothing but imagine wings were sprouting from my shoulder blades. I was free, naked. I was flying. I moved into profile knowing that, in this position, on all fours, shoulders higher than the curve of the bottom, a girl looks her very best, a healthy young animal, natural, earthy, deeply erotic, yet deeply feminine.

I went back for another turf, and another. The sun grew hotter and sticky rivulets of dirt ran between my breasts, over my tummy, into the crack of my bottom, the earth turning to mud as it touched my skin. I recalled reading that Einstein got more pleasure making his own bookshelf than penning his theory $E = mc^2$ and I was conscious of the same satisfaction, the patchwork of grass growing as my wet body became an atlas of oozing slime.

Dr Goetz watched me as he spoke on his mobile,

and I tried to see myself as he was seeing me, a bare grubby girl with breasts slicked in mud from where I supported the turfs, my knees pitted. I felt natural, primeval, the narcissism of my nakedness before the eyes of the doctor sending shivers of inexplicable pleasure up my spine. That shivery feeling reminded me of the way Dr Iliescu had played me like a musical instrument, and I remembered Professor Martin following her into the night as if lured by a spell.

The moment Professor Martin popped into my brain, his head popped around the French doors. He gave me a wave, then sat beside Dr Goetz.

I am not sure why I was embarrassed, but my cheeks turned to fire and I was aware of my breasts jiggling as I bounded back to the stack of turfs. Dr Goetz with his beard shaped like pubic hair was a paradigm of the perverse, but my tutor was really rather boyish with his long nose and big teeth, and it was only at that precise second that I knew why my tutor had sent me to Dr Goetz in the first place.

The two academics in their Sunday shorts and sandals sat in the shade watching me move across the garden as if they were spectators at a cricket match on a village green. The sun grew bigger and hotter. The piles of turfs slowly went down and, by the time I had set the last one in place, I was no longer a nude girl. I was an earth maiden, a fertility symbol, something primitive and wanton, every orifice filled, every crease and crack slippery with perspiration. I felt like a healthy little animal, my limbs tired, my heart beating evenly in my chest, my breasts standing out as proud as the prows on a pair of pirate ships.

Dr Goetz came closer to look. 'Well done, Milly, that's a lovely job,' he said and patted my bottom in the friendly way you might pat a pony. I felt awfully proud for some silly reason.

The doctor went and found a flat sheet of board from the garden shed and my tutor helped him place it over the newly laid grass. They walked up and down, settling the turfs in.

'Nice job,' said Professor Martin. 'It's very dry, though.'

'It just needs a good wetting, Andy,' he replied. 'Go and get the hose, my dear,' he added, turning to me.

The hose was attached to a spool on the side of the shed. It needed all my strength to unwind the green snake across the garden. I turned on the tap and the men sat back below the canopy mopping their brows with white handkerchiefs while I gave the grass a good dousing. When that was done, I tried to wash the earth off my body, holding the hose in one hand, but it required two hands to do a decent job. I needed to stand under the spray and spent ages trying to hook the hose over the overhanging bough of a tree, throwing it up again and again, the water swishing backwards and forwards like rain on a car wind-screen, the men observing my clownish performance like children at the circus. Finally, the hose hooked and I wriggled and squirmed under the cold water. I got most of the mud off, but it was really caked on in some places and wouldn't budge.

'Here, let me give you a hand,' Professor Martin said, approaching and pulling the hose down from the tree.

He held his thumb over the nozzle and I danced around under the spray.

'That's never going to do it, Andy,' said Dr Goetz. 'I'll get the bucket.'

The doctor collected the bucket from the shed and placed it in the middle of the patio tiles. Professor Martin filled it, and I stood there submissively as he washed me down with a big yellow sponge, first my back, under my arms, deep in the creases of my bottom and down my legs. I lifted one leg at a time, he cleaned between my toes, and I rinsed my feet in the bucket, which he emptied and refilled with clean water.

He hosed down the parts he had cleaned, wrung out the sponge several times and I turned round. He dipped into the wells below my collar bones, discreetly lifted my breasts to wash underneath, then spent ages down on his haunches scrubbing my pitted knees, his long nose so close to my wet pussy it was in danger of slipping inside. He sluiced the dirt from my pubic hair and ran his fingers between the open lips of my vagina. As my tutor, his role was to cleanse my mind of preconceived ideas, although I must say he did a good job running the sponge through the lips of my vagina to cleanse away any lingering motes of earth.

He revolved the head of the hose against my labia, giving everything a good rinse. My lips puckered open, sucking at the tube so that a fountain of water gushed up inside me, teasing every fold and nerve ending. I wasn't conscious that I was lowering myself over the tip of the hose, but I did so, and my tutor responded to my movement, easing it up and down, up and down, soaking his leather sandals. My eyelids closed. My bottom contracted, the breath caught in my throat, and then I gasped, my wet orgasm exploding like a champagne cork, warm juices flooding my thighs, and I was aware that the hose was like the tail attached to the girl in the photograph by Man

Ray, that everything was elaborately connected, an erotic puzzle still taking shape.

Dr Goetz emerged from the house with a length of white rope and two canes.

'Would you believe it, this girl broke one of the antique frames,' he said, addressing Dr Martin. He looked at me, standing there dripping wet in the autumn sunshine. 'Do you remember what I told you, Milly? Like a sailing ship, a good house is driven by the winds of discipline.'

He coiled the rope efficiently around my wrists as he was speaking and I found myself being led docilely back to the same overhanging bough where I had hooked the hose. Dr Goetz tossed the end of the rope over the branch in one throw, looped the end through the knots about my wrists and hauled my arms up above my head. He secured the end of the rope around the trunk of the tree. Stretched up on my toes, wet and naked, I was a ripe shapely girl of eighteen who had known the first moment I had seen the whips and canes and crops on the wall that one day I would taste them upon my flesh. What man could resist striping my backside with a cane? What girl could resist such flattering attention?

'Six each, I think, Andy,' Dr Goetz said thoughtfully, and my gasp was so loud he seemed suddenly surprised that naked girls made noises and caned girls were likely to give full throat to their gratification.

He hurried back into the house and returned with a leather gag containing a ball about the size of a golf ball attached at the centre and straps that he buckled at the back of my head. 'We don't want the neighbours to hear, now do we, they'll only complain that they weren't invited.'

He stood back and glanced around the garden, at the new turfs glistening with beads of water, the turned flowerbeds waiting to be replanted, the sky as blue as a robin's egg. My tutor came and stood beside Dr Goetz and they studied me as if I were an exhibit in a gallery, my breasts, my well-defined rib cage, the sensuous turn of my hip bones, the isosceles triangle of my pubic hair. I felt like a work of art, a new sculpture released from an ancient mould. I was connected to a primordial tradition that went back to the beginning of time. The two academics with their bare legs and me, naked, hanging from a tree, my toes just touching the ground, was an exact representation of the cave drawing in India, a tableau vivant carefully replicated by some Victorian clergyman.

Dr Goetz ran his hand down my back and over the curve of my bottom. 'I told you about my research into the frescos at the Ellora caves,' he said and Dr Martin leaned forward with interest. 'The intriguing thing is, Andy, the girl in the photograph is identical to the girl painted on the cave wall. And our Milly is a mirror image of them both, the full breasts, the slender waist, the shapely hips, her mica-dark eyes and long tresses.'

'An Indian deity, quite astonishing.'

'Not exactly,' said Dr Goetz. 'It conforms to my theory, as I told Milly, man's idea of beauty, the shape and form, and man's aspiration to beat the object of his desire, has remained unchanged throughout time. It is, if you like, the very definition of reincarnation.'

I would like to have joined in the discussion, but I couldn't speak through the gag, and it was a shame because I had a lot to say on the matter. I had spent some time contemplating why men wanted to beat girls and had come to the conclusion that it was because they wanted to own them and, while we practised obedience and thrived on discipline, while we relished being objects of desire, objects so desirable men were moved to chastise that object in the most agonising fashion, they could never truly possess the object. Land and gold, yes. The souls of girls never.

The poet Sappho wrote that *what is beautiful is good*, and Schiller said *physical beauty is a sign of interior beauty, a spiritual and a moral beauty*. The nuns at Saint Sebastian's had the same view, or at least it always seemed to be the pretty girls who were made team captains and prefects.

I had never really thought of myself as being beautiful, that was Binky's domain. But I had blossomed under Jean-Luc Cartier's hand and my being there that day in the garden, bound and naked, was a sign of my inner purity, my earnest struggle to be true to myself, a stepping stone on the path of my destiny. Freedom is being yourself, knowing yourself. That moment when Jean-Luc held a glass of water to my mouth and the water gushed over my front was a Zen awakening, and I had relived it in my imagination many times since. I had never been caned before. I knew it would hurt, it would hurt a lot, and I knew, too, that I could mutate the pain into pleasure. I sucked on the rubber ball and it was soothing.

'After you,' Dr Goetz said.

My tutor stood back on the wet grass, took a practice swing with the cane and brought the beast down on my proffered bottom. I bit down hard on the ball and a tear squeezed from my eye. Sweat gushed from my armpits. My shoulder blades cracked. My knees trembled and my backside burned like the fires of Valhalla as the flames whipped up my spine and down the backs of my legs.

The way my hands were suspended, my toes were scarcely touching the ground and, as I wriggled, my body turned and surely looked more appealing, my dancing thighs inviting attention and that's where the second stripe came, across the soft flesh below the pouting lip of my bottom. I screamed in silence, sucked the rubber ball and pirouetted on the tips of my toes.

'I don't recall ever seeing anything quite so lovely,' I heard Dr Goetz say, but the words faded at the sound of the cane slashing the air and printing a third stripe across my inflamed posterior, the line slicing the first two and scorching shiny stars of tenderness where they crossed.

My whole body was on fire, my pink nipples tingling, my shoulders taut, the provocative globes of my rump like red-hot coals.

'Three,' the doctor said, and I really didn't think I would make twelve.

I noticed Dr Martin change position. The fourth crack of the cane was another diagonal, scoring my bottom from the top of my left cheek to the place where my right cheek curves into my thigh. I wriggled as if to escape the blows knowing that my wriggling bottom would be all the more enticing, and knowing that there was no escape. I had without protest allowed myself to be tethered to a tree. I had imagined it the very moment I gazed down at the photograph of the girl in the cave painting in India. I had willed it. I was in a position of total servitude, total surrender, and with that thought the pain was more tolerable. My tutor took up his position once again, and once again the cane seared my moist folds of flesh. One more, I thought, one more and we are halfway. Sweat glistened from my body and, as the cane came down, I was aware of the sweet musky smell of my own arousal.

'Very nice, Andy,' said Dr Goetz.

I opened my eyes and my gaze met the cool marble stare of Luther Goetz.

'This is going to hurt, Milly,' he said. 'Your tutor is a new convert to our calling, but I am experienced in the art.'

He stood back and gave several practice swings. I heard the thin cane cut the still air and the sound was like cotton being ripped asunder, like an axe splitting wood, like the sigh of the sky at night. I closed my eyes and tried to remain still. I would absorb the pain. I had done it before. But the pain when it came was like no pain I had ever experienced, like nothing I could imagine. The cane burst upon my bottom like an explosion, like the invasion of a foreign army. Tears pressed from my tightly closed eyelids. Sweat ran down my back and dried the instant it reached the furnace of my burning bottom.

The cane came down again and again. I was sure I would be marked forever and I didn't care. I just wanted it to be over. Two. Three. Four. Each worse than the one before, the doctor picking his spot and finding unmarked flesh to brand, lines of fire crossing lines of fire. It was nearly over. I had done it. I would take the beating as the girl in the cave in India must surely have done more than two thousand years ago, like the girl in the amateur photograph. We were sisters in an eternal tradition. It was something to be proud of and, with that thought floating into my mind, the fifth strike of the cane didn't seem quite so painful.

In spite of my resolve, I had been wriggling non-stop and determined to remain still, to take the twelfth stroke of the cane with dignity. My body was ablaze with new feelings, new sensations, and it was with complete horror and even embarrassment that as the cane crossed my flesh one last time I felt a contraction inside my sodden pussy and sighed silently through a long smouldering climax. How? Why? It was something to ponder later and now I hung there suspended from the bough of a tree feeling deeply debauched and deeply satisfied.

I used what strength I had left to stretch up, my feet left the ground, and I swung backwards and forwards, the movement of air cooling my poor little bum, my scored thighs, my burning pussy. When I opened my eyes, the two academics in their short trousers were studying me with what I thought was awe and respect. Could they have done what I had done? I didn't think so.

'Take her down, Andy, I won't be a moment,' Dr Goetz said and went hurrying back across the garden to the house.

Dr Martin untied the rope from the tree and I came slowly back down to earth. He freed my bonds, released the gag, and I collapsed in his arms. I was trembling, aftershocks of my orgasm clenching my insides. Dr Martin carried me back to the shade below the green canopy and, at that moment, Dr Goetz reappeared with a tub of ointment. He sat in his chair.

'Here, Andy, over my knee.'

Dr Martin did as he was instructed. He lowered me to my feet and bent me over Dr Goetz's knee. I thought I was going to be spanked and was too weak to argue. I was wrong. The doctor removed the top from the tub he had brought from the house and I flinched as he soothed ointment into my fiery cheeks.

'Witch hazel,' he said. 'It will smart for a moment, then the pain fades.'

He was right. After the initial moment, the sting went away and I felt a wave of pleasure course through my body. The sun was slipping towards the horizon, scoring orange stripes on the pale blue dome of the sky, and I remained stretched over the doctor's lap as he spread the ointment over the orange stripes on the dome of my bottom. I was a well-beaten and satisfied girl at one with the universe.

It was almost dark and getting chilly when I came to my feet. Dr Martin had thoughtfully gone to get a towel and I enclosed myself in its folds.

'Thank you,' I said, and walked slowly back into the house.

I thought about taking a shower, but the witch hazel was so soothing I decided to stay sticky. I lay on my tummy on the unmade bed and called David. I told him what had happened that day in the garden and, the moment I had finished telling him my tale, he asked me to tell him again.

'Why?'

'When people tell their stories they always remember more details the second time,' he replied. 'It's a writer's trick.'

I could hear his breath race.

'David, are you masturbating?'

'Are you joking? Of course I am.'

'Slowly, slowly,' I said. As my fingers slipped up inside my wet parts I understood the pleasures of phone sex for the first time.

* * *

Over the coming weeks I watched the grass grow greener as it slowly knitted together and, like the lawn, the welts on my bottom slowly healed. The caning had left me poised, calm and focused. My gaze was clearer, my mind sharper. I could remember every detail in the books I was reading for my course and my essay on the role of castratos in Renaissance opera received an appraisal from Dr Goetz that made my tutor so proud he sent me a dozen roses that I stood on the shelf below the window in my room. I had never received roses from anyone before.

I joined the philosophical society and met up with several Old Bashers at Tamara Tucker's gunpowder, treason and plot party. As a good Catholic girl, Tamara found it *fwightfully wisqué* burning Guy Fawkes on a pyre of packing crates. The garden was filled with rowing blues and rugger toffs, young men with floppy hair and girls who reminded me of Mummy in their designer shoes and Tiffany bracelets. Fairy lights like falling snow glimmered in the trees and the retro band playing music by The Who kept conversation at a minimum.

I drank too much champagne and went home with a scrum half named Guy or Oliver or James, something historic. In the hall outside his room, he pulled off my clothes in the way you might toss items in a laundry basket, dropped his trousers and hoisted me like a trophy on to his erection. As my feet left the ground his firework exploded and he was too inebriated to be embarrassed. I got a taxi home.

The petals fell from the roses. The days were growing shorter. I went Christmas shopping between lectures and was packing to go home for the holidays when Dr Goetz invited me to join the coven in the country to celebrate the winter solstice. It would mean delaying my return to London, but activities surrounding Luther Goetz were likely to be educational and would almost certainly be more interesting than the student parties punctuating the days.

The doctor drove an old maroon Bentley and I enjoyed sinking into the wrinkled leather seat at his side. We collected Professor Martin and one of the wan women, who appeared dressed from head to toe in black with a black veil and whose name as if by some literary convention was Dr White.

We sat in silence, mesmerised by the lap of the tyres on the road. The buildings thinned and disappeared, the country lanes became narrow, the headlights making amber haloes on the hedgerows. Tall trees with bare branches patterned the sky and in the crepuscular light it felt as if we were moving through a dark tunnel of time. After this, the shortest day, the days would grow longer, the cycle would continue. I felt connected to that cycle, a tiny dot in the portrait of time.

We passed through high gates set in thick privet. The track descended into a valley and in a cleft between the hills stood a Gothic mansion with towers and turrets, arched windows and gargoyles leaping from the corners of the roof. Dr White led me to my room and stood on the threshold gripping my arms with trembling hands and staring into my eyes as if I was about to go into hospital for an operation.

'I love the full moon, don't you?' she gushed, but didn't wait for an answer. 'You'll find your costume on the bed,' she added and glided along the corridor on feet dancing to music only she could hear. Academics are by nature weird and the women are the worst.

A nun's habit lay on the eiderdown. Black candles lent the room an eerie glow and adorning the red

189

flock wallpaper were prints of prehistoric creatures in repeating patterns that reminded me of Escher, but the drawings were peculiarly unsettling and androgynous, lizards eating little girls who are defecating little boys who in turn are eating lizards. They were signed *Pandora* and I imagined that the room with its blood-red ceiling and red carpet was the very box from which sprang all manner of depravity.

The black habit was made of the same fabric as the maid's uniform. As I peeled off my clothes to try it on, a slice of moonlight entered the glass doors like an ethereal hand that beckoned me to the stone balcony outside. I thrust back the doors and, protected by the birds of prey guarding the balustrade, I stood in the lunar glow breathing the intoxicating air of the solstice.

It was December 21st but I didn't feel cold. My flesh was feverish. A ray of milky light entered the top of my head and shot through my body. My bottom was tingling with pins and needles. I ran my fingertips over the fine lines left from the caning. I looked back over my shoulder and, in the reflection of the glass windows, I could see a pattern scorched into my skin. Like moonlight on moving water, like a photograph emerging in a developing tray, the pattern took the shape of a pentangle, the silver scars, invisible by day, illuminated by the ghostly light of the moon. I was branded by the moon. People through time have worshipped the sun but I from that day on would always belong to the moon.

I left the doors open and went to dress in the nun's habit, the garment making me feel both religious and sacrilegious, each containing a shade of the other, needing the other. I was tingling and moist, my thighs prickling. The white cap covered my head, framing my face, and the habit clung to my full breasts. I looked sexual, predatory, and it occurred to me as I gazed into the bevelled mirror that nuns must know the effect they have.

There was a knock on the door. I turned and Dr White entered, costumed now as a Druid in white. She led me through the labyrinth of stone corridors that were rather similar to those in the dream I'd had that night when I drank too much Peralada cava, the night of the soirée.

We arrived at a hall where the rest of the group were similarly dressed, some with their hoods in place, their eyes like black holes as they followed my entrance. The sky was lit by a sprinkling of early stars and all eyes flickered frequently towards the moon as it climbed through the heavens beyond the high arched windows.

A bent waiter with a club foot was passing flutes of fizzing cava and laid out on a table was a selection of food, all in black and white: little rings of goat's cheese dotted with caviar, quails' eggs in black pepper, black olives, black rice with slivers of cuttle-fish, aphrodisiac selections from Gala Dali's surrealist cookbook, said Dr White, although my tummy was too tense for anything except champagne.

My tutor approached across the room wearing his hood, but he was taller than everyone else and I knew it was him by his sloping, slightly diffident walk. The moment he joined me, one of the ghostly figures peering from the window called, 'It's time,' and everyone hurried to deposit their plates back on the table. Professor Martin took my elbow and guided me towards the door and outside, on the stone flagging, we formed two ranks. I was positioned immediately behind the first two and we set off in a snaking file towards a low, perfectly round hill we approached up a stone path. The Druids chanted as they went.

Waiting at the top of the hill was a man I assumed was Dr Goetz, dressed in black, his face hidden in a hangman's hood. Beside him stood Alba Iliescu, wearing devil's horns that extended from her headdress and a black cape that swirled around her body in the evening breeze. A pentangle of white stones was laid out on the top of the hill and I noticed three wooden stakes were set in an isosceles triangle within the pattern.

Heaven In Is It As Earth On . . .

I tried to make sense of the words but my attention was fixed on Dr Iliescu. She removed her cape and stood there naked except for the devil mask, her white breasts gleaming, her hand supporting the huge penis strapped about her. She appeared to be masturbating, stroking the phallus like a man, but this I realised was an optical illusion: she was wearing the double-headed penis from Dr Goetz's study and was driving the concealed half of the phallus up inside her. The chanters were still chanting . . .

Done Be Will Thy Come Kingdom Thy . . .

I noticed Dr Iliescu's chin go back, her mouth fell open and she let go of the rhinoceros horn to stop herself climaxing. At that moment, the full moon reached its apogee and became a ball of white fire over the horizon.

The black-clad Druid bent forward and lifted the hem of my nun's habit. He ripped it along the seam, tearing it from me like he was skinning the forbidden fruit. I was wearing pink panties which he cleaved apart, one side, then the other. He turned me round and the chanters chanted even louder as they gazed upon the pentangle gleaming upon the moon of my white bottom.

Name Thy Be Hallowed Heaven In Art Who Father Our . . .

The man in black looked up at the sky, then urged me to enter the stone pentangle. I was made to lie down. My arms were lashed to the stake above my head and my legs were spread out, my ankles tied to the two remaining stakes.

The chanters were chanting, but all I could focus on was Alba Iliescu lowering herself between my spread thighs, her lips slightly parted, her eyes gleaming like two black stars, like portals into another dimension, the devil horns piercing the moon above.

Alba Iliescu held herself steady with one hand and, with the other, guided the snake head between the lips of my vagina. A flood of warm juices swept through me and the beast throbbed with life as Alba drove the phallus in and out, in and out. There was a gush of wind which could have been a collective sigh, or a collective orgasm. The worshippers murmured their mantra, their voices growing in volume as Alba drove the rhinoceros horn deeper into my secluded places. I screamed, I screamed in pain and pleasure and knew that these two sensations were one and the same, that one doesn't exist without the other, that I must pursue both to be everything I could be.

A little pebble from a dam broke loose inside me. Liquids seeped through the gap, the gush became a tide, a torrent, a flood, and it was biblical lying there in the lunar light climaxing with Alba coming in a deluge. Her Dracula blood was boiling and she was shrieking like a werewolf.

When she caught her breath, she started again, slowly now, the twin snakes greased by our girlie jism. The Druids began a different chant, just softly, and she continued rocking back and forth, each seesaw of the phallus filling me and filling her, and the harder she thrust into me, the more the snake wound its way up inside her. Her eyes sparkled like moonstones above me and as she sank her teeth into my exposed throat I erupted in a second vast and gratifying climax.

The chanting came to an abrupt stop and Dr Iliescu drew back, easing the snake from me. She stood over me, masturbating again, very slowly, and in the background the Druids started removing their robes. They tossed them to one side and moved around me in a circle, the men gripping their cocks and masturbating, the women squeezing their nipples and thrusting back their heads. They moved closer and closer and, one after the other, the men released their orgasms and spurts of spunk like gleaming ectoplasm coated my face and breasts, the hollow of my tummy, and I remembered that day when Dr Goetz had said they all wanted me to do my best, and I was doing my best, and it was a relief to know that at Cambridge I would get the best education in the world.

6

The Garden of Eden

Around the corner from the Majestic on La Croisette in Cannes is a club called the Garden of Eden. Outside, along the edge of the pavement, a blue velvet rope hangs from chromium posts. Gorillas in dinner suits guard the entrance and, behind the rope, hundreds of wannabes stand night after night hoping to be admitted, the intense young men lugging bags full of film scripts, the girls close to naked and some terribly young. 'Sluts in training,' Binky remarked as we turned the corner and saw the usual line up.

We had left David in the bar at the Majestic surrounded by admirers and journalists. *Cheats* didn't win best short film at Cannes, but being nominated is recognition in itself and David was being hyped as 'on the way', an auteur with a personal signature. He was 24 and awfully handsome, all the more so with the new confidence gained from his film. Other writers were now giving him feature projects to read and, with Hermann Mann his tutor, he had abandoned his own bag of scripts and acquired a Hugo Boss black linen suit.

When you imagine the Cannes Film Festival, the first thing that comes to mind are the stars in starry glitter walking the red carpet to premières, the phallic lenses of the paparazzi, the ravenous eyes of the watching crowd. Of course, that's all very important, glamour sells, but beyond the bright lights in smoky screening rooms, Cannes is a casino, a thieves' market where fortunes are made and more often lost. A Korean who has had good sales at home will sell his feature at Cannes to small-time distributors who put on subtitles or dub the voice track before seeking a release in their own country. Big studio films get automatic distribution, but indie movies have to fight for screens in the marketplace.

It is at Cannes where miracles happen and dreams break on the rocks of cold hard reality. *Cinema Paradiso*, a nice little film hardly seen in Italy, was discovered in some dive miles from the palm-lined promenades, repackaged and screened all over the world. In counterbalance, there's a forest of film scripts that remain unread, a million miles of unseen film that will remain unseen, and the movie business is all so nebulous that when I'm grown up I shall probably go into something secure like the art world or politics.

I was surprised to learn that more than half the business done at Cannes is in the porn market, erotica, hard core, snuff flicks from Brazil, bestiality from beastly places. Glamour sells, but porno seems to sell even more and, while I had been freeing my mind of unyielding opinions at uni, David had been sitting in the editing suite with Sacha Vance cutting the twenty steamy minutes of Stephanie Jones tonguing my shorn pussy into a five-minute short that he screened to distributors, not to get a release – Stephanie would have sued to be sure – but to show he had more than one string to his bow. David Trevellick would do *anything* to make a feature and, while I wasn't entirely sure that such overt ambition was an attractive quality, what I did know was that successful artists, successful people, are sure of their goal and follow its trajectory until they get there. They don't have a bow with many strings but an arrow they fire into the heart of their vision.

At least David had paid my expenses to attend the festival. As Binky had a gap in her exam schedule, she came, too. Except for Christmas, we had spent little time together, although I had kept up a constant email appraisal of her revision. She had, as I expected, applied to King's College and, when I told Dr Goetz, he stroked his beard in the reflective way that showed his mind like a search engine was scanning the spiralling helixes of probability and chance.

'Does she have the right attitude for King's?' he enquired.

'If you mean does she enjoy being spanked, the answer is yes,' I replied, and he promised to have a word in the right ear.

Nothing is ever as it seems. Thank goodness.

Under the doctor's tutelage, I had become more confident. I knew how to hold my own in discussion. I knew how to walk, how to dress, how to present my chin, raised slightly, turned to one side. I had abandoned my wardrobe of jeans and trainers, ragged skirts and slashed shirts. I wore dresses that clung softly to my curves, stockings held by thin elastic garters, no knickers except on the odd occasion each month. I looked more refined, more sophisticated, more elegant. I looked older. I was older. I was nineteen, my body smooth and graceful, my thin arms like the necks of swans, my legs long and tapered in needle heels. A naked woman feels fully dressed in high-heeled shoes.

This sense of being older wasn't something friends would have observed, but a change I could see in the mirror's reflection, in the subtle depths of my dark eyes, in the serene curve of my lips, in the retroussé slope of my little nose. I had lost all need of haste, all feelings of anxiety, and experienced a curious pleasure being in the midst of my contemporaries knowing that below my clothes I wore a badge of moonlight, that I had knowledge of things that few of them would ever know. The rowing blue named Guy or Oliver or James who had taken me home and plonked me down on his oar had no notion of what pleasure he may have had. What pleasures he may have given. The students talked about current affairs and fashion, skiing holidays and idle caprices. I had tasted the forbidden fruit and that night, as if drawn by fate, I would enter the Garden of Eden.

As Binky and I clipped along in our heels towards the club, a limousine pulled up and a group of *very* important people stepped out. I knew they were very important by the way the faces of those queuing behind the blue rope lit up like the lamps on the seashore at twilight, the way tears fell from their eyes, the way they elbowed each other as they pressed forward. They waved their arms, the little girls showed their breasts, and the gorillas in dinner suits, film grips moonlighting by the look of them, pressed back like rugger props in a scrum, punching teary faces, manhandling slices of bare flesh and allowing one or two ragged nymphets to enter the hallowed portals of paradise.

Two silky women in capes slid from the limo behind a tall man with silver hair in a ponytail and another, younger man, who had won best director for

A Girl's Adventure. His name was Van Van de Vere, and although the alliteration was becoming the soul of all that was cool, vogue and sexy, as I had yet to see the film, and as I only knew it was Van Van by the breathless chant of the fans, I didn't get that heart-moving blast of adrenaline people seem to experience when they are confronted by the famous.

Van Van was the rising star in whose slipstream David was setting out to follow, a pioneer taking high-concept erotica mainstream. Had David left the Majestic with us and remained with us that evening, he would have felt as if he had died and gone to heaven; at least he would have gone to the Garden of Eden. Such are the laws of probability and chance.

I wasn't drawn to celebrity in the same way and considered fame abstract and undependable. Imagine being famous and not being recognised. Imagine being known by reputation only and having to explain yourself all the time. I was once at a dire dreadful luncheon at the Tuscan villa where Daddy had grown up. Sitting at the long table under the lemon trees was an oil engineer from Texas who turned to the English woman at his side and asked in a voice to awaken the dead, 'So, tell me, honey, what do you do?' Her eyebrows shot up like arrowheads. 'I am,' she said, 'the Minister of Health in the House of Lords,' and the Italians all had a good giggle. They were not impressed by such things. The Italians at the table were all counts and princesses. Everyone in Italy has a title and, if they don't, they do the courteous thing and make one up.

I was only a little girl at the time but the brief exchange came back to me as the man with the silver ponytail marched along the pavement away from the screaming horde and placed his arm around my waist. He was tall, he was wearing a white suit and he had a Texan accent.

'I've seen you somewhere before,' he said.

'I don't think so.'

Like a giant octopus, he engulfed Binky in his free arm.

'I see everything at Cannes. Everything,' he said. 'You girls trying to get in?'

We were now walking towards the club entrance, the fans screaming and crying, the girls tearing off their clothes, the boys tearing scripts from their shoulder bags.

'Actually, no,' I said.

'Actually, no! Hey, Van Van, don't you just love that accent?'

'British,' he said.

Binky glanced at me and shrugged. She was dressed in a black backless shift with a neckline that hung in swags and showed her long white neck to best effect. As a blonde she looked well in black. I was wearing a Diane von Furstenberg dress revealing one shoulder, the slant of the neckline repeated in the angle of the hemline, those 26 grams of golden thread complemented by Jimmy Choo shoes, a chain-mail evening bag shaped like a new moon and earrings consisting of three rings of gold, each containing a shifting universe of glittering stars, a Christmas gift from Dr Martin.

The dress, as Mummy remarked when she bought it for me at Christmas, was not designed so much to be worn as to be taken off. Now that Mummy had lost the parental fear that her daughters were going to rush out and get pregnant, something that happens for some arcane reason on council estates in the North of England, she was making a superhuman effort to treat Binky and me more as apprentices than rivals, and saw herself as the master of seduction. Except for dipping each day into the *Daily Mail*, Mummy was not burdened with the ordeals of a formal education and believes girls should know how to ride, how to dress, how to cross their legs, when necessary and with elegance, and how to flirt in at least two languages as well as English. 'Anyone who doesn't know one of the three really isn't worth speaking to.'

Was Mummy proud of us? I think she probably was.

I smiled back at Binky and the Texan tightened his grip around us. We were birds of paradise and he was the king of the jungle.

The dinner suits parted like a black and white tide and, to the tune of the hiss and whistle of those still behind the blue rope, we entered the Garden of Eden, something of a misnomer, I thought. The club was dark, smoky and vast, like a railway station, with French rap screeching from big speakers and endless avenues of arches like a Giorgio de Chirico painting, the colonnades disappearing into the foggy ruins of time, a phrase I remembered from somewhere and which seemed terribly apt. Creepers climbed the columns supporting the arches and from the overhanging branches shiny red apples hung just above my head. They were made of plastic.

One of the girls who had slid in with us was on her knees before the biggest of the big doormen, her mouth stretched in a rictus over the bulging head of his manhood, the gorilla clutching the girl's hair in the same fist that had been pummelling the eager faces outside and driving his erection into the delicate tissue of her gaping throat. This was her price for entering paradise. After choking down the doorman's stuff, she would wipe her lips, hook her little bra back in place and be free to pursue the stars, the producers, the directors, the men in suits.

'That's how Marilyn got started,' the Texan said.

He had been watching me watching the girl's oral exercise and although I couldn't see myself booking my passage in this way, a girl in a man's world does what she has to do to get where she wants to go. The Texan shoved a folded bank note into the doorman's top pocket and, as if this were a cue on stage, he leaned back, pulled the hose from the girl's mouth and sprayed her face in a wash of thick milky gruel. The girl stuck out her tongue and shook her head as if in religious ecstasy as she lapped up the last hesitant squirts.

From my chain-mail bag I produced a Kleenex and, as the girl wiped her face, she couldn't take her eyes off the man whose hand was still around my waist.

'Is that Tyler Copic?' she asked, her eyes glazed, her mouth still open.

'I've no idea, we haven't been introduced,' I replied.

The Texan found this amusing and steered me away from the girl as you would from a beggar on the King's Road.

My companion was indeed Tyler Copic, which he revealed in the modest way of someone who antici-pates being known and, in spite of my dearth of film knowledge, the result of a boarding school education, I did recall having seen his credit on cinema screens on several occasions. Now that Tyler Copic was focusing on me more fully, I was focusing on him and realised that while his hair was prematurely silver, his face was young, a long, fine-boned, finely sculpted face with carved cheek bones, a Roman nose and resourceful, pale-blue eyes that could have been copied from the blue of Wedgwood china.

In his white suit, white shirt and white Cuban-heeled cowboy boots, Tyler Copic could have been the high priest of a New Age religion, and it occurred to me that film *is* the new religion, that in a fragile society shorn of traditional values and lacking traditional close-knit communities, film stories like campfire stories provide the tribe with morals and meanings, the good guys tend to triumph and the villains meet a deserved and ghastly end. You can learn how to persevere, practise patience, be a good buddy and how to hold a knife and fork properly from watching movies. More people go to the cinema than go to church. Film is the culture. As the producer of Van Van's *A Girl's Adventure*, Tyler was showing us new ways to live, new ways to love, new relationships, true liberation. Amélie Ames and Greta May, striding ahead in their capes, were the two actresses whose *selfless* performances would take the erotic to a general audience. To the world. In my Diane von Furstenberg silk dress I was caught in the vanguard of Cannes magic.

'What did you think of the film?' Tyler asked, pulling me closer, his large hand gripping my side.

'I haven't seen it,' I replied.

'You haven't seen it? I thought everyone had seen it. I'll get a copy sent over to you. Did you see *Brokeback Mountain*?'

'Yes . . .'

'*A Girl's Adventure*'s better.'

'I'm sure it is.'

'You did that short, what was it called?'

'*Cheats.*'

'Yeah, that's right. Did you fuck the old guy?'

'I beg your pardon?'

'Come on, there's no secrets in the movies.'

'A lady,' I said, 'never explains.'

He grinned and I thought I was going to crumble into dust as his big hand squeezed down like a vice on my hip bone.

I had almost lost sight of Binky and the rest of our group. The Garden of Eden was in permanent twilight and they were all dressed in black, Van Van in the same sort of suit that David had chosen, Amélie and Greta in velvet capes that had a metallic blue tinge and gave them the look of blackbirds in flight. As we caught up with them and made our way through the colonnades I heard voices softly whisper *Tyler Copic, Van Van de Vere, A Girl's Adventure* like a chant, like a mantra, and I thought if I ever became famous I would disguise my name and wear a mask.

We moved into an alcove with a domed roof and an oval table encircled by a red velvet banquette. It was like being inside an egg. A waiter appeared with a fizzing magnum of champagne.

'It is the first law of the universe,' Tyler Copic remarked, 'never say no to champagne.'

'I never do,' I replied.

'Hey, I like you, what was your name?'

'Milly Petacci.' I glanced at Binky. 'My sister, Roberta.'

'Binky,' she said, and raised her glass.

'You're so British,' said Van Van.

'Italian, actually,' she told him.

He grinned. 'That's just what I mean.' Van Van stroked a blonde curl from her eye and she purred magnificently.

With her hair in waves about her wide cheekbones and her eyes half-shaded by long lashes, my little step-sister had quietly gone retro. She had borrowed all the Brigitte Bardot films in Daddy's collection and had analysed the discreet charms of BB's body language, every shrug and pout, every turn of heel and toss of her golden mane. I was growing very fond of my sister and was glad she would be coming up to King's.

The actresses had settled beside me on the curve of the banquette, their movements studied like mime artistes, their hoods framing chalk-whitened faces with elliptical eyebrows and carmine lips. Like well-brought-up children in olden times, they lowered their heads and bowed slightly as they said their names. When they cast off their capes, I all but lost my poise. Words rose to the tip of my tongue where they withered to silence. Amélie Ames and Greta May were all that is desirable, tempting, illicit, the fruit in the Garden of Eden.

My gaze went from Amélie to Greta and back again. They straightened their shoulders and sat erect as if posing for a photograph. The girls were identically dressed, a mirror image in a gorgeous assembly of black leather leashes and straps that buckled about their throats, wrists and ankles. A harness crossed their breasts horizontally in such a way that their nipples were permanently erect, the upper strap of the harness connected to the ring in the throat band. In the ring was a silver disc that, as I would later discover, spun on a central axis and, when spinning, revealed a name. Around their waists, the girls wore studded belts that supported a fringe of leather thongs that danced and slithered midway down their slender thighs. They were not clothes they were wearing, not costumes, but the livery of display.

It was bad mannered, I'm sure, but it was hard for me to take my eyes off Amélie and Greta, at the deft arrangement of black leather crossing their skin, at their pink rosebuds emerging like spikes from the gap in the harness and reversing the tired cliché of revealing the breasts while concealing the nipples. Amélie wore tattoos on her shoulders and legs. Unlike the snake in my little movie, the tattoos were real, a hawk, a lizard, a dragon with a fiery tongue, words in Gothic script I couldn't read. Greta May had unblemished skin the colour of cream. But virgin pure or esoterically illustrated, the girls were coolly exotic, their outfits exhibiting all the pleasures of paradise and warning, too, that only the initiated should dare approach. They belonged to a world that I didn't know and would glimpse that night for the first time.

As they moved, the thongs parted to expose on Amélie the clipped stripe of fur ornamenting her mount. Greta was sitting with her chin resting on her knee, her left foot in gladiator sandals raised on the banquette, her legs open to reveal the silver rings piercing the lips of her shorn vagina. I gazed down at her moist gash and she pulled at the rings, opening the lips still wider and showing me the pink fruit within. I glanced up and, when our eyes met, I caught a glimpse of her features behind the mask of chalk. I knew Greta May, I knew her from somewhere. But where?

'Have we met before?' I said.

'On the hockey field. In the swimming baths. At pony club.'

She smiled. Now I remembered. Greta had gone to Saint Sebastian's like Binky and me. She was much older, 22 or 23, but I could recall the willowy girl in the sixth form when I was in the third taking the lead role in school plays. She had been everything I wanted to be and it felt that night as if fate had drawn us together, that I was exactly where I was supposed to be. Greta slid her bottom towards me on the banquette and I couldn't resist leaning forward and teasing the rings glittering between her legs. She closed her eyes as a wave of pleasure coursed through her body.

I glanced at Binky, but she was engrossed in conversation with Van Van. As I had observed before, my sister was more concerned with being admired than experimenting with the erotic, and it was Tyler Copic who woke me from this moment of disorientation by tapping the rim of my champagne glass with his own.

'Do you like what you see?' he asked. He flashed a glance at the two girls.

I nodded slowly, judiciously. 'Yes,' I replied.

He leaned closer. 'They belong to me,' he said.

Tyler was wearing a signet ring with a backward C and a regular T that stood out above the dull silver band. He pressed the ring against my arm and his initials, TC, were printed on my skin, white for a moment then fading back to the brown of my suntan. The backward letters reminded me of the scene when Ricky first sees the tattoo in the mirror in *Cheats*, and again I had the sensation that everything was linked and that everything was how it was meant to be.

They belong to me.

I didn't know what he meant, not exactly, and felt breathless trying to imagine things beyond my imagination.

I took a sip of champagne and Tyler refilled the glass.

207

Beyond the egg, figures drifted by like phantoms in the swirls of smoke. I saw faces I recognised and faces I thought I recognised. I saw young men carrying bags filled with film scripts and was reminded of the Pleiades, those wayward sisters in Greek mythology punished for killing their husbands by being forced to carry water in vessels so artfully holed they are always empty when they reach their destination. The Pleiades were more than mere stars. They were a constellation.

I saw girls with silicone-frozen pouts, silicone-frozen breasts, Cannes suntans. It was the hottest spring on record and news teams from across the globe were capturing the outbreak of nudity claiming the town. Girls were leaving the beaches and cruising the Croisette in nothing but Prada shades and sometimes in nothing at all. They were making the updates on Korean TV, Venezuelan TV, Albanian TV, CNN, and no one they knew would see their segment, and they wouldn't see their segment, but it didn't matter. For a second, just a second, they *were* the news.

Young men stopped to shake Tyler's hand, to pay obeisance to Van Van de Vere. They praised Amélie and Greta, who closed their eyes behind fluttering eyelashes and turned unsmiling back to each other.

A dwarf wearing a mortar board stopped and held out his little hands as he spoke.

'*Voilà!*'

On the black surface of his headwear were shiny pills of many colours. I didn't try them. I didn't want to. Nor did Binky. To be who I am I did not need drugs, if that was what the little pills were. I had in Cambridge been taken to the edges of my own reality, to that place where you are able to look below the surface of things, and what I had seen made me realise that life is too brutal and fleeting to do anything other than what pleases you and what pleases me is best viewed through unclouded eyes.

My old friend Aristotle said the only rational course to pursue in life is the path of happiness and I reminded myself of his advice as if his words were a prayer that needed to be repeated often. The nuns at Saint Sebastian's would say that if what you are doing makes you happy and what you are doing harms no one, it must logically be the right thing to be doing. A girl at school when I was fifteen died of head injuries after diving into an empty swimming pool. Another, a promising ballerina, lost her leg in a car crash. Disaster can catch us at any time. Plane crashes and cancer, tragedy and loss. Life is an obstacle course. There is only this moment. It is brief and precious. Only when you appreciate that are you, philosophically speaking, truly alive and truly free to be yourself.

Did Tyler Copic comprehend these things?

I'm sure he did.

Did Amélie and Greta not belong to him?

Some men can see into the mysterious core of the feminine psyche. They understand the ambiguity of our deepest needs and, as I sat in the Garden of Eden in my golden frock, my mind floated on the champagne bubbles back to that Gothic mansion on the Isle of Skye where I had finally lost my virginity and become a woman. Binky and I had returned home with red bottoms and a secret so terrible and marvellous we could never have told anyone because no one would have believed us. We had peeled off our clothes. We had been smacked and cropped. We had without urging fallen on each other in a frenzy of wild lesbian sex, and we had then been simultaneously serviced across the dining room table. We had reached the outer limits of unimagined pain and a deep, unknown sense of gratification. We had drawn the sweet nectar from chalices so similar to our own it was like making love to yourself. As the Laird broke my maidenhead it was as if the blinders had been taken from my eyes. It was the moment of awakening. It was as if my virginity had been sacrificed on the altars of my own subconscious desires.

What was so shocking, so shameful, so revealing, and the reason why it was something Binky and I had never talked about, was that once we had got over the embarrassment of removing our clothes we had relished every moment of our humiliation. We were stark naked, our proud bodies glistening with nervous sweat in the firelight, our nipples smouldering with tension, our pussies growing damp under the watchful eyes of the two strangers. We were miles from anywhere, cut off from London, from school, from parents, from the past, from our own reality. In the Laird's island redoubt we were free like birds to forget ourselves and just be ourselves. We had been frightened, yes, petrified, but like the moth drawn to the candle flame, it is fear of the unknown that draws you into the unknown.

We had slept that night in the stable and didn't get our clothes back until the following afternoon when a driver appeared with Binky's little pink car. The Laird paid for the repair and we paid him back by collecting eggs, feeding the chickens, sweeping out the barns and outhouses, buildings filled with poo and fetid straw that hadn't been cleaned for years. The Laird believed young girls should be strapped, span-

210

ked, mated and kept naked at all times. They are wee animals who find true contentment when they get back to nature.

Were you to say such a thing in the cold light of a Chelsea cocktail bar it would sound absurd, but on that brisk summer's day as I walked around the farmyard covered in mud and dust, my pussy and armpits moist and smelly, it felt completely natural and not at all unpleasant, a rehearsal, in fact, for my turf-laying adventures in the garden of Luther Goetz.

As I looked back over the months since leaving school and going up to Cambridge, I felt fortunate to have met Jean-Luc, Hamish the Black Watch, Dr Goetz, and felt sorry for girls who had not had the same opportunities as me. David Trevellick had warmed to the enchantment of strapping me with his belt, but I had come to see that the pleasure, my pleasure, comes not from leading but from being led, from being in a position where I become a part of something outside myself, in a state where I am an empty vessel ready to be filled with every extreme of sensation. I understood, too, I understood now, that every smack and spank, every caning and whipping was more than an indulgence for those administering the chastisement, it was an indulgence for the one receiving it. It is in this state of submission that I pass from the shadows of confusion and insecurity, the human condition, the human dilemma, and find myself in pure radiant sunshine, in a crystal light.

I turned to look again at Tyler Copic.

They belong to me.

What did he mean? Amélie Ames and Greta May were under contract? Now they had made one film for him they were obliged to make another? Or was it more literal? Or more ambiguous? His blue eyes

211

were turquoise in the foggy ruins of the light. He was listening with apparent fascination to a young man revved up on false confidence who had stopped to pitch a film idea, which he did in thirty seconds. The boy produced from his pocket a single sheet with his concept in 150 words, shook Tyler's hand, said *way to go* as he held up a fist in an anarchist salute to Van Van de Vere and disappeared back into the river of lost souls drifting by our booth.

Tyler dropped the film idea on the floor.

'*An Officer and a Gentleman* meets *Reservoir Dogs*.'

'*Star Wars*.'

Tyler and Van Van spoke a private language, a code. Tyler came to his feet, the sign for us to move on.

We abandoned the champagne and wandered the colonnades between womb-shaped niches where girls in various states of bondage and nudity sat and perched and lay spread out on the oval tables like objects in a museum, like models backstage at a fashion shoot, like dolls being constructed on a conveyor belt, like actresses preparing for *Titus Andronicus* or *Satyricon.* There were girls on their knees performing fellatio, girls in chains, *à quatre pattes,* white bottoms showing between the banquettes and the tables, their two orifices invitingly open, one pink and slippery, the other violet and all the sweeter, forbidden fruit graciously offered. There were girls on laps, legs spread, vaginas spread, anuses spread, heads thrown back, breasts free, so much sex and so open, and so public, I realised I was on a journey of one thousand miles and had barely taken the first step.

The Garden of Eden was a house of many rooms and moods. It would, I thought, be easy to become lost in the maze, to move from one erotic scene to the next, one womb to the next. People here felt safe as I'm sure the first people felt safe before temptation and Flood. I could see it in their eyes, in their graceful unhurried movements. It was hot. Sticky. Girls as girls do when they see other girls naked were stripping down to the bare essentials, getting out of themselves. Being themselves. Something printed in invisible ink in the depths of our subconscious was coming to light. In the new millennium girls were growing taller, fitter, our own atavistic genes taking us by surprise. My body was the treasure chest that held all the pleasures of original sin. I was in my golden slippers with my full breasts and dripping pussy the quintessence of sex. I could smell sex on me. I could smell sex in the air, spicy and faintly vegetal, the aroma of male sperm pooled with the scent of girlie excretions, sweet and oily to the tongue, the stuff of life, a heady mixture that made my heart beat faster. Film people talked the talk but the labyrinth to me was a place for being not talking and I had an intuition that it was those who kept silent who made films.

The arches were evenly spaced, identical whichever way you turned, and I was reminded of a school trip to Córdoba when we visited the Mezquita, the mosque so vast and perfect the cathedral built in its interior at the time of the Inquisition is dwarfed to insignificance. Was this significant of something? Did it resonate with my life? I had yet to discover who I might be, what I might be, but at nineteen I was in the process of choosing and as we weaved our way through the twists of the maze it was like turning through my mind's web of neurons and synapses and for some reason hard to explain I could feel rising in me like mercury in a thermometer a bubble of pure contentment, that special intense joy that comes from living totally in the present.

My skin prickled in the golden dress and I understood as Tyler stroked my hip bone in the patient way of the faithful counting prayer beads that I would be taking it off for him before the night was through. He moved his hand to the curve of my bottom and I wondered if through the sheer fabric he could sense the marks of the pentangle.

I adored being a girl and I adored being surrounded by girls. They were everywhere. Like the dancing fairies in *A Midsummer Night's Dream*. Like gilded butterflies. Like angels with gossamer wings fitted on harnesses and on these wings they were flying through the arches like genies escaping bottles. There were girls on tables, kissing in corners, their mouths filled with smiles, with filmmaker appendages, their nude bodies landscaped with glittering seas of semen. There were girls I'd seen on magazine covers, models from the catwalks of Paris, from the silver screen, stars whose names I knew, their slender perfect bodies they had worked so hard to create finally liberated from the stifling prison of their costumes and their clothes. Mirrored balls turned on the ceiling picking out our faces, moving impetuously on to the next and the next. People alone and in pairs were dancing to the throb of the music. It came at us in ebbs and flows as we grew nearer and then drew away from the speakers, French rap, free-form jazz, discordant, unfamiliar, mesmerising. We stopped at one of the oval niches where the dwarf joined us.

'*Voilà!*' he announced.

The men inspected the confections laid out on his mortar board.

'M&Ms,' Tyler said.

He chose several of different colours and tossed them back into his throat. He closed his blue eyes, then pinned me like a knife thrower in his gaze as he opened them again.

'You like it here,' he said. It was a statement, not a question. He had read my mind.

'Yes, I do.'

Suspended from the arch before us like a figure in a painting by Brueghel was a girl in a black hood, hands stretched above her head, her feet resting on the stone capitals at the place where the columns turned into the arch. I noticed that around her wrists, ankles and neck were black straps similar to those worn by Amélie and Greta. The split between her legs was at head height. Van Van paused, held her thighs and, as he slid his tongue up inside her, I thought how pleased she would be should someone tell her that the best director at Cannes that year had shared her wet parts. The director's tongue was going in and out like a piston, the girl's breasts were bobbing and swaying with the centrifugal force, and I could hear her wailing in ecstasy inside the hood.

'Who are all these people, where do they come from?' I asked, turning to Tyler Copic.

He didn't answer straight away. He took my two hands and looked me in the eyes. 'They are film people,' he said. 'People who make films. People who want to make films. People who want to be in films. Making films is a mission, a crusade, a journey through an impenetrable jungle. You're never quite sure why you start making a new film and once you start you can't imagine you're ever going to finish. When you do finish, you have to slake off your old skin like a serpent and renew yourself. The people who come here understand that.' He paused. 'Do you understand that?'

'I think I do,' I said.

He let go of my hands and looked at me for a long time in my little gold frock. 'How old are you?' he asked.

I pressed my finger to my lips and thought carefully before I answered. 'Ancient,' I said, and he nodded without smiling.

'So am I.'

His voice was little more than a whisper and in our few words was a complicity, a contract. Tyler Copic was a man who would expect a woman to abandon all sense of herself and surrender to his will, to be his slave, his property. I glanced back at Amélie and Greta, erotic handmaidens following in our wake.

They belong to me.

He ran his palm slowly down my back and under my skirt. As he stroked the bare skin of my bottom I trembled. I wasn't wearing knickers, naturally. This seemed to satisfy him enormously and I was pleased to have provided him with this unexpected pleasure.

Beyond the arch was another niche and as we moved on through the legs of the girl in the hood, I saw the girl who had gone down on the doorman as we were entering the club. She was lying across the table, her arms lashed at the wrists by belts that curled around the table legs. Her knees were spread so lithely they were touching the table top and a broad-shouldered man with a beard was lapping like a hungry bear from the lips of her vagina. He threw back his head, roared like a beast in the jungle, and then saw our little group around his alcove.

'Tyler,' he said. 'Thought I'd see you here.'

'Is there anywhere else to be?'

216

The two men hugged like lovers. The girl grinned at me. The man with the beard was an Oscar winner, a household name, and her little pussy was the fount of his inspiration.

'Sweeter than maple syrup,' he said, his fleshy lips obscene as they opened behind his beard. The wiry bristles were drenched. 'I'll catch you downstairs.'

Tyler glanced at me. 'We'll be there.'

The bearded man leaned closer to Tyler Copic. 'Prizes mean zilch, what I want to know is are you taking any money?'

'The film's not on release yet.'

'Yeah, but how are the rights going?'

Tyler shrugged. 'We've sold *A Girl's Adventure*, well, everywhere.'

'The United States?'

'Every territory.'

'You're always ahead of the trends.'

'Is there anywhere else to be?'

The bearded man threw up his hands and was shaking his head as he turned back to the ingénue on the table. She lifted her rear from the surface, bowed her spine and her sopping pussy opened, pink and shiny as a sea shell.

'You have to finish what you start,' said the beard and dipped back down into the silky sea.

We continued on from the egg room beneath the arches and came to an arena lit by a cat's cradle of criss-crossing lights. The arena was high with a domed roof like a bird's cage and suspended from the darkness above on long ropes were a number of trapezes where girls in the masks of different birds were flying through the beams of light. The trapezes hung just above our heads and in the shadows a crowd had gathered, everyone peering up with the

217

absorbed expressions I imagine people would have in the presence of a miracle. The masks fitted neatly over the heads of the girls, disguising them completely and giving them the look of mythical creatures from a new and better world. In a mask, in a disguise, I thought, there is no need to explain anything to anyone.

Nearly all the girls were naked, their lithe bodies varnished in sweat and shimmering like silver needles as they traced a path through the spotlights. Girls were slipping from one bar to the next and from the bars into the arms of waiting men or waiting women. Other girls as they appeared from the dark recesses around the sides of the arena were lifted up, they swung back and forth, back and forth, twisting one way and the other, passing like acrobats in the circus from trapeze to trapeze and I thought the feathery masks gave them more élan and I'm sure more confidence. The fragrance wafting about the arena was a heady elixir and I took a deep breath, filling my lungs with the perfume of girls, that ripe, lusty odour, spicy perspiration on perfect flesh, sticky with exercise and lust. I could smell the cologne of their oily discharges, the pre-orgasm scent of desire, rich as a drug. I could smell sex and the smell sharpened my senses and made me wet.

There were girls in bondage, in fetish, a girl in skin-clinging latex wearing the head of the phoenix. I admired two black girls in sumptuous corsets cinched so tight it made their waists surrealistically small. Their breasts were pushed forward like polished aubergines and their long ebony legs were swinging rhythmically to and fro below the cross-spar of the same trapeze. Their heads were in the masks of mynah birds and through the pale-orange beaks I could hear them softly cooing.

A golden girl with gilded breasts likes the domes on a cathedral glided by and I felt the wind-rush from her golden feathers. I saw a girl with an aviary of birds tattooed over her entire body. There was a girl with piercings in her cheeks and nipples, the silver chain clipped to the lips of her vagina twisting in circles like a Catherine wheel as she sailed overhead. I watched a petite blonde wearing white wings and a swan's head that perched gracefully on her long neck. Her skin was diaphanous, her feet perched on the trapeze and her tiny bottom looked like the moon rising over some distant horizon.

The girls were so comfortable with their nudity I realised fully, and with some relief, that when I first visited Jean-Luc's office my intense desire to cast off my school uniform was completely natural. I was stepping out of my old skin, my old self. I was stripping away the bridle and bonds of the convent girl to dress in the costume of my naked flesh. I understood, too, that Jean-Luc, the Laird and Luther Goetz were guides leading me on a journey to find a master. I glanced sideways at Tyler Copic. Was he the one? *They belong to me.* The notion was quixotic, energising. The girls on the trapezes, Amélie and Greta, they belonged to a special world, a secret world, my world. I felt like Alice about to begin my adventures in Wonderland.

Like the motions of the universe, the display above us was continuous and ever-changing, the black ropes and spars of the trapezes vanishing in the darkness, the glittering girls like a flock of muses appearing and disappearing through the lights like apparitions, like distant memories caught in a camera obscura. I saw a raven, a magpie, a parakeet, a falcon, a yellow-plumed bird of paradise whose display appeared to have been choreographed and whose small, perfect white breasts seemed familiar.

I glanced from side to side. Amélie and Greta were standing tamely beside Tyler watching with glowing eyes. Van Van, too, alone now, his hands thrust in his jacket pockets, his neck bent, his mouth open. Binky had left the flock and I realised that my sister had been reborn as the bird of paradise. She had been the best gymnast at school and was the most exotic object of desire in the pleasure dome. She moved from trapeze to trapeze, her long thin arms churning the air like a swimmer in the sea, like a bird on the wing, her naked body glowing in the lights as white as a sail. Tyler must have sensed that I was tempted to join her and placed his hand over my bottom to hold me still. This was performance, he seemed to say. It was for the crowd, not for him.

When Binky had tired of her routine she dropped into Van Van's waiting arms and he carried her to the side of the arena where birds of every hue were preening and flapping as they opened their bodies to the men in suits who had slipped from their suits to connect one to the other in a continuous circle of sexual congress, cocks in bottoms with mouths on the next cock connected to the open legs of the next exotic bird, one after the other like a tableau on an erotic temple and I remembered the frescos from the walls of the Ellora caves. As my sister in her beautiful mask joined the orgy I realised she had found herself. This was what she wanted, an eternal circle of sex with her the centre of attention. The circle extended around the curve of the arena and into dark passage-ways that I would have enjoyed exploring, but Tyler Copic led me and the actresses away from the display towards an arched door in the opposite direction.

Four doormen were guarding the archway. One of them swung the door open and, as we made our way in darkness down a curling flight of steps, I was conscious of the beat of my heart and the sound of my heels echoing over the stone walls. In my mind I could see flying, spiralling birds in a gilded cage, and I thought I would remember what I had seen that day for the rest of my life and for the rest of my life I would be drawn back again and again to the Garden of Eden.

We reached another door and entered a cavern where the silence was so severe you could feel it on your skin. Around the walls, below the curve of the vaulted ceiling, was an elongated wine rack that stretched into the distance, thousands, tens of thousands of bottles of wine layered in dust and ancient cobwebs. Facing the wine rack were barrels, taller than a man, with small cups suspended from taps and, as we passed, each cup like the basket below a hot air balloon would faintly quiver.

'Shoes,' Tyler said softly, and I slipped them off.

We were far below the streets of Cannes. It was cold and a shiver ran through me as we made our way through the ranks of wine. We reached an arched niche where we sat before a glass table on leather sofas, Amélie and Greta on one, Tyler and me on the other. Tyler was quiet for a long time. He just sat gazing along the length of the dimly lit cellar, at the barrels and bottles.

'The wine sleeps like children and no one knows its dreams.'

His voice was soft. I had to lean closer to hear him. He ran his hands through his silver hair.

'Ten years ago I stood with the world at my feet on the summit of Mount Everest,' he said. 'I have tasted the meat of an albino elephant and eaten the brains of a Himalayan monkey. They say the creature's brains will awaken your dreams.' He showed his empty palms. 'Like Bigfoot and the Abominable Snowman, we find the footprints, never the myth.'

He paused and turned the silver ring he was wearing around his finger.

'Did you know Spanish fly is actually the dried body of the Cantharidin, a green beetle, not a fly at all? In Gujarat, ground rhinoceros horn is a speciality. An aphrodisiac?' He shook his head. 'Just another story. They should leave the horns where they are, where they belong, on the rhinos. Once we kill all the animals, as we surely will, we will be humans without humanity. It is the animals, the fish and the birds that remind us we are human.'

He gazed off again into the distance.

'Amélie, the '47 Saint-Emilion,' he then said and she slipped off obediently along the line of waiting bottles.

'I have trained ten thousand girls,' he continued. 'I have turned girls into stars and turned them into black holes, empty spaces. I have seen the Aurora Borealis, the sun setting on Kuta Beach. I have rattled the keys to paradise and when you see the flying birds in the Garden of Eden life is almost bearable.'

Our eyes met. Had he read my thoughts? Had he planted his thoughts in my mind?

He looked back at the sleeping wine and a feeling of melancholy in that hushed silent place touched me like a cold hand. I glanced at Greta. She was sitting with one leg over the arm of the sofa, the pads of two fingers teasing the rings in her labia. Her chalk-white face was untouched by emotion and I coveted her poise, her acquiescence, the silver charms like silver fish in the pink pool of her open body. My tranquillity was disturbed by the Himalayan monkey, the hunted rhinoceros, but as Greta May smiled the melancholy lifted and I understood that like her my role was not to fret on matters over which I had no control. I had been made the way I am for another purpose. If Tyler Copic was the high priest of cinema it followed that I, as the naked girl in *Cheats*, was an acolyte, a disciple, an extra in this new world religion.

Greta continued to smile, she continued subliminally to nurse the rings in her exposed cleft, and I admired her equanimity, her complete acceptance of everything. It had seemed an odd coincidence that, like me, Greta May had been a pupil at Saint Sebastian's, but in that quiet place, on that black sofa with Tyler Copic, nothing seemed strange and everything was magically real.

He put his hand on my leg, just above my knee.

'Every night when I sleep I am robbed of the opportunity to travel to faraway places, to have an adventure, to be someone else or something else. I come here to listen to the wine dreaming and believe that one day I, too, will be visited by dreams.' Tyler paused and looked at me once more. 'For a man for whom no pleasure is denied there is only the subconscious. He who sleeps without dreaming, for all that he has in the waking world, he is a man deprived of one third of his life.'

Amélie returned with the wine opened and four crystal glasses on a tray. She placed the tray on the table, filled the glasses equally and sat again beside Greta.

'The secret of wine is patience,' said Tyler. 'The wine has waited for us. Now we shall wait for the wine. Let it breathe.'

We waited. The minutes passed. Tyler then came to his feet and offered me his hand. I stood. So did the girls. He turned me around to lower the zip on my dress. He turned me back to face him and peeled the gold silk from my body as if it were a cover over an oil painting. As I stepped from the material, the last traces of melancholia drifted away and a wave of contentment passed through me. I was in my natural state. A fragile smile flickered in Tyler's eyes. He appreciated my full breasts that defied gravity, firm and erect, my pert nipples, dewy-pink like rosebuds. My hips were miniature boomerangs that inscribed arcs like bookends edging the plain of my tummy and my dark pubic hair was a verdant mat smelly, I'm sure, with the carnal thoughts in my mind.

Tyler held my shoulders. He turned me into profile. He turned me again and, like a man reading Braille, ran the tips of his fingers over the curvature of my bottom. The fine lines crossing my flesh were only visible in moonlight, but as a man who surely knew how to administer those subtle scars he must have sensed their presence. As if by a force of will, the cheeks of my bottom parted and his hand slipped in the slot, sliding through the curve and into my wet pussy. I was dripping, dripping, on the verge of rapture, and his finger caressing the star of my clitoris was racing me all too quickly to climax. As the air caught in my throat and my heart swelled in my chest, he stopped and stroked my bottom until the sensation passed.

. I know, I know I have said it before, but I adore being a girl and nothing at that moment would have given me more pleasure than for Tyler to have bent me over the sofa and tanned my bottom until it was the same shade of red as the wine standing on the

224

glass table. I knew, too, even as the thought was running through my mind, that for a man like Tyler it is the anticipation of pleasure more than pleasure that he seeks. He took his hand away and Greta licked the juice from his fingertips. Tyler was staring into her eyes and the ellipse of her raised eyebrows as she sucked his fingers gave her the look of a Japanese Geisha and I suppose that was her role.

Amélie passed each of us a crystal glass. As we touched the rims the sound resonated like a high-pitched bell over the ceiling.

'Shush,' Tyler said, 'the wine is sleeping,' and we smiled.

We slowly drank the Saint-Emilion. I know nothing about wine except the delight it stirs on my taste buds, but I cannot imagine a vintage with greater depth, more sensitivity. As the dreamy liquid coursed through my body, I got a sense of the rolling hills of Bordeaux, sunlight on vineyards, the rich harvest of 1947. I sipped my wine until it had gone and the teardrop that remained in the well of the glass was too deep for me to reach with my tongue but I tried anyway. Tyler saw me.

'Shall we open another bottle?' he asked.

'No,' I said. 'One dream is enough.'

'To begin with,' he said.

The girls replaced their empty glasses on the table and we watched them strip from their costumes, first Amélie, then Greta. It was like a performance, and although Tyler had been everywhere and tasted every fruit, I was sure this show he would always enjoy. Greta slid the strap from the buckle holding Amélie's harness, Amélie pirouetted on her toes and her costume stripped away from her body in a continuous ribbon of black leather. She did the same for Greta

225

and as Greta turned in a circle I could see a shiny scar at the pit of her back.

Before I could look closer, Greta showed me the silver disc that turned in the ring she had been wearing at her throat. On it were little ticks and scores like hieroglyphics.

'Blow,' she said, and when I did so the spinning symbols spelled the name Tyler Copic.

Greta turned so that I could see her back. So did Amélie. Each had the identical scar immediately above the crack in their bottoms.

'You can touch,' said Greta.

The scar consisted of the letters TC.

I looked at Tyler. He was holding his wine glass and I could clearly see on the dull silver ring he was wearing his initials in reverse.

I touched the scar on Greta's back. It was smooth and must have been scalded into her skin with the ring heated until it was white hot. It was hard to imagine what agony it must have been, but pain passes, it is the sister of pleasure, and as the girls turned back to face me I wasn't surprised to see how inordinately proud they were with these tokens of belonging.

We stood there quietly, the silence in some way drawing us closer. Tyler had said little about himself. He had asked nothing about me. But as a man who had seen everything, he must have perceived in the erotic outtakes from David's film something in me that could reach its full potential were the ring that he wore to sign a contract on my flesh. Was it chance that his limousine should have pulled up at the moment when Binky and I were approaching the Garden of Eden? Perhaps so, and perhaps there is no such thing as chance, that each coincidence, each

226

random encounter has been plotted by the stars and destiny is how we respond to that coincidence, that arbitrary encounter.

I glanced at Greta, at Amélie, two naked girls with finely drawn features on painted faces, and it occurred to me that for Tyler Copic, a man for whom no pleasure is denied, a man who can make the dreams of others come true, the one true pleasure he had was to have complete power over girls who are young and malleable and at their very best, the moment when they are in full control of their own power. Power meeting power is the unstoppable force of the film world. Tyler's brand on Greta and Amélie was an outward sign of who he was, of what he could do. Greta and Amélie were girls who knew what they wanted. They wanted careers. Now, they belonged to Tyler Copic. One day they would be stars. They would leave him, perhaps, find other men to serve, but the brand on their bodies would remain, a reminder that wherever they went and whatever they did, he would always be their master.

'Come,' he said, still whispering. 'We have one more surprise for Milly.'

Tyler ducked out of the niche and we followed him to another door in the opposite direction to which we had come. The door was made of dark wood and studded in black iron rivets. Tyler turned the round handle and motioned for me to lead the way. We left the crypt of dreaming wine and, as I made my way down a spiral of stone stairs, I imagined I was a reproduction from Marcel Duchamp's *Nude Descending a Staircase*. We had analysed the painting in art class, a small canvas depicting successive movements of a single body, and though I had looked at the print on countless occasions only now, naked on a spiral staircase, did I recognise that just as art does not depend on an established set of rules, nor does life. I understood, too, that my lack of desire to be famous, to be a star in the movie firmament, gave me an unfettered sense of freedom. I was a Duchamp ready-made, a functional object with a fresh aesthetic.

I wasn't cold now. There was a smile touching the corners of my lips. My breasts moved just slightly with my movement and I could see in my mind's eye facets of my naked form in constantly moving shadows. I enjoyed that sense of the scene before me appearing and disappearing with each curve on the spiral. The staircase ended in another domed arena where, at the centre, there was a circular pool with water shivering on the surface like molten gold. The pool was shallow and around the perimeter, sloping up from the edge, was a bench two metres wide covered in what appeared to be fur the same lustrous colour as Binky's blonde hair.

Both in the pool and stretched around the circular bench were naked girls, girls swimming, making love, in twos and threes. I could smell the pungent scent of desire. I could hear the irrepressible gasp of girls in ecstasy. In Dante's inferno the denizens descend into deeper layers of hell. In the Garden of Eden, I had a sense of entering paradise.

Tyler Copic left us and climbed the stairs to the gallery above the pool. I noticed the bearded man, the Oscar winner, at a table with two other men and Tyler went to join them. I glanced from table to table and, as I did so, Greta told me who they were. I didn't know all their faces, but I knew their names. They were the producers, agents, screenwriters, the directors, famous actors, the men in suits. I remember David telling me the first filmmaker was Georges

Méliès, a Frenchman. The movie business began here, in France, in Cannes, and those men on the gallery were the chosen few who made the films that guided our lives and shaped our thoughts. There were no women on the gallery, no men in the pool, just a sea of beautiful girls all perfectly formed and full of grace, sculptures come to life from a pagan temple. The gilded roof of the dome warmed the light into a golden glow that gleamed like oil on their naked flesh and seemed to give those girls an inner radiance.

As we moved towards the pool, I noticed that each girl stood very straight when she walked and when she swam in the golden water her long limbs made barely a ripple. I saw when their eyes met mine that their gaze was clear, sharp, unclouded by doubt, and what was most striking was the sense of abandon, the shameless lack of inhibitions, the way that one girl would sink her tongue into the intimate parts of another, take her to orgasm, and move on to the next. There were girls who were well known, actresses and models from the pages of magazines, the girls I had seen walking among the arches above us, but here beside the pool they were starkly, nakedly themselves. There were no divisions, there was no sense of competition, just an inexorable desire for pleasure.

Greta took my hand. We slipped into the pool. It was shallow at the edge and, as I waded towards the centre, brushing shoulders with all those divine beings, my feet were nursed in fur, a moving carpet like reeds on the bed of a lake, an immense pelt from a woolly mammoth. The water was smooth like an unguent and, as I began to swim, I savoured the syrupy tang of girls, their slippery essence softening the water and igniting my senses. Greta followed and, as I climbed from the pool, we slipped down together on the yellow fur, two sacred creatures discovering the universe.

We kissed. Her lips were full and the white chalk on her face had vanished in the oily balm of the pool. I licked her cheeks, the hollow of her throat, I slipped her breasts into my mouth, first one then the other, biting down on the crimson buds until she squealed with delight. Her breasts were small and muscular, her ribcage well defined, her stomach concave as she lay with her legs stretched out on the bench. Her pussy was open. The silver rings were slicked in juice. I caressed them with my tongue and pulled them with my teeth. As I did so, Greta May writhed under me, shivering with satisfaction. I swivelled round. I sank my tongue deep inside her creamy wet cleft and, at the same time, I felt Greta's tongue reach into the core of my body. We were joined. Two convent girls from Saint Sebastian's.

While I was sliding my tongue around Greta's bejewelled lips, a tongue pressed into my bottom and though I thought it was probably Amélie who had joined us, I wasn't certain and that sense of not knowing was all the more exhilarating. Greta began to climax below me, she raised her bottom from the furry bench and as she exploded in orgasm, I did too, and we rolled over in a mass of arms and legs. It wasn't Amélie who had joined us. It was the girl with an aviary of birds illustrating her flesh. She lowered her sex over my waiting mouth while Greta opened my knees and pushed her tongue back inside my pussy. I felt complete, joyful. There is something reassuring about the feel of the whip and the cane, but for heavenly bliss there is nothing like the taste of girls.

I swam in the pool. I kissed girls as they floated towards me. We climbed out of the creamy water and

230

probed each other's secret places. In this hall of paradise I would be presented with every manner of indulgence and realised that however far I was taken I was sure I would go further. I was grateful to Tyler Copic for having shown me the world of film the camera never sees, but my destiny was not to wear his brand. I was, I realised, not born for fame but for the anonymous realms of unknown pleasure.

7

The Prize

David was impressed and a little resentful that I had
made the acquaintance of Tyler Copic and Van Van
de Vere. There are no secrets in the film industry
except, perhaps, the golden pool below the Garden of
Eden. David had been given a grant by the Film
Council to develop a feature; there are blind babies
and homeless people on the streets of Kensington,
but filmmakers have to be supported, too, and using
the Film Council award prudently, David asked me
to go with him to Agadir for a week so I could add
my input to the script. I was down from Cambridge
and June was the perfect time to add a new layer to
my Cannes suntan.

We stayed in a bungalow on the beach. I stretched
my limbs below the sun in a black bathing suit. I let
the sand trickle through my fingers and the days
trickled by in the same leisurely way. We avoided the
Europeans. We were travellers not tourists. We ate in
the old town with its smell of spices and couscous, the
women in veils, like shadows in the night. Men in
turbans played backgammon, throwing the dice and
stamping counters noisily over wooden boards. David
handed out cigarettes and joined in, cupping his hands
and blowing on the dice, bathing them in magic.

Beyond David, across the bar, I became conscious of the man who I would come to know as Omar watching me as I raised a glass of mint tea to my lips. He was standing with the light behind him in a pale linen suit, his hair sleek and shiny, his eyes endless as tunnels. I was sucked into them. David played for just a few dirhams but his winnings paid for our roast lamb, and he still had a little wad of grubby notes when we left the bar to wander back to our compound on the beach.

We are drawn to routine, to creating patterns. I ate fresh mangoes and watched the sun warming the sheet of African sea. Girls with covered heads and kohl-farded eyes sat at my feet with beads and sugared almonds as I read David's crime caper set in East London, a sort of *Lock, Stock and Two Smoking Barrels* meets *Swimming With Sharks* and wisely not too original. Tinny music seeped from the minarets around the mosque and in the cheerful chaos of the kasbah I gazed at the violently-coloured sweets and nougat, woven rugs, brass hookahs, money belts with hidden pockets, men selling loose cigarettes, blind beggars with jostling hands. I found a carved alabaster atomiser filled with oil of frankincense, then I found two more and bought one each for Mummy and Binky.

We went that night back to the same little eating house. David played backgammon with a man with small impish eyes and a long white turban. Omar watched from the distance, tall in the background like the minaret above the mosque. I smiled at him with a sense of familiarity, but he didn't smile back. He just stared at me and my neck grew pink under his gaze. The man in the turban played recklessly. I told David this later, when we were alone, but he assured me that I didn't understand the game. He knew what he was doing. It was good research. Anyway, he had won the equivalent of $50 and next day in the kasbah he bought me a sequinned silver dress that shimmered like fish scales.

The week had flown by. I liked the warm dry air. The smell of the desert. The feel of the waves on my skin. I washed my hair in rose water and shaved the down from my armpits. I sprayed oil of frankincense into the air and it fell in a haze that coated my skin. I dabbed the fragrance behind my ears and below my breasts. Loose strands of my dark hair hung negligently about my face when I pinned it up and my lips were shiny as apples when I painted them red. My skin was lustrous, warm and damp, my appearance provocative in this land of invisible women. When in Rome, do as the Romans, I thought, slipping into a white bra and pants before stepping into the silver dress.

I was the only woman in the little eating house. David had already won a pile of dirhams from the old men, $50 or more, and that was the stake Omar suggested across the table when he approached. Strict rules. It was a large sum, and for the first time the special dice was brought into play, a dice with the numbers 2, 4, 8, 16, 32 and 64, a doubling device. Either player could double the stake at any time, and his opponent either accepted, or conceded the game.

I gripped David's arm. 'Don't,' I said.

He shrugged me away. Omar was holding out his hand. He was urbane, gracious, looking down as if from an ivory tower.

'Omar,' he said, introducing himself.

'David.'

They shook hands. I was not introduced. I have no name. I am an object. A silver fish.

'We will play three games,' Omar continued, and I marvelled at his good English.

He sat. David sat. The men in the bar moved closer to watch, and I watched them, pulling on cigarettes, rewrapping their turbans.

David started with a double four. He tossed a succession of high numbers, secured a stronghold and, after rolling a double three twice in a row, doubled the stake. The move was ambitious, aggressive, a filmmaker's move. Omar rattled the two dice in his open palm as he studied the board, then conceded.

As they gathered the pieces David tried to hide his smile. He glanced at me and a trickle of sweat ran down my back into my knickers. The room was full of smoke. Someone offered me a chair, but I preferred to stand. In my heels I was taller than most of the men. Height gives you confidence. The dice danced across the board, the counters changing patterns like chips of glass in a kaleidoscope, and it is all so meaningless this winning and losing, I thought. The second game was closer, first one then the other moving ahead, and only with the last throw of the dice did Omar win without doubling. David remained $50 ahead.

They lined up the counters. Omar looked at me for the first time, looked closely, his steady gaze validating me as a woman, and it occurred to me that he was challenging David on a level too subtle for David to understand. Like a good film script, the game wasn't about what it was about; it had undertones, subtext: desert man against city man, the third world facing the developed world; it was the past in stasis viewing the glitzy future across history and tradition, and I grasped that in this battle of cultures I was the prize. Did the Greeks not launch their fleet in pursuit of Helen after she sailed to Troy?

'Good luck,' I said to David but I was looking at Omar.

'Inshallah,' he said. 'God willing.'

David threw first. He quickly moved ahead and after throwing two doubles in a row he set the doubling dice on two. The stake was now $100. It was time for Omar to forfeit the game. He played on. His expression was unchanging. His eyes turned to me as he slid his counters forward.

When David moved half his pieces into the home stretch he doubled again to $200. The amber dice thudded like drum rolls as they bounced from the sides of the board, arranging themselves enigmatically. I could smell mint tea and sweat, the frankincense on my skin. I was hot and tired. I wanted to sleep, wake with the sunrise, swim once more in the sea before flying back to London. I watched David turn the doubling dice to eight and knew that my life was about to change, completely, and forever.

Omar threw three doubles in a row, two sixes, two fours, two fives. They were level suddenly. Either could win. I was cupped like the dice in the hands of fate. David tossed a weak two and a one. Omar looked closely at the board before turning the double dice to sixteen – sixteen times $50.

I could hear the beat of my heart. My breasts were rising and falling like waves inside the sequinned dress. Before Omar's gaze I felt naked. I tried to swallow the lump in my throat and watched his hand open like the pages of a book, the dice springing from his long fingers, juggling themselves into the numbers he needed.

Omar could have doubled again before the end of the game but settled on winning $800.

There was a long sigh around the room. Then silence. There was no question of David not paying. It is something men understand. There is a code. Debts must be honoured. He looked from Omar to me, then back again. The shiny eyes of the watching men followed. Omar's expression remained unaffected.

David's voice was a whisper. 'I don't have the money, actually. Not exactly.'

'You play without money?' Omar looked surprised.

David shook his head. 'Well, yes, sort of.'

There was another silence. My underarms were damp. I glanced down at David. He seemed to have shrunk in his chair.

'You are a stranger here?' Omar said.

David nodded.

'Then I must give you one more chance. It is our custom.'

The men nodded. They understood. Omar placed the two dice in David's hand.

'What?'

'We each have one throw. If you win, we shake hands and say goodbye.'

David was relieved but unsure. This was a lifeline. 'And if I lose?' he asked.

Omar's eyes brushed over me momentarily. 'Then she is mine.'

David was gripping the dice tightly in his hand. His knuckles were white. His fist was shaking. I could see his Adam's apple bobbing up and down. He didn't know what to say and looked to me for guidance.

'Until midnight,' Omar added.

David glanced at his watch.

It was three hours before midnight.

I remained very still. I looked at David looking at his watch. Slowly, he looked up at my eyes. The

237

blood was racing in my veins. The flush rushed up my neck, over my cheeks. It was as if a sheet of paper had been placed on hot coals, warming and curling before bursting into flames. We waited for something to happen. There is no rush in the desert. David didn't know whether to look at Omar or at me.

'But what for?' he said finally.

'That is for me to decide.' Omar looked down at his watch. It was gold. A Rolex. 'It is nearly nine.'

David came to his feet and took a step towards me. He laid his hands over mine. I could feel them tremble.

I nodded, solemnly, and the men in the room nodded also.

I am worth $1,600.

We watched David blow into his cupped hand. He let the dice run across the board until they settled on a six and a three: nine, a good score. The men in the bar sighed, drew breath.

Omar scooped up the dice. He had no tricks, no spells, no entreaties. He looked into my eyes, and we both looked down at the black and red points marking the backgammon board. The dice caught the light as they tumbled melodically across the wooden surface, and it was as if time was standing still, the dice turning over each other until they stopped abruptly. On each of the faded amber faces were five spots, a double five. We were silent for a moment, as one is after dramatic events. David was white, drained of colour. The watching men returned to their own tables.

'Come,' Omar said, and I followed like a sleep-walker out from the bar into the hot night. We climbed into a black Mercedes and I watched the buildings of Agadir vanish as we drove into the desert. David held my hand in the back seat. He didn't know what to say and didn't say anything. I watched Omar watching us in the rear-view mirror. There were other cars behind, hidden by dust.

No one seemed surprised when we arrived at the encampment, an oasis around a well with a few date palms. Tribesmen with biblical faces and dark secretive eyes sat in the shadows beside a log fire and I wondered where the logs came from; except for the few palms there were no trees. I heard the sound of camels, goat bells, barking dogs. Some musicians smoking kif in hookahs sat with legs crossed, observing me with the transient interest of people in the bazaar idling away time with no interest to buy. Not that they can afford me. I am worth $1,600, an expensive piece of merchandise. More so here.

The sand ran between my toes as I stepped away from the car. David's weak smile said he was with me; we are in this together. He had no idea what awaited me. Neither did I. That was the wager he had made with Omar, and to which I had agreed.

Omar sent an older woman off to one of the tents, his words in Arabic like the phrases of a song. Several younger women followed. The musicians gathered up their instruments, flutes carved from gourds, a lute, a drum, the skin stretched over a clay pot, an ancient man with empty eye sockets bent over a zither.

'She will dance,' Omar said, his orders directed always to David, and David nodded his assent.

The music was mesmerising, sensuous, primeval, slow at first and slowly gaining in tempo. My shoulders lifted and fell automatically, my hips swayed. It was the music of a belly dance, not that I had a belly to display, just thin arms and sharp bones, a reed caught in the wind. I was unable to hear what

Omar was saying to David, but understood when David caught my eye and pulled at his shirt.

'Your clothes,' he whispered.

Of course. My clothes. The roll of the dice was a contract. The future had been set in stone. My fingers found the zipper running down my side and the silver dress fell from me like the skin of a tropical fish, glinting in the firelight as it slipped to the sand. The pulse of the music was growing. I moved to the beat, swivelling my hips, lowering the thin straps on my white bra, revealing my breasts. They felt hot in my palms, hot and sticky with frankincense. My nipples were taut and my breasts swayed sensuously as I lowered my panties over my thighs.

I moved to the beat of my heart, to the sound of the music. I was Helen, the face that launched a thousand ships. I swirled like a Dervish and below the black sky I could see across the desert as far as the horizon. The moon was silver, curved like a sword, the stars close enough for me to reach out and touch. They shifted and sparkled, more than you can count, the constellations so vivid I could predict my future in their shapes and motions. The fire burned with green flames, the logs snapping, the shadows of the date palms swaying almost imperceptibly. I was bathed in moonlight, naked as a flower, the warm wind faint as breath on my skin.

I raised my hands to the stars and it felt right somehow that I should be dancing like this, my body bared. Something awakens in me when I am naked before unknown eyes. I feel liberated, more alive. I was dancing to the music, not for the musicians, not for the tribesmen with flames in their eyes. I was dancing for him. Just him. My skin was dewed in perspiration, warmed by the fire. I could hear the crackle of the logs, the eternal, hypnotic sound of the zither. I danced and kept dancing and when the music stopped the silence was as vast as the desert.

The old woman who had hurried into the tent before I began to dance poked her head out and called, her tongue clucking. I glanced at Omar, then David, docile at his side, his features shaped by doubt, by insecurity. I had never danced for him, and I caught in his look the vague regret that though he had entered my body, beat me with a belt, with his hand, with his tongue; though he had watched me making love with Roddy Wise and Stephanie Jones, he didn't know who I was or what I might become.

One of the dogs growled, the sound muffled, deep in its throat. The other dogs joined in. The camels languidly raised their heads, firelight reflecting in their glossy eyes. I like the stillness of the desert, the silence, the purity. It felt as if I was beginning a long journey that must be taken alone and without fear. I wondered what the time was and glanced up at the stars as if they might tell me. I recalled a birthday card I had tucked away in a drawer to save. It had on the front a Chinese sage wandering beside a blue river and inside was the adage: To go wrong and not change course can truly be described as going wrong. The words came to me as I approached the tent and like a prayer I found them a comfort.

I imagined that a bed had been prepared, that Omar was going to ravage me.

I was wrong. I would be wrong again many times that night.

Several women were waiting. Dark hands patterned with henna reached for me and I was draped over a low divan. The smell inside the tent was ripe and pungent, the odour of women who rarely wash,

241

the fear prickling my armpits, something spicy and unknown that was cooking on a primus stove. Two girls raised my legs in an arch as if I were about to give birth. Others held my shoulders and the old woman who had been sent to make these preparations approached snapping at me with a pair of scissors, the sort of scissors you would use to shear a sheep. I wriggled but in vain. I was afraid for the first time. Tears filled my eyes. I stared up at the girls, murmuring unintelligibly, and they saw my tears, but they didn't see me. They had their ritual, their task, whatever it was, and they were too strong for me to fight.

The old woman was growing impatient, the blue tattoos on her face giving her a demonic appearance as she loomed over me, the scissors glinting, and for a sickening moment a vision too barbarous to contemplate ran through my mind. She pressed down on my stomach until I was still. I sucked air through gritted teeth, held myself rigid, and watched with a feeling of reprieve as she snipped away at my pubic hair. She pulled and poked, her eyes squinting malevolently in the glow of the lamp a young girl was holding, her gaze above her veil fixed on the gaping lips of my vagina.

A woman wearing lots of bangles ran her palm over my thighs, my thin arms. There was no hair to remove. My underarms too were as smooth as porcelain. I had prepared myself without knowing for what. She moved on to my breasts, her bangles jangling as she tugged at my nipples. She teased them out, pulling viciously as if at the udders of a goat. My nipples grew firm between her fingers and I envisaged milk pouring from the swollen buds. The dreamy-eyed girl holding the lamp lowered her veil. She was

242

no more than fifteen, intense and curious as she ran her hand down my side, over the curve of my waist, across my hipbones. The old woman hissed through blackened teeth, pinching me as if there were insufficient meat for a decent meal, and I couldn't help wondering if I had fallen among cannibals.

Now that that first wave of fear had passed I observed the girls observing me, studying my body with indifference. The aloof way in which they touched my breasts made me think of women buying live chickens in the marketplace. I was until midnight their prisoner, and as I looked up into their dark eyes I wanted to know what they were thinking, their secrets, the meaning of the henna swirls covering the backs of their hands.

The snipping was soon over. My triangle of pubic hair was a patchwork of stubble. I had no idea why this had been done to me and remembered a year ago making *Cheats* and doing the same for David Trevellick, for his vanity and pleasure. The old woman stretched my thighs and before I was aware of what she was doing she ran her finger through the spread lips of my vagina, rubbing it back and forth. She held her finger up to the oil lamp and the girls clucked their tongues when they saw it glistening in the dull light.

The girls were saying things in Arabic, their voices like ripples in a pool, and I watched the old woman crossing the tent to the iron pot bubbling on the stove. She gripped the handle in the folds of her skirt, and returned, placing the pot on the floor beside the divan. The mixture had the yeasty smell of pitta. As if some message passed between the women, their grip on me grew tighter, their weight leaning into my shoulders, my legs parted, held still, my white skin patterned with their dark hands.

The old woman grinned as she stirred the mixture. I watched, terrified, as she ladled the stuff from the boiling pot to my pubic bone, the burning as it touched my skin like the touch of fire, the kiss of the devil. It was a pain beyond pain. My body shook and grew wet with fear. My scream was so shrill it was hard to believe the sound had came from my throat. I wriggled, but the hands holding me were strong, they were women who milked goats and carried pails of water in the desert, women who worked like men. The old woman was going back for more, digging the spoon in the pot, spreading the paste over the delicate lips of my sex. Tears fell from my eyes. But the pain was less intense. My senses were numb. Sweat glossed my skin and with my sobs I rocked uncontrollably.

The old woman's tattoos turned her face into a mask as she smoothed the mixture into the crack of my bottom. The young girl seemed fearful, the lamp swaying in her trembling hand, the shadows dancing just as I had danced in the firelight. The others watched as if it were a rite of passage. Still I had no notion of what they were doing to me. Or why. But the pain was passing and it didn't matter. The holiday with David was a luke-warm bath, not fiery and steaming like the poultice setting as solid as a chastity belt between my legs.

I had agreed to Omar's challenge knowing how it was going to turn out. I had once watched David play blackjack in the casino in Cannes and no matter how much he won he always lost. I had been waiting it seemed with a sense of destiny for the pattern to recur once we had arrived in Morocco.

There was pressure again on my arms and legs. The old woman started picking at the poultice. She teased back the edge across the top of my pubic bone until she had a ridge wide enough to grip in her fingers. She looked into my eyes and I looked at her fading tattoos as in one swift movement she snatched off the compress, the stubborn tufts of hair ripping out and again I screamed in agony.

'Cluck. Cluck. Cluck,' she said, tapping my thigh.

Struggle was pointless. I opened my legs wider, proffering myself, pushing up my bottom, and the old woman picked away at the dried mess, pulling out the last strands of hair as she did so. My pubic mount was bare. I was as smooth as an egg, ripe as fruit. A virgin. My vagina stung but the old woman produced some talcum that eased the pain as she upended the tin and let it snow between my legs. She dusted away the powder and the young girl with the lamp leaned forward to admire her handiwork.

The woman with the ringing bangles prised the lid from a pot containing a buttery ointment with a harsh, faintly rancid fragrance and all the dark hands dipped in at the same time, scooping out the stuff, spreading it over my skin, my arms and legs, my breasts and tummy, between my thighs. They turned me over, massaged my back, rubbing in the cream, their busy fingers strangely hypnotic. I wriggled like a fish.

The hands of the women grew still. My skin was coated, every plane and angle, every crack and crevice smooth and oiled. I sat on the edge of the divan and the young girl leaned forward, the lamp lighting my features, her own face illuminated with anticipation and curiosity. I was being prepared like a bride, I realised. The girl had this to come. I was the echo resonating her future.

The older woman pushed her to one side and opened an earthenware pot that she stood beside me on the divan. The pot contained kohl, black and shiny, which she dug out with a long fingernail. I leaned back. I opened my eyes as wide as I could, and they smarted with tears as the woman sprinkled the coal dust below the lids. The tears spread the kohl around the eyes, the mixture making them shine, even in the dark. Women have always suffered for their beauty, high shoes, bustles and girdles, bare legs on cold days. From another jar, the old woman produced a dry hard pellet of rouge which she warmed between her palms, rubbing it until it was soft before applying it to my nipples.

They dressed me in silver bracelets and anklets with discs that shivered when they moved like the wind through sand. It was what a bride wears on her wedding night in the desert. I was ready. Almost ready. The old woman threaded leather thongs through the clasps on the bracelets and led me out from the tent to where Omar stood as if he had been waiting, the same look in his dark eyes as he had worn earlier that evening when he approached David in the bar.

Had it been an hour ago? Two hours ago? I looked up at the stars.

I wasn't sure why I felt more naked with my pussy shorn. I noticed David in the distance, smoking, staring at me as if at a stranger. A camel had been hobbled behind the fire. The dogs tethered beyond the camel were howling at the moon. Two of the men led me from the tent and the silver discs rattled on my wrists and ankles.

The women followed and sat beside the fire. They watched impassively as the men coaxed me to lie face down across the body of the camel. With the leather thongs in the bracelets they lashed me to the beast,

246

my left wrist to the beaded necklace around the animal's throat, the right to the harness over its tail. I didn't struggle. I was bound by fate. The camel stared at me briefly before laying its head back again in the sand. Its stomach throbbed as it drew breath, bobbing me up and down with the movement.

The men were no longer silent. Their words I did not understand but it sounded like pub chatter, odd phrases ending in laughter. They moved closer and I tried to see myself as they saw me: a skinny girl tied in this bizarre way, my arms stretched out, my head over the camel's hump, my bottom pushed up and out, moving with the beat of my own breath.

Hands stroked my skin. Were they his hands? I had no way of knowing. My legs were pulled further apart and in one awkward movement a man still clothed spread himself across me, his cock driving through the swollen lips of my vagina, and as he pumped into me the pressure made the camel push back. I was trapped between opposing forces. I closed my eyes. I thought of nothing, nothing but the movement, and in a few seconds hot sperm was shooting up inside me, and the man pushed himself away.

There was a froth of noise. Laughter. The man seemed to have done well and another hurried forward. The camel groaned under his weight. His cock slipped inside me, greased by the semen from the first man, and the camel pushed back, rocking him to orgasm. I was an object to be used in any way and there was some small satisfaction in my humiliation.

One of the boys stepped around the camel. A dewdrop glistened on the end of his penis, sparkling in the firelight. I licked it off with the tip of my tongue and took the shaft into my mouth. His body trembled, his knees shook, and his thrusts grew faster

247

until he came, emptying himself copiously into my throat.

Another man was stretching apart the cheeks of my bottom. Something slippery and cold filled my crack and a finger teased its way inside my anus. I gritted my teeth. The finger became two fingers, widening the hole, and he gasped with pleasure as his cock split me in two. The pain was insufferable, but I had learned over the knee of more than one man that pain passes and turns to pleasure.

When he had finished his turn, filling my bottom with hot sperm, another took his place. There was a murmur of satisfaction when a sticky cock pushed between my teeth and I gathered by the faintly soiled taste that it was the same man who had just buggered me. The thought was passing, ephemeral. I wrapped his penis in my tongue and nursed it back to strength until with what I was sure was pride, he leaked another speck of sap into the back of my throat.

As he moved away, the one in my backside touched orgasm and I felt the drool squelching warmly out of me as another man took his place. The men sweated and dribbled across my back. The stench of the camel tainted my perspiration with a lusty, lurid smell and my skin was hot and chafed where I was pushed and bounced against its vibrating body.

Another man used my mouth, vacating his bitter load over the walls of my throat. As he moved away I saw a shadow across the desert. I thought for a moment it was David, wandering off in shame, but the man was taller. As he drew closer, I realised it was Omar. He was carrying a bowl which he placed at his feet and the sound of the dogs lapping up water was an echo of the man thrusting frantically between my sopping legs.

One after the other, after buggering me, the men found pleasure using my tongue to make them clean. I was growing sore, but there was no pain and oddly no shame, no regret. I had saved David from dishonour and my being used in this way I realised again had always been in the dark heart of my own subconscious. Tyler Copic had offered me his seal, his promise of success. Omar had offered nothing and as I lay there tethered in the desert I imagined he could take me to places outside my experience, outside my imagination.

The camel turned from time to time, stared at me with bored glossy eyes, and gnashed its teeth as its head returned to the sand. Its sloping stomach held me perfectly, displaying my rounded bottom, my shaved pussy pushed through my thighs, the discs murmuring about my wrists and feet. I tried to glance back, but I couldn't see the women, and I tried to keep count of the number of times I had been pierced, the number of times those men had left their sticky mess slurping through my crack. It was just a number. It made no difference to anything. I wasn't aroused or stimulated, or even afraid. I was a backgammon board and they were dice running over the surface.

My three openings were used repeatedly. Suddenly they stopped. I pulled my head back to look up at the stars. It must be midnight, I was thinking, it is over. I heard the men shuffle back. There was silence except for the sound of muffled footsteps. It was Omar. He stood in front of me and removed what I realised was a whip from the harness around the camel's neck. The whip had a short handle and dozens of long thongs that ended in tiny knots.

He glanced at his watch, glanced into my eyes, and moved back around the camel. I was spread white as

249

snow in the desert night, the marks of the pentangle vivid in the moonlight. The sound of the whip as it came down on my bare flesh was like the sound of thunder on a still day. I screamed, my voice rippling and resonating across the desert.

The camel rolled unsteadily, tossing me about like a ship at sea. Before I could catch my breath, the whip came down again, the knots on the thongs like darts piercing my skin. The pain was excruciating but the bite of the whip through some strange alchemy turned into something I could never have imagined or expected. It felt as if a velvet fist was gripping my intestines. My stomach vibrated with contractions. I pushed up my bottom involuntarily to meet the third strike of the whip and, as those leather thongs met my soft flesh, my body erupted, not in agony but in shocking, unadulterated ecstasy, my orgasm exploding from me in undulating spasms as endless as the waves on the desert sand.

My body was wet, ripe, aching, oozing with my own juice, slimy with sperm. The camel rocked as if waiting for more. But it was midnight. It was over. The bindings holding my wrists were released. I came shakily, proudly to my feet. Omar gave instructions to the old woman and, when she returned from the tent with a white sheet, he wrapped me tenderly before carrying me like a bride in his arms. He placed me in the back of his car. David sat beside him in the front and in silence we drove back to Agadir, the cool wind blowing through the open window.

There were single beds in our bungalow and I sensed as I lay wrapped in the white sheet that David wanted to crawl in beside me. I slept like a child dreaming the dreams of the wine sleeping below the streets of Cannes and the salt sea healed the wheals from Omar's whip as I slipped at sunrise into the waves.

Like a shimmering fish I slid back into the silver dress. David kept looking at me as if I were an invalid requiring help. He needed reassurance. A taxi arrived and the driver loaded our suitcases filled with souvenirs in the back. The road uncurled into the heat and dust of Agadir. I could smell sugared almonds. Omar's black car was parked outside the same eating house where the men played backgammon. I tapped the driver on the shoulder.

'Stop,' I said. He did so without question.

David touched my hand as I opened the door. 'I don't understand,' he whispered.

'Nor do I,' I told him.

I stepped out of the car and closed the door behind me.

'What about . . .' he paused. 'What about your things?'

'I won't be needing them.'

'What about me?'

I didn't know what to say, and didn't say anything.

nexus

The leading publisher of fetish and adult fiction

TELL US WHAT YOU THINK!

Readers' ideas and opinions matter to us so please take a few minutes to fill in the questionnaire below.

1. Sex: Are you male ☐ female ☐ a couple ☐?

2. Age: Under 21 ☐ 21–30 ☐ 31–40 ☐ 41–50 ☐ 51–60 ☐ over 60 ☐

3. Where do you buy your Nexus books from?
☐ A chain book shop. If so, which one(s)?

_____

☐ An independent book shop. If so, which one(s)?

_____

☐ A used book shop/charity shop
☐ Online book store. If so, which one(s)?

_____

4. How did you find out about Nexus books?
☐ Browsing in a book shop
☐ A review in a magazine
☐ Online
☐ Recommendation
☐ Other _____

5. In terms of settings, which do you prefer? (Tick as many as you like.)
☐ Down to earth and as realistic as possible
☐ Historical settings. If so, which period do you prefer?

_____

☐ Fantasy settings – barbarian worlds
☐ Completely escapist/surreal fantasy

☐ Institutional or secret academy
☐ Futuristic/sci fi
☐ Escapist but still believable
☐ Any settings you dislike?

_____

☐ Where would you like to see an adult novel set?

_____

6. In terms of storylines, would you prefer:

☐ Simple stories that concentrate on adult interests?
☐ More plot and character-driven stories with less explicit adult activity?
☐ We value your ideas, so give us your opinion of this book:

_____

_____

_____

7. In terms of your adult interests, what do you like to read about? (Tick as many as you like.)

☐ Traditional corporal punishment (CP)
☐ Modern corporal punishment
☐ Spanking
☐ Restraint/bondage
☐ Rope bondage
☐ Latex/rubber
☐ Leather
☐ Female domination and male submission
☐ Female domination and female submission
☐ Male domination and female submission
☐ Willing captivity
☐ Uniforms
☐ Lingerie/underwear/hosiery/footwear (boots and high heels)
☐ Sex rituals
☐ Vanilla sex
☐ Swinging

☐ Cross-dressing/TV
☐ Enforced feminisation
☐ Others – tell us what you don't see enough of in adult fiction:

_____

_____

_____

8. Would you prefer books with a more specialised approach to your interests, i.e. a novel specifically about uniforms? If so, which subject(s) would you like to read a Nexus novel about?

_____

_____

_____

9. Would you like to read true stories in Nexus books? For instance, the true story of a submissive woman, or a male slave? Tell us which true revelations you would most like to read about:

_____

_____

_____

10. What do you like best about Nexus books?

_____

_____

11. What do you like least about Nexus books?

_____

_____

12. Which are your favourite titles?

_____

_____

13. Who are your favourite authors?

_____

_____

14. **Which covers do you prefer? Those featuring:**
    (Tick as many as you like.)

☐ Fetish outfits
☐ More nudity
☐ Two models
☐ Unusual models or settings
☐ Classic erotic photography
☐ More contemporary images and poses
☐ A blank/non-erotic cover
☐ What would your ideal cover look like?

_____

15. **Describe your ideal Nexus novel in the space provided:**

_____
_____
_____
_____

16. **Which celebrity would feature in one of your Nexus-style fantasies?**
    We'll post the best suggestions on our website – anonymously!

_____

THANKS FOR YOUR TIME

Now simply write the title of this book in the space below and cut out the
questionnaire pages. Post to: Nexus, Marketing Dept., Thames Wharf Studios,
Rainville Rd, London W6 9HA

Book title: _____

nexus

NEXUS NEW BOOKS

To be published in September 2007

LONGING FOR TOYS
Virginia Crowley

Robert and James are upstanding members of the community. They are young professionals with bigoted, conservative upper middle class girlfriends. When Michele – a gorgeous stripper at the notorious club Hot Summer's – sees Robert's shiny red new roadster, she is overcome by a desire to possess it. Manipulating his friends and neighbours with offerings of ever more sordid sexual delights, she engineers Robert's descent into a tangled world of erotic temptation. As his character degrades from that of an altruistic medical researcher into a drooling plaything around the manicured fingers of his keeper, Robert's fiancée and best friend try to help him; unfortunately, their involvement also subjects them to the irresistible lure of pretty toys.

£6.99   ISBN 978 0 352 34138 9

To be published in October 2007

LUST CALL
Ray Gordon

Attractive, blonde Sarah lives happily with her husband in a state of suburban bliss. Until she receives a salacious e-mail from a man called 'Brian', who knows intimate details about her. It suggests she is being watched. More mails arrive admiring her sexy outfits. Her bemusement soon turns to curiosity and she begins a correspondence with Brian. Convinced the writer is her husband, she begins to follow the requests in the emails and engages in sexual games with her husband. Hooked on the game, the requests become more extreme and she engages in affairs with other men. It is only then that she becomes aware that the identity behind Brian is not her husband. A stranger has transformed her from a loyal loving wife, to an insatiable adulterer.

Swamped by an overwhelming desire not only to discover who Brian is, but to find gratification from outrageous sexual acts, she begins to seduce the men she suspects are Brian. Time after time she attempts to solve the mystery of Brian, but fails, while slipping further and further into shame and depravity. And all the time, he watches, until . . . finally, he is revealed.

£6.99   ISBN 978 0 352 34143 3

CUCKOLD
Amber Leigh

A little knowledge is a dangerous thing. But that's all Edwin Miller wants. He has a good job, a pleasant home, and is married to the beautiful and loving Des. All he needs to make his life complete is the answer to one question:

Has his wife made him a cuckold?

Not sure if the idea is the sum of his fears, or the revelation of his true desire, Edwin struggles to uncover the truth. But the answer could mean his life is never the same again.

£6.99   ISBN 978 0 352 34140 2

If you would like more information about Nexus titles, please visit our website at www.nexus-books.com, or send a large stamped addressed envelope to:

Nexus, Thames Wharf Studios,
Rainville Road, London W6 9HA

NEXUS BOOKLIST

Information is correct at time of printing. To avoid disappointment, check availability before ordering. Go to www.nexus-books.com.

All books are priced at £6.99 unless another price is given.

NEXUS

☐ ABANDONED ALICE   Adriana Arden   ISBN 978 0 352 33969 0

☐ ALICE IN CHAINS   Adriana Arden   ISBN 978 0 352 33908 9

☐ AQUA DOMINATION   William Doughty   ISBN 978 0 352 34020 7

☐ THE ART OF CORRECTION   Tara Black   ISBN 978 0 352 33895 2

☐ THE ART OF SURRENDER   Madeline Bastinado   ISBN 978 0 352 34013 9

☐ BEASTLY BEHAVIOUR   Aishling Morgan   ISBN 978 0 352 34095 5

☐ BEHIND THE CURTAIN   Primula Bond   ISBN 978 0 352 34111 2

☐ BEING A GIRL   Chloë Thurlow   ISBN 978 0 352 34139 6

☐ BELINDA BARES UP   Yolanda Celbridge   ISBN 978 0 352 33926 3

☐ BENCH-MARKS   Tara Black   ISBN 978 0 352 33797 9

☐ BIDDING TO SIN   Rosita Varón   ISBN 978 0 352 34063 4

☐ BINDING PROMISES   G.C. Scott   ISBN 978 0 352 34014 6

☐ THE BOOK OF PUNISHMENT   Cat Scarlett   ISBN 978 0 352 33975 1

☐ BRUSH STROKES   Penny Birch   ISBN 978 0 352 34072 6

☐ BUTTER WOULDN'T MELT   Penny Birch   ISBN 978 0 352 34120 4

☐ CALLED TO THE WILD   Angel Blake   ISBN 978 0 352 34067 2

☐ CAPTIVES OF CHEYNER CLOSE   Adriana Arden   ISBN 978 0 352 34028 3

☐ CARNAL POSSESSION   Yvonne Strickland   ISBN 978 0 352 34062 7

☐ CITY MAID   Amelia Evangeline   ISBN 978 0 352 34096 2

☐ COLLEGE GIRLS   Cat Scarlett   ISBN 978 0 352 33942 3

☐ CONCEIT AND CONSEQUENCE   Aishling Morgan   ISBN 978 0 352 33965 2

☐ STRIPING KAYLA	Yolanda Marshall	ISBN 978 0 352 33881 5
☐ STRIPPED BARE	Angel Blake	ISBN 978 0 352 33971 3
☐ TASTING CANDY	Ray Gordon	ISBN 978 0 352 33925 6
☐ TEMPTING THE GODDESS	Aishling Morgan	ISBN 978 0 352 33972 0
☐ THAI HONEY	Kit McCann	ISBN 978 0 352 34068 9
☐ TICKLE TORTURE	Penny Birch	ISBN 978 0 352 33904 1
☐ TOKYO BOUND	Sachi	ISBN 978 0 352 34019 1
☐ TORMENT, INCORPORATED	Murilee Martin	ISBN 978 0 352 33943 0
☐ UNEARTHLY DESIRES	Ray Gordon	ISBN 978 0 352 34036 8
☐ UNIFORM DOLL	Penny Birch	ISBN 978 0 352 33698 9
☐ WHALEBONE STRICT	Lady Alice McCloud	ISBN 978 0 352 34082 5
☐ WHAT HAPPENS TO BAD GIRLS	Penny Birch	ISBN 978 0 352 34031 3
☐ WHAT SUKI WANTS	Cat Scarlett	ISBN 978 0 352 34027 6
☐ WHEN SHE WAS BAD	Penny Birch	ISBN 978 0 352 33859 4
☐ WHIP HAND	G.C. Scott	ISBN 978 0 352 33694 1
☐ WHIPPING GIRL	Aishling Morgan	ISBN 978 0 352 33789 4
☐ WHIPPING TRIANGLE	G.C. Scott	ISBN 978 0 352 34086 3

NEXUS CLASSIC

☐ AMAZON SLAVE	Lisette Ashton	ISBN 978 0 352 33916 4
☐ ANGEL	Lindsay Gordon	ISBN 978 0 352 34009 2
☐ THE BLACK GARTER	Lisette Ashton	ISBN 978 0 352 33919 5
☐ THE BLACK MASQUE	Lisette Ashton	ISBN 978 0 352 33977 5
☐ THE BLACK ROOM	Lisette Ashton	ISBN 978 0 352 33914 0
☐ THE BLACK WIDOW	Lisette Ashton	ISBN 978 0 352 33973 7
☐ THE BOND	Lindsay Gordon	ISBN 978 0 352 33996 6
☐ THE DOMINO ENIGMA	Cyrian Amberlake	ISBN 978 0 352 34064 1
☐ THE DOMINO QUEEN	Cyrian Amberlake	ISBN 978 0 352 34074 0
☐ THE DOMINO TATTOO	Cyrian Amberlake	ISBN 978 0 352 34037 5
☐ EMMA ENSLAVED	Hilary James	ISBN 978 0 352 33883 9

☐ EMMA'S HUMILIATION	Hilary James	ISBN 978 0 352 33910 2
☐ EMMA'S SECRET DOMINATION	Hilary James	ISBN 978 0 352 34000 9
☐ EMMA'S SUBMISSION	Hilary James	ISBN 978 0 352 33906 5
☐ FAIRGROUND ATTRACTION	Lisette Ashton	ISBN 978 0 352 33927 0
☐ IN FOR A PENNY	Penny Birch	ISBN 978 0 352 34083 2
☐ THE INSTITUTE	Maria Del Rey	ISBN 978 0 352 33352 0
☐ NEW EROTICA 5	Various	ISBN 978 0 352 33956 0
☐ THE NEXUS LETTERS	Various	ISBN 978 0 352 33955 3
☐ PLAYTHING	Penny Birch	ISBN 978 0 352 33967 6
☐ PLEASING THEM	William Doughty	ISBN 978 0 352 34015 3
☐ RITES OF OBEDIENCE	Lindsay Gordon	ISBN 978 0 352 34005 4
☐ SERVING TIME	Sarah Veitch	ISBN 978 0 352 33509 8
☐ THE SUBMISSION GALLERY	Lindsay Gordon	ISBN 978 0 352 34026 9
☐ TIE AND TEASE	Penny Birch	ISBN 978 0 352 33987 4

NEXUS CONFESSIONS

☐ NEXUS CONFESSIONS: VOLUME ONE	Ed. Lindsay Gordon	ISBN 978 0 352 34093 1

NEXUS ENTHUSIAST

☐ BUSTY	Tom King	ISBN 978 0 352 34032 0
☐ CUCKOLD	Amber Leigh	ISBN 978 0 352 34140 2
☐ DERRIÈRE	Julius Culdrose	ISBN 978 0 352 34024 5
☐ ENTHRALLED	Lance Porter	ISBN 978 0 352 34108 2
☐ LEG LOVER	L.G. Denier	ISBN 978 0 352 34016 0
☐ OVER THE KNEE	Fiona Locke	ISBN 978 0 352 34079 5
☐ RUBBER GIRL	William Doughty	ISBN 978 0 352 34087 0
☐ THE SECRET SELF	Christina Shelly	ISBN 978 0 352 34069 6
☐ UNDER MY MASTER'S WINGS	Lauren Wissot	ISBN 978 0 352 34042 9
☐ THE UPSKIRT EXHIBITIONIST	Ray Gordon	ISBN 978 0 352 34122 8
☐ WIFE SWAP	Amber Leigh	ISBN 978 0 352 34097 9